A Sweet Summer Camp Romantic Comedy

LOVE AT THE LAKE

JULIE MILO

www.juliemilo.com

For Gabriel

My own golden retriever puppy. You are my sunshine.

Author's Note

This novel is light, sweet, and funny–it's a rom com after all–but the characters deal with tough things in their lives just like real people.

First and foremost, one of the main characters in this book is an adult adoptee. I purposefully wrote the character to honor the adoptee perspective, which is the one most often overlooked in media portrayals of adoption. This story does not take a rose-colored view of adoption, even adoption under the best circumstances, but I hope it portrays adoption honestly.

Second, a character in this book struggles with trauma around their experiences with dyslexia as a child and continuing into adulthood.

This book contains no sex on the page, very limited swearing, and no deaths (animal or human).

Chapter One
Olivia

I slump against the passenger seat of my best friend Annie's car, exhausted and restless.

"You ready for a summer of surprises?" Annie asks brightly, in acute contrast to my energy levels.

She's driving us home from the airport. It's a late Sunday afternoon in early summer and we just got back to Austin, Texas, from northeast Florida where we'd been attending my older sister Nicole's wedding. Annie was my plus one—there are certainly no men in my life worth the title. Not that I needed a man. Annie was the perfect date, and we had a blast, hence my exhaustion.

I look at her now, sliding my sunglasses down my nose and scrunching up my face. "Surprises? If by surprises you mean sleeping in a cabin and keeping sunburnt, hyperactive kids occupied, then sure. I guess so."

Annie quickly glances at me in the passenger seat before returning her eyes to the road. She smiles, but there's an uneasiness behind it.

"It'll be fun," she insists, drumming her fingers against the steering wheel. "Maybe even the best summer of your life."

I take my sunglasses fully off now and stare at her profile. "Best summer of my life?" I repeat.

I leave tomorrow to work as the activities director for a kids' sleepaway camp about two hours east of our hometown. I'll be there for thirteen weeks. Working at a summer camp is a fun way to earn money for the next few months—and definitely beats the patchwork of jobs I've been working for the last year—but I'm not sure why my friend would prophesy it being "the best summer of my life."

I fold my arms in front of my chest. "What's going on?"

Annie shrugs, conspicuously keeping her eyes facing forward. "Nothing. I'm happy for you—heading off on a new adventure. New experiences. You know?"

"Hmm," I hum as I slide my sunglasses back on my face.

Annie's being weird. Actually, she's been a little weird for six months now, ever since we got home from an ill-advised trip to New Orleans. We stayed with my oldest sister, Molly, and hung out at the Halloween parade with Annie's twin brother, Gage, and his girlfriend. I wonder if maybe something's going on with Gage that has her so restless, but I can't ask her.

Annie and I *never* talk about Gage. It's been an unspoken rule of our friendship ever since the *event* that happened right before our high school graduation. We've both silently agreed to never mention it again. So her cryptic behavior now makes me think whatever she's hiding is Gage-related. We don't have secrets from each other that don't have to do with Gage.

Annie pulls into the driveway of my house in southwest Austin. Well, my parents' house, though they're still in Florida for a couple more days. I moved back home after I graduated college. A year later, I'm embarrassed to still be here with no plans or directions beyond this summer.

In a way, I kind of hope Annie's right, and it will be a summer of surprises. My life could use some upheaval. Some direction. Some motivation. And yeah, some romance if it's not asking too much. A summer fling could be exactly what I need. Or maybe that's the last-single-sister melancholy talking.

Both of my older sisters—my smart, beautiful, successful older sisters—are married and thriving in their careers. Nicole, who married her husband, Adam, yesterday, is an academic librarian at a cute little college in Florida. Molly, who surprised everyone by eloping with her husband, Jonathan, in Las Vegas last Thanksgiving, started a new job a few months ago. She's a coastal environmental scientist running her own lab with the National Centers for Coastal Ocean Science in Charleston, South Carolina.

Meanwhile, there's me: a single serial dater teetering on the cusp of unemployment after barely graduating with my bachelor's degree.

I'm happy for my sisters and so proud of them. They're amazing. But I can't help but look at their lives and look at my life and feel ... deficient.

All through high school and college, playing soccer was my passion. I was the captain and best striker on my Division I college team, thriving on the pulse of the game, the consistency of the workouts, and the camaraderie of the team.

When that last season ended my senior year, I felt listless and directionless. I scraped through my last semester to graduate with my degree in exercise science, but I don't know what to do with it.

I don't know who I am now that I'm not a soccer player.

I've gotten by coaching weekly classes for a kids' soccer program here in Austin, but the hours are limited, and the pay is low. I definitely don't make enough to move out of my childhood home into my own apartment.

So when Annie found an ad from a sleepaway camp looking for an activities director for the summer and encouraged me to apply, I figured *why not?* It's temporary, but it gives me more time to figure out my next step and a blessed reprieve from living with my parents.

I twist in my seat and grab my bag from the backseat of Annie's car. Before I can reach for the door handle to get out, Annie stops me with a hand on my arm.

"Good luck tomorrow," she says. "I'll miss you this summer, but I know you'll do great." She pauses, her nose scrunching up as if considering how to word what she says next. When she speaks, it sounds suspiciously like a pep talk. "Promise me you'll keep an open mind about anything ... unexpected that may happen. And call me if you need anything or want to talk anything through. You know I love you and want you to be happy."

I stare at her. It's a supersweet sentiment and of course I love Annie, too, but everything about this conversation and her mannerisms screams suspicious. "What unexpected things are you expecting will happen?"

She darts her eyes away. "I don't know. Poison ivy. Homesickness. Awesome camp crafts. A summer romance, maybe?" She laughs, but it's pitched too high, the way she laughs when she's nervous.

I narrow my eyes. I had a long day of travel after waking up a little hungover this morning from yesterday's festivities. I need to unpack, do laundry, and repack before I have to get up early tomorrow to drive to Camp Prairie Star. I'm going to let this go for now. Annie is not as sneaky as she thinks, so I'm sure whatever she's hiding will come to light sooner rather than later.

"Okay, I promise."

Annie grins. "Thanks. Love you, Delaney." She calls me by my last name, which she's done since high school when I first asked her to.

"Love you, too." I sigh and open the car door, dragging my overfilled duffel bag behind me.

The next morning, I toss the same equally overfilled duffel bag into the backseat of my hand-me-down sedan and drive east.

My parents bought my pale-blue clunker fifteen years ago when my oldest sister started driving. Molly passed it down to Nicole, who passed it down to me. A perk of being the youngest is that I get to keep the car, even though it had definitely seen better days by the time I started driving it.

I pat the dashboard. High mileage or no, Cammie has been good to me and is saving me from a car payment in my current era of underemployment. *At least the Bluetooth connection still works*, I think as my audiobook plays through the car speakers.

The drive to Camp Prairie Star takes about two hours, and when I spot a Buc-ee's less than an hour from camp, I stop to fill up on gas for the car and snacks for me.

I notice a text notification on my phone. It's from the group chat with my sisters. Considering Nicole got married less than forty-eight hours ago and is currently on her honeymoon, I hope it's Molly texting.

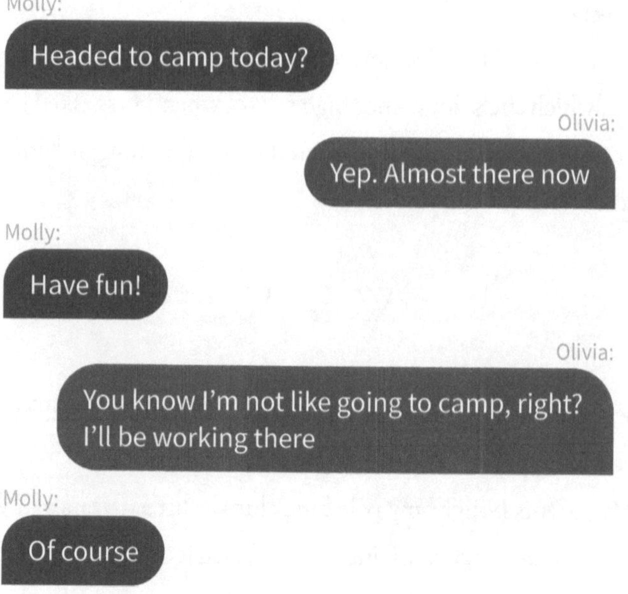

I sigh in frustration. Panda is a stuffed animal I've had since I was a baby. It's a panda, obviously. I was not a kid who was very creative with names.

Right after Molly claims to know that I'm an adult, she asks about my old security stuffie. Figures. Of course, Panda *is* in my duffel bag, obviously, but still.

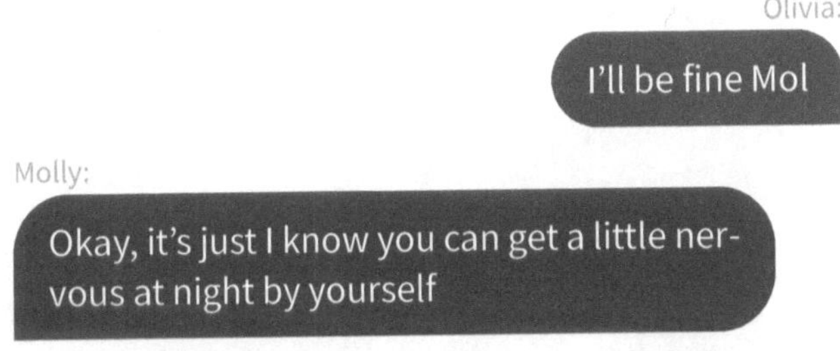

I lean my head back against the headrest and groan, closing my eyes. I swear, it's like I have two moms. Hazard of having a sister seven years older.

I chuckle at their reactions. Messing with them never stops being fun. I think it's a little sister thing.

Chapter Two

Gage

*D*on't panic, I tell myself. *You probably misheard.*

Surely I misheard Linda, the camp director at Camp Prairie Star, when she announced the camp activities director's name. I look at the faces around me and breathe a sigh of relief. She's not here.

This summer is about preparing for grad school in the fall, getting my body out of an office and into the fresh air, and, most of all, connecting with my biological family. The last thing I need is Olivia Delaney twisting up my emotions until I can't think straight.

Then Linda repeats herself. "Our activities director, Olivia Delaney, will be here tomorrow morning."

Okay, so I didn't mishear, but it could be someone else—a different Olivia Delaney.

"She's at a family event this weekend and will be driving in from Austin. She goes by Delaney."

I groan. Nope. It's my Olivia Delaney. I mean, not *mine*, of course. Never mine. But the Olivia Delaney I've known half my life, who is at her sister's wedding in Florida this weekend, lives in Austin, calls herself Delaney, and is best friends with my twin sister, Annie.

Speaking of Annie, there's no way she didn't know that both Olivia and I would be at Camp Prairie Star this summer. The little sneak.

As soon as the meeting is over, I duck outside to text my traitor of a twin.

Do you want to give her a heads up?

Well, okay then. This will be fun.

Olivia and I have a history that's ... complicated. From the time Olivia's family moved into our neighborhood during sixth grade, she and my sister were inseparable. Before that, it was always me and Annie.

Not that I didn't have guy friends. I had a lot of them, but Annie had a harder time making friends, and we'd always been each other's person. When Annie and Olivia latched on to each other, it could have been my opportunity to ditch my sister guilt-free and focus on my other friends. Instead, the three of us became the three musketeers.

As we got older and headed to high school, something shifted, at least for me. My feelings for Olivia became less friendly and more romantic. Olivia changed, too. That's when she started going by her last name. She was almost two different people. At school, she was Delaney, aloof, shallow, and unattainable, but after school she was herself, Olivia: confident, fun, and a little snarky.

At school she was queen bee, but on the weekends, the three of us would still run around the neighborhood, climbing trees in the woods behind Olivia's house, lounging on the couch to binge-watch Netflix, and playing video games.

I remember this one Saturday around tenth grade when Annie, Olivia, and I rode our bikes to a shopping center near our houses for ice cream. As we stepped outside with our cones—Olivia wearing cut-off jeans, an old T-shirt, and ratty sneakers, her beach-blonde hair braided down her back—two girls from school exited the big makeup store next door. I recognized them as two of the girls Olivia usually sat with at lunch. I've long since forgotten their names.

When Olivia saw them, she ducked behind a cement pillar. As soon as she did, the girls looked over at us and squealed my name, waving me over. I chatted with them for a few minutes, and they left. Only then did Olivia come out from behind the pillar, like she couldn't let these girls who knew her as Delaney see her being Olivia.

"Embarrassed to be seen with us?" I teased her.

She shook her head, green eyes flashing. "Never. But I *am* embarrassed to be seen like *this*." She waved a hand in front of herself. I knew she wasn't dressed as stylishly as she would be for school, but she looked amazing. She always did.

Anyway, while Annie and Olivia are still close, I haven't spoken to her in years. Not really.

I know what Annie's trying to do. She'd love to go back to the years when it was the three of us united against the world, when she didn't feel constantly torn between her brother and her best friend. I get it, and I know the schism between Olivia and me has been hard for Annie.

I head back to my cabin before the next part of orientation starts—a walk-through of the daily camp schedule once the kids arrive. I duck into the bathroom that next week I'll be sharing with eight ten-year-old boys. I scrub my hands over my eyes and splash water on my face. I stare at my reflection in the mirror for a few minutes. Quietly, I give myself a pep talk.

"You're at this camp for a reason this summer. Focus on that, and it won't matter where Olivia is. She doesn't have a hold on you anymore. You're over her."

Even as I say the words, a niggling voice in the back of my mind asks how true they are. But of course I'm over her. How could I still be holding onto feelings for a woman I don't even know anymore?

And yet, after the rest of the day's orientation meetings, including a welcome bonfire and our first introduction to the Camp Prairie Star traditional camp songs, I lie in bed and can't sleep. Each time I shift to a new position, the plastic mattress protector crunches under the bamboo sheets I brought from home. The cabin is quiet and dark, and my mind is racing.

I've gone on dates with plenty of women since high school, even had a couple of serious relationships, but every time I think my heart has finally escaped Olivia's influence, she creeps back into my head. It doesn't matter that she broke my heart and cut me out of her life; I still look for her in every woman I meet. Most have a few of her characteristics—a sharp wit, sparkling eyes, fierce loyalty—but none have it all. None but Olivia herself.

Knowing I'll see her tomorrow is equal parts dread and excitement.

Bright and early the next morning, a bugle calling out Reveille wakes me. I groan and press the pillow against my ears. That's going to get old real quick if they plan to wake us up with a bugle call all summer.

I roll out of bed to shower and get dressed before breakfast starts. A chill lingers in the air this morning—though I know it won't last long—so I throw my burnt-orange Longhorns hoodie on over my T-shirt before walking to the mess hall, my fitted black UT baseball cap turned backward on my head.

After breakfast, Linda asks me and another counselor, Brynn—a woman who looks to be in her early twenties, like me, and has dark brown hair that's cut short around her warm, beige face—to follow her to the main office.

Linda is chattering about the orientation activities we'll be doing today as she ushers us into the office to help her carry the boxes of supplies. Before I step inside, I spot a beat-up pale-blue sedan rolling toward us down the dusty road in the distance. I recognize it immediately from my high school days. *She's still driving that old thing?*

I watch the car from the office window as it gets closer and closer, finally pulling into one of the parking spaces in front of the building.

"Gage," Linda calls. I pull my gaze away from the clunker outside and turn toward her. "Can you please grab that box in the back corner?"

"Sure thing," I respond, stepping away from the window to retrieve the box.

The office door opens with squeaking hinges and a jingling bell.

"Hi!" That all-too-familiar voice threads through my body as I stand frozen in the corner. "I'm Delaney, the activities director for the summer."

She's talking to Linda, her face turned away from my unobtrusive hideout in the corner. She hasn't seen me yet. I study her. Her blonde hair is lighter than I remember, almost silver in the harsh fluorescent lights of the office. She's wearing it on top of her head in a long sleek ponytail. Her face, or what I can see from this angle, is bare: no makeup. Her green athletic tank accentuates the lean muscles and golden tan on her arms. My gaze continues down, taking in her silver-and-black-patterned leggings. I force my eyes back up to her face, so I don't linger on the view of her backside like a creep.

The last time I saw Olivia was in October, nearly seven months ago. We all met up in New Orleans for the Halloween parade. I thought I'd be okay hanging out with Olivia—it had been almost five years since high school after all, and I had a girlfriend I really cared about—but I wasn't okay, at all. She wore this sexy colorful peacock costume, complete with a Mardi Gras-style mask that made the green of her eyes glow. Fortunately for me, she ended up going back to her sister's house early with food poisoning or something.

Linda's voice cuts through my thoughts. "Welcome, Delaney! I'm Linda, the camp director. Let me go get your welcome packet."

Linda steps into the other room, and Olivia takes the opportunity to scan this one.

She smiles at Brynn, and the two exchange introductions. Meanwhile, I consider ducking under the desk. But this forced reunion is going to happen sooner or later, so I might as well get it over with so I can get back to my summer.

Finally, Olivia's gaze turns to me, blank for a split second before recognition makes her stumble back a step, and her eyes bulge.

"Gage," she chokes, my name pulled from her throat like an involuntary tic. "What are you doing here?"

I spread my fingers in front of my chest in an awkward wave. "Hey, Olivia."

Brynn's head bobs between us with interest. "Do you two know each other?"

Dazed, Olivia murmurs, "He's my best friend's brother."

"We've known each other since we were kids," I add.

Brynn laughs. "Really? How funny that you're both working here this summer."

Olivia's eyes snap to mine, sharp and stormy. "You're working here?"

I chuckle nervously. "I'm a counselor all summer."

She lifts her eyebrows nearly to her hairline. I shrug.

Yep, this is totally uncomfortable.

Chapter Three
Olivia

Ten Years Ago

"Pull over here," I instructed my sister Nicole. It was nice of her to offer me a ride to my best friend Annie's house, but that didn't mean I wanted everyone to see me getting dropped off by the goth queen over here. Her naturally blonde hair was dyed black, her clothes all black, and her fingernails? You guessed it, black.

I could have walked the two blocks from our house, but I had my overnight bag stuffed to the seams and didn't want to carry it even that short distance, especially because I was running late.

Nicole parked at the curb three houses down from Annie's. As I climbed out, dragging my duffel with me, I waved to my sister. "Thanks, Nicole!"

"No problem." She waved back. "Have fun."

I shut the door of the car—a light blue sedan that would be mine in three long years when I was finally old enough to drive. Grinning, I walked across the lawn to the Carters' house.

Annie and her twin brother, Gage, were having a pool party for their fourteenth birthday. It felt weird that they had just turned fourteen considering I turned thirteen only two months ago. I had a summer birthday and theirs was in September, which put us all in the same grade at school even though I was nearly a year younger.

When my family moved into this new neighborhood last summer, Annie was one of the first kids I met. She was quiet in a way that paired nicely with my loudness, and we became best friends right away.

Annie was excellent at making up elaborate stories for the games we played in the woods behind my house, and I was always ready and willing to act the stories out.

So, because we were best friends, not only did I get to join the pool party, Annie also invited me to spend the night, hence the duffel bag.

We'd started eighth grade together a few weeks earlier, which meant high school was around the corner. Thinking about it made my stomach churn. School was ... not my favorite.

But today was Saturday, it still felt like summer in central Texas, and I refused to think about school.

Instead, I dropped my duffel bag off in Annie's bedroom and headed to the backyard. Kids I knew from school and church were scattered across the Carters' yard—splashing in the in-ground pool and running on the deck, hanging on the tire swing tied on the huge oak tree near the back fence, sitting in deck chairs eating pizza and chips. Only the treehouse in the oak remained off limits, the rope ladder pulled up to discourage entry. Annie and Gage didn't even let *me* go into the treehouse. It was their own private clubhouse.

Their backyard was chaos, and I loved it.

I spotted Annie, dangling her feet in the water in the only quiet corner of the pool. Her light brown hair was tied up in a ponytail, and her blue eyes matched the pool water with their sparkle. She wore a long gray T-shirt, but I could see the straps from her swimsuit tied behind her neck.

I might have thrived off this kind of lawless energy, but I knew Annie hated it. She'd rather be curled up on the couch watching a movie and eating popcorn, which was what we'd do later that night, I was sure. The crazy party was undoubtedly Gage's idea.

I shucked off the shorts covering my bathing suit, and with a piercing yell, I ran full speed toward the pool, leaping into the air as I reached the edge. I tucked my knees up to my chest and crashed through the surface of the water in a cannonball. I came up laughing and swam toward Annie's corner.

Hanging on the wall, I looked up at her. Her T-shirt was dappled in water droplets.

She wiped the water from my splash off her forehead, a wide smile on her face. "Olivia! You're here!"

I threw both hands in the air and shouted, "I'm here!" while treading water with my legs to stay afloat.

Gage paddled over on a giant inner tube shaped like a flamingo. "Nice entrance!" he called to me before adding a quiet, "You good?" to his sister. His hair, normally a sandy blond only slightly darker than mine, looked nearly the same shade as his sister's when wet and tousled like it was. His eyes matched hers, too—one of their only physical similarities.

Annie nodded, flashing him a thumbs-up. Unsatisfied, Gage placed both his hands on top of my head and dunked me underwater.

I spluttered to the surface, ready to tip Gage's stupid float over. But he grinned at me from his flamingo perch. "Don't splash Annie," he ordered. "She doesn't want to get wet."

I turned my head toward Annie, who waved away her brother's concern. "It's fine. I'm having fun."

Gage shrugged and paddled away.

I set my hands on the side of the pool and hauled myself up to sit on the wall next to Annie. "Are you really okay with this loud party?" I asked her.

She tilted her head. "I am. It's what Gage wanted and, to tell you the truth, no one's paying attention to me anyway, only to him." She smiled. "It works for both of us."

"Well, I'll pay attention to you," I promised. "I don't care about Gage."

Annie grinned and laid her head against my shoulder. "He's actually pretty entertaining." She lifted her head and pointed to Gage on the far side of the pool, standing on the pool deck. "Watch this. He's been obsessed with his abs for weeks, ever since his baseball coach told him he's a power hitter because of his strong core." She rolled her eyes.

I watched as Gage approached a group of girls from school. I couldn't hear what he said, but he gestured with his hands, made a fist, and pantomimed punching himself in the stomach. "What is he doing?" I asked.

Annie giggled. "He's trying to get someone to punch him in the stomach to show how strong his abs are. So far, he hasn't had any volunteers."

I laughed, still watching Gage across the pool. "I'll do it."

Annie looked at me. "Do what? Punch my brother in the stomach?"

"Sure." I shrugged. "Why not?" I was pretty strong, mostly in my legs because of soccer, so it'd have been better if I could *kick* him in the stomach, but I bet my punch could do some damage, too. Plus, he deserved it after dunking me underwater like that.

I hopped up and held out my hand to Annie. "Come on."

She grabbed my hand and let me pull her to her feet. Giggling, she followed me around the pool until we stood behind Gage, who was entertaining half a dozen other kids.

I propped a hand on my hip and tapped Gage on the shoulder. He turned around.

"Aren't you going to ask me?" I said.

His eyes darted over my shoulder to Annie and then back to me, his forehead pinched. "Ask you what?"

I smiled brightly. "To punch you in the stomach. You haven't asked me yet."

His eyes widened, but he quickly crossed his arms over his bare chest. He raised his eyebrows and smirked. "*You* want to punch me?"

I nodded my head slowly, eyes narrowed.

Sensing something about to happen, kids came from all over the yard to circle around us. The girls were giggling, while the boys nudged each other and laughed about Gage fighting a girl.

"Fine." Gage dropped his arms to his sides. "Go for it." He pulled his shoulders back and tensed up his core.

I pulled my fist back and then quickly shoved it forward into Gage's stomach. It did feel pretty solid. I had to hide my wince as I pulled my hand back. Gage, on the other hand, could not hide the shock on his face when my fist crashed into him. I smirked.

Gage doubled over, trying to catch his breath. My smirk turned into full-on laughter. I stepped back and glanced over at Annie. She laughed so hard that literal tears ran down her face. Gage finally straightened back up to his full height, his cheeks red as his friends elbowed him, laughing and teasing.

None of it fazed him, though. He shook his head and laughed with other boys. He caught my eye and grinned, highlighting a row of freckles across the tanned skin on his nose and cheeks. A flurry in my stomach caught me by surprise. My heart almost leapt out of my chest; it was beating so fast. I took a deep breath and slowly smiled back at him.

I was so distracted by my body's new reaction to my best friend's twin brother that I didn't even notice that he had crept back to my side. Next thing I knew, his arms were around my waist for a moment before my body blasted through the surface of the pool water. I came up sputtering. Again.

"Oh, you're asking for it now!" I shouted to Gage, who stood smugly on the edge of the pool, hands on his hips. Annie rammed a shoulder into his back, and Gage was soon submerged next to me. He came up grinning. He put up his arm and one of his friends tossed him a water gun, which he caught easily.

"Water fight!" Gage called gleefully.

Soon, every kid at the party had a water gun or bucket, splashing and tossing water at everyone else. Even Annie joined in. She ran to the side of the house and turned on the garden hose, aiming it at Gage and laughing.

I made my way to her through the crowd of kids and water.

"This is the best birthday ever!" she squealed in my ear above the chaos.

I grinned back at her. It was a great day, one I would always remember. It was the day I fell in love with my best friend's twin brother.

Chapter Four
Olivia

When Linda steps back into the room, she hands me a packet of papers and asks Brynn to give me a tour of camp on the golf cart. Thank the Lord she doesn't ask Gage to take me.

Why is Gage here?

I ask Brynn to give me a minute before the tour, escaping outside ahead of her. I glance around before I scurry behind the camp office building with my phone.

I call Annie, and as soon as she answers, I hiss, "Anaya Gwendolyn Carter. What did you do?"

I was blindsided, seeing Gage here at Camp Prairie Star. With no time to prepare before seeing him, hearing his voice, it was like the air was sucked out of my lungs. I'm lucky I didn't pass out.

He looks good, though. Too good with his hat on backward and those gym shorts that show off his muscular legs. Gage played baseball all through high school and college, and I always appreciated how all that conditioning honed him into the perfect eye candy. *Look but don't touch.*

Annie's words yesterday about "keeping an open mind" about anything "unexpected" that might happen this summer all of a sudden make sense.

"What do you mean?" she asks, a cautious note to her voice.

"Oh, you know exactly what I mean!" The volume of my voice rises, but I catch myself and return to a stage whisper so that no one overhears the conversation. "You're supposed to use your plotting skills for your novels, not for my life."

There's a pause on the other end of the line. "Would you believe it's a coincidence?"

I laugh wryly. "Not for a second."

"Okay, okay," she admits. "After Gage got the job at Camp Prairie Star, I suggested that you apply without telling either of you about the other."

Gage didn't seem surprised, though. Or he hid it better than I did.

"And *why*, exactly, did you do that?" I demand.

"Because you two like each other, and this nonsense of keeping me in the middle has gone on long enough."

I gasp, but try to keep my voice down. "We *do not* like each other!" I've barely seen the man in the last five years. I dart my eyes around now, as if he's lingering nearby, listening to my every word.

"See, I didn't think so either until ..." She pauses dramatically. "Exhibit A: New Orleans!"

Internally, I groan. Seeing Gage with his handsy girlfriend at the Halloween parade had gutted me. I was glad he was happy. I wanted him to be happy. Maybe just not so in my face.

"What do you mean Exhibit A? Your brother and I hardly interacted on that trip."

"Exactly! I saw the way you were watching Gage and his girlfriend at the time, whatever her name was, together before you *claimed* you had a stomachache and left the parade early. And I saw the way he looked at you."

"He didn't look at me in any kind of way," I protest. "He had a girlfriend."

"Yeah, who he broke up with the very next week after seeing you!"

That gives me pause. "Did he say something to you about me after New Orleans?"

"No! Neither of you ever talk to me about the other. Exhibit B!"

I sigh heavily. "I think all those rom-coms you read are going to your head."

"Could be," she allows, "but even if the two of you end up at least being friends again after this summer, I'm still winning."

"Annie, this is … a lot. I wish you hadn't let him catch me unaware like that. You should have warned me."

When Annie answers, her voice is curious. "Why do you need a warning before you see my brother?"

"No, well … you know, because of everything that went down at graduation," I stammer.

"Leave it in the past. I'm serious, Delaney. That was five years ago. You've both dated tons of other people since then. Surely you can try to be friends now."

Gage has dated tons of women? I shake off the discomfort of that revelation.

"Okay, I'll try," I promise, "but I'm still mad at you."

I hang up with Annie and meet Brynn back out front by the golf cart. I settle into the passenger seat and Brynn hits the gas, pointing out the sites around Camp Prairie Star. My mind wanders.

Unfortunately, I already gave up all my coaching time slots for the summer at my other job and I need the money, so leaving camp really isn't an option. But I can't be here with Gage all summer because here's the thing—Gage is exactly my idea of the perfect man. He's smart, playful, caring, handsome, athletic, protective, ambitious, and loyal. I've seen the way he takes care of his sister, how he used to take care of me, too. But I'm pretty sure I am *not* Gage's idea of the perfect woman. At least, I shouldn't be.

"So is Gage your ex?" Brynn asks as if reading my thoughts.

"No, we never dated," I mumble.

"But not for lack of trying?" She must pick up on the ... is that bitterness? ... in my voice.

"Something like that."

"Trying by who?"

"Him. Him trying. Me refusing. And pining."

That's not the whole story, but it's plenty to tell a stranger.

I could never even tell my best friend I was in love with her twin brother. No. Not love. We were in high school, for crying out loud.

It was a crush, I guess. What do you call it when you're desperate to kiss someone's face off but also really respect who they are as a person and know they're too good for you?

Yeah, pining works.

"Olivia?" Brynn cuts through my thoughts.

"It's Delaney," I correct.

"Oh. Gage called you Olivia."

"Yeah, he does that," I mutter.

When I started high school, I decided to start going by my last name—Delaney. It was an easy enough transition for the most part. The only kids I knew well in our freshman class were Annie and Gage. I asked Annie to start calling me Delaney and she did, no questions asked. She slipped a time or two—breaking habits is hard—but she would quickly correct herself.

When I asked Gage to start calling me Delaney, he gave me a look of disgust and asked why. As I tried to come up with a lie that would satisfy him, he wouldn't break eye contact. I swear it was like he was staring into my soul and seeing all my secrets, all my insecurities. When I finally stuttered out some sort of half reason, he nodded his head.

"See you around, Olivia," he said. He's stubbornly refused to call me Delaney ever since.

Again, Brynn's voice reminds me that I'm not alone. "Well, Gage is super hot. Are you going to try to get with him this summer?"

"Get with him?" I echo.

"Yeah. Do you have dibs? Or would it be cool if I gave it a shot?"

No! I want to shout. *I have all the dibs on Gage Carter.* But that wouldn't be fair.

I turn my head to the right, away from Brynn, and stare at the trees in the distance. "Go for it," I say flatly into the wind.

Chapter Five

Gage

Five Years Ago

The last month of senior year of high school was really one party after another. We had some last-minute schoolwork thrown in there, but mostly we were celebrating.

Senior prom was three weeks before graduation and felt a lot like a last hurrah with my friends before we all went our separate ways for work or college. Annie and I would be separated, too, for the first time in our lives, because we were going to different colleges. Not until the fall, but still. These were the last few weeks of being in school with my sister.

I got a baseball scholarship locally here at UT Austin, and Annie would be moving three hours east for school. At least Annie got to stay with Olivia, who accepted a spot playing Division I soccer at the same school.

But that meant I wouldn't be seeing Olivia every day anymore either. As much as I hated the idea of being separated from my twin, my heart literally ached when I thought about being away from Olivia. Not seeing her smile or her electric green eyes. Not hanging out with her after school or cheering her on at her soccer games.

I really hated being apart from the people I loved, and as stupid as it sounded, I knew I was in love with Olivia. My feelings developed slowly, almost without me noticing. Through middle school and starting high school, she was my sister's best friend, one of my best friends. I always knew she was cool and funny, and pretty, once I started paying attention to that sort of thing.

In tenth grade, I was dating a girl named Chelsea. She was nice. Cute. We got along well. A month into the relationship, I realized that I spent way more time thinking about Olivia than I did about Chelsea. I broke things off, knowing it wasn't fair to her.

But I didn't make a move on Olivia. I mean, it was *Olivia*. What if she didn't feel the same way? What if I admitted my feelings and it made hanging out awkward? What if Olivia and I dated, and it turned Annie into a third wheel and made her feel left out?

So, I kept my feelings to myself. I didn't even tell Annie. I watched for any sign that Olivia might consider me as more than a friend, too.

And now we were going to senior prom together. Well, sort of.

Annie, Olivia, and I were all going together. The Three Muske-teers. The Three Amigos. The *Three's Company* roommates. Luke, Leia, and Han from *Star Wars*. Hey, that one was actually a pretty good fit. Boy-girl twins and a love interest, except that would make *me* Leia, Annie Luke, and Olivia Han.

Anyway. The truth was that I'd rather go to prom with Olivia as "friends" than go with anybody else as a real date.

I had no idea how she ended up dateless, though. Every guy in school would have killed to take her to prom. Their loss was my gain.

The girls didn't want a fuss, so the plan was for Olivia to meet us at our house to get ready with Annie, and then we'd drive over together in my Jeep.

I was ready way before the girls, so I put the Texas Rangers game on the TV in the living room while I waited for them.

Annie came downstairs first, in a pretty black dress with a halter top neckline and lace accents around the waist. Her brown hair was down but pulled back at the top, with loose curls that fell around her shoulders.

I stood up. "Nini, you look great," I told her, using the nickname I'd had for her since we were learning to talk, and I couldn't quite say Anaya, or even Annie.

At the bottom of the stairs, she twirled, giggling as she showed off her outfit. Our mom came out from the other room with her phone.

"You both look so good!" she gushed. "Let's get a few pictures. Is Delaney coming down?"

Annie nodded. "She's almost ready. She's finishing her makeup."

"Okay, I'll get the two of you first then." She lined us up in front of the fireplace mantel in the living room. Our mom had been taking photos of us our whole lives; we knew the drill by now. We smiled as she took at least ten identical shots.

Distracted by movement in my periphery, I looked away as she was taking at least her twentieth picture. Olivia descended the stairs, an absolute vision.

I thought I was going to pass out—forgetting how to breathe, I got lightheaded, my eyes fixed on Olivia. Finally, I felt a jab in the side, courtesy of my sister, and I took a breath and closed my mouth.

I want to be clear: Olivia always looked beautiful. Wearing her soccer kit or dressed up for church, in jeans and a T-shirt or in sweats. But this ... this was something else entirely.

Her dress was jade green with a deep V-neck and spaghetti straps. The material was something flowy and kind of gauzy, with a criss-cross pattern across her midsection where the skin of her stomach showed under several layers of sheer fabric. The skirt was long, reaching all the way to the floor, but with a slit on one side where almost her entire leg—long and muscular—peeked out as she walked.

Her hair was down, flowing past her shoulders, but with some of it up in the back in complicated-looking mini braids that formed sort of a crown. She wore more makeup than usual, and I wasn't sure if it was the makeup or the dress, but her eyes were electric—a deep green that sparkled like emeralds.

I couldn't look away.

It was an outfit designed to grab and hold the attention of everyone around her. Well, she certainly had mine. Then again, Olivia always held my attention, whether she knew it or not.

Olivia reached the bottom of the stairs, and both Annie and my mom immediately started fussing over her.

"You look so beautiful!"

"Come on over here, now, Delaney. I promised your mom I'd take some pictures for her."

Laughing, Olivia looked up and met my gaze. Her smile softened as I watched her scan me from head to toe and back up again. Her cheeks were flushed when she focused back on my face.

Olivia allowed my mom to pull her over to where I was still standing by the fireplace. Mom lined all three of us up, nudging Olivia closer to me on one side, while arranging Annie on my other.

While my mom was fiddling with Annie's hair, I leaned close to Olivia's ear. "You look amazing," I whispered.

She tilted her face toward me, pursing her dark red lips. I wanted to kiss the gloss right off them.

"So do you," she murmured.

Our eyes locked. She had never looked at me like that before—a mixture of awe, happiness, and desire. It was hypnotic.

"Okay, smile!" my mom called, breaking the spell.

After a few more pictures, we left for the dance. Inside the hotel ballroom, the space was crowded with our classmates and chaperones. The music pulsed, the beat syncing up with the pounding of my heart.

If Olivia feels something more than friendship for me, I could find out tonight, I thought.

We found a table to be our home base for the night, and Annie sat down. She wasn't big on dancing, or really anything that might draw attention to her.

Olivia tugged on Annie's hands. "Come dance with me. Please?"

Annie shook her head.

"I'll dance with you," I found myself volunteering.

Annie smiled. "Ooh, good idea. You both love to dance. Go ahead. I'm going to check out the food."

I held out my hand to Olivia. She looked at it, biting her lip as if she wasn't sure she should take it.

I wiggled my fingers. "Come on, Olivia. It's not a snake."

My teasing comment must have put her at ease because she smirked and put her hand in mine. It was warm and soft, and I immediately intertwined our fingers as we walked to the dance floor.

With ideal timing, the fast dance song that was playing came to an end, and the DJ switched to something slower paced.

I dropped her hand, and we faced each other, laughing awkwardly. I raised my eyebrows. "Shall we?"

Olivia smiled, slipping her arms around my neck. I set my hands on either side of her waist, above her hips. The warmth of her skin seeped into my fingers, even through the fabric of her dress.

Before I could stop it, a contented sigh escaped my lips. Holding her, having her this close, felt so right.

"Why didn't you have a date tonight?" I asked suddenly.

She ducked her head and glanced away. "I don't know."

"I bet you had at least a dozen guys lined up to ask you. Why did you tell them no?"

She didn't answer, just kept staring across the dance floor, leaning in so that her cheek rested against my chest.

I dipped my head so that my mouth was right next to her ear. "Olivia," I said huskily.

She turned her head, tilting her chin up to meet my eyes. Her gorgeous green eyes that were so familiar to me harbored a timidness I'd never seen on her before.

"I didn't want to go with any of *them*."

My ears heard the words, my brain decoded them, and still, I couldn't believe the implication. *Did she … did she want to go with me?*

My slack-jawed reaction seemed to give her confidence. She moved her fingers up my neck and played with the hair at my nape. Instantly, my whole body reacted. I felt every point of contact between our bodies and craved more. I shifted my hands off her waist and around to her back, pulling her even closer. She fit perfectly against me.

"What about you?" she asked softly.

"Hmm?" I answered, like an idiot. With the feel of her fingers in my hair and her body against mine, my brain was mush.

"I never see you dating."

I forced myself to focus on her words. "I date some."

"Do you?" She smirked at me.

I shrugged, holding eye contact. "I guess I was waiting for the right girl," I said meaningfully.

Her cheeks turned an irresistible shade of pink. She tilted her head. "Why did you have to wait?"

"I didn't think she felt the same way." I was sure she could feel my heart pounding.

"But now you do think so?"

I brushed back a strand of hair that had fallen across her forehead. I let my hand linger, running my fingertips lightly across her cheek. She shivered.

"Yeah," I finally answered. "I do." For the first time, I felt confident that even if Olivia's feelings weren't as deep as mine at this point, she was feeling something more than friendship for me. It was a starting point.

I smiled down at her as the song ended and a high-energy dance song started playing. Instead of letting her go right away, I pushed her out and spun her, finishing in a dip. She was laughing when I set her on her feet again, and I reluctantly let her leave my arms.

But she stayed close, and we danced together through the fast songs, laughing and shouting to hear each other over the music.

After a few songs, I felt guilty leaving Annie alone for so long, so I told Olivia I was going to sit down for a while.

"I'll come too. I could use a break."

We found Annie where we left her, but she wasn't alone. She was talking to some guy. I couldn't see his face.

I was about to join them when Olivia grabbed my arm.

"No, leave her. That's Carlos. She wouldn't want us to interrupt."

I whipped my head toward Olivia. "Who the heck is Carlos?"

Olivia laughed. "A guy she's interested in. He's in art class with her." She pulled my arm back toward the dance floor. "Let them talk."

I allowed Olivia to tug me away, but I kept glancing back to check on my sister. She was laughing, and the guy—Carlos apparently—was smiling at her. Seemed innocent enough.

Olivia wrapped her hand around my chin and moved my head, so I faced her again. Without letting go, she said, "Hey, she's fine. I promise. He's a nice guy." She smirked. "Focus on me."

She didn't have to tell me twice.

I floated through the rest of the weekend. Olivia definitely gave the impression that she wouldn't hate the idea of pursuing something more than friendship with me.

The only question remaining was how Annie would feel about the whole thing.

I put off asking her through the weekend and most of the school week. In the meantime, I tried to play it cool with Olivia, but after how closely I held her at prom, it was like I couldn't stay away.

I finally cornered my sister in the kitchen Friday after school as she poured herself a bowl of cereal.

"What would you think of me asking out Olivia?"

Annie scrunched up her face as she considered. "It would be kind of weird at first, but I like the idea of you two together."

That settled it. I was going to tell Olivia how I felt, hopefully kiss her, and ask her to be my girlfriend.

Chapter Six

Gage

After I carry the boxes to the mess hall for Linda, I slide my phone out of my pocket and text Annie.

Gage:
She's here

Nini:
Just got off the phone with her

Gage:
She was mad?

Nini:
You could say that

Gage:
I don't know what you were thinking

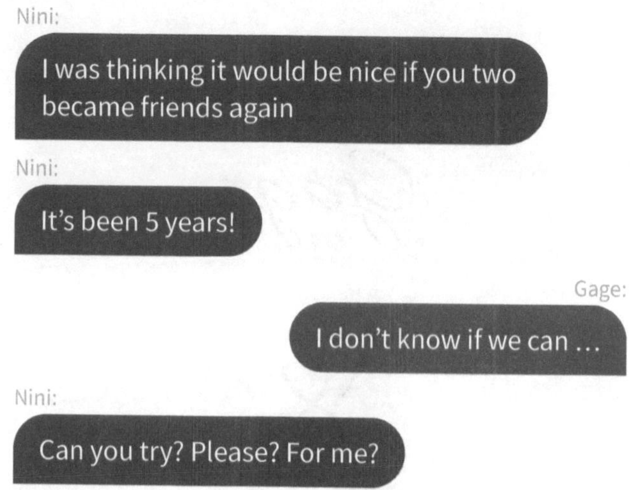

I sigh to myself. Annie doesn't ask for much, and I could never deny her anyway.

I sigh again and take off my hat to run my hand through my hair. *But how? How can I be friends with Olivia?*

Before long, the other counselors start trickling in for the first orientation session of the day. Camp Prairie Star hosts around one hundred campers a week, divided into twelve cabins—six cabins of about eight girls each and six cabins of about eight boys each. The kids are all between the ages of eight and fourteen.

In addition to the twelve counselors—one for each cabin—the staff includes the activities director, nurse, cooking staff, lifeguard, craft counselor, nature counselor, assistant director, and of course, Linda, the camp director. The nurse and cooking staff are exempt from the whole orientation rigmarole, so there are about sixteen of us seated around the mess hall waiting for Linda to start the session.

Olivia sits as far away from me as possible, which is fine with me. Still, no matter how hard I try to pay attention to what Linda is saying about ... homesickness? conflict resolution? ... my eyes keep wandering to Olivia.

She catches me staring more than once. The first time, she quickly looks away. The second time, she lifts her eyebrows and points toward the front of the room where Linda is standing. The third time, she glares at me.

By lunch, I determine that it would have been easier if I'd promised Annie to be creepy rather than friendly. I've got creepy on lock.

I shuffle through the food line, picking up a turkey sandwich wrapped in plastic, two apples, and a bag of crunchy Cheetos and placing them on my tray.

I find an empty table. I'm usually Mr. Sociability, but I'm not in the mood today. Even though I was expecting her, seeing Olivia this morning was a shock to my system. I've been drawn to her all day like a mosquito to a bug zapper. It's the same way she used to capture and dominate my attention back in high school. Was she ever drawn to me the same way? Is she now?

A tray plunks onto the table next to me. I look up to see Olivia settling onto the bench.

"Hi," she says.

"Uh, hi?" Her arm brushes mine as she gets situated, and the goosebumps are immediate.

"Annie made me promise to try being friends with you this summer," she explains.

I shake my head at my sister's plotting. "She made me promise, too," I admit.

Olivia raises her eyebrows. "And I made the first move? Excellent. Let's be sure she knows that."

I hold back a smile. Everything's a competition with Olivia, although I could say the same for myself. Rather than engaging, I change the subject. "How was your sister's wedding?"

She tilts her head as she considers. "Beautiful. Odd. A little drunk, but that was just me."

I chuckle. "Odd how?"

"Well, they're both librarians, you know? So, they had the wedding ceremony in this beautiful courtyard on the college campus where they work, and then they had the reception in the library itself. Where they work. They timed the wedding so that it fell during the semester break. It was a beautiful library, but still. A library." She shakes her head.

"Sounds like it suited them perfectly."

"Oh, it did. Nicole was very happy. It was nice to see." Olivia's expression goes soft, her eyes misting.

Nicole has chronic depression, and I remember Annie telling me that Olivia's sister had a major depressive episode while we were in college. Olivia has always worshipped her older sisters, so I can imagine Nicole's struggle was hard for Olivia.

She clears her throat. "Anyway. What are you doing working here this summer? I figured you'd be climbing the corporate ladder at some important job or another postcollege."

"Actually, I've been working in my dad's office since graduation, saving up money. In the fall, I start a graduate program in occupational therapy. A doctorate. I want to be a pediatric OT."

Warmth wells in my chest as I think about my plans. There's no doubt in my mind that it's the best path for me.

Olivia sets her sandwich on her plate and wipes a napkin across her mouth. "Annie didn't tell me that." She watches me with a mix of curiosity and ... could be awe, but I'm probably projecting.

I shrug. "She doesn't tell me a lot about you either."

"There's honestly not much to tell." She snorts and picks up her sandwich again.

"Didn't you lead your soccer team to the D1 championship senior year?" Now I set *my* sandwich down to study *her*.

She waves her hand in the air as if swatting away my words. "Yeah, but that feels like ages ago. I haven't done much since. Nothing worth mentioning."

This self-deprecation is new. I mean, we all had our self-esteem issues in high school, but I remember Olivia as being confident and untouchable.

"The D1 championship is pretty impressive. I think you can afford to rest on your laurels a while. Being a student athlete at a D1 school is no easy task. I should know."

I played baseball all through college at UT Austin. We were good, but never good enough to make the College World Series, or even the tournament some years. I never really considered going pro—I knew it wasn't the lifestyle I wanted—but my college performance clinched it. I peaked in high school. I still had a lot of fun playing college ball, though, and formed great friendships with my teammates.

"Thanks," Olivia murmurs.

School has never been Olivia's favorite. She has dyslexia and has always had to work harder than everyone else to score average grades. If she wasn't so smart, she would have struggled even more. I don't think she even really wanted to go to college, except that it gave her the chance to keep playing soccer.

We keep talking as we finish lunch and walk together to the next orientation class. The conversation somehow turns to professional soccer and Olivia's favorite team, Chicago.

I scoff. "Bella's overrated," I say, referencing one of Chicago's best players.

She gasps, eyes widening. "You shut your filthy mouth!"

I shake my head, grinning.

"Marco Bella is a *god*. He's a lockdown defender who always wins 1v1 situations. The Chicago front office would be idiotic not to re-sign him with a huge raise before his developmental contract runs out." She pauses. "Plus, mmm, the quads on that man!" She fans her face with her hand.

A bolt of jealousy shoots through me, which is insane because first of all, *my* quads happen to be pretty nice, too. I mean, I could definitely go harder on leg day, but the definition is good. Second, because what do I care what Olivia Delaney thinks of Marco Bella's quads or my quads or anybody else's quads for that matter? I *don't* care. Haven't for a long time.

I exaggerate a gag. "I think you might have forgotten that you're talking to me, Gage, and not my twin sister, Annie." She rolls her eyes. "And anyway," I continue, "do you want to play him or date him?"

She stares over my shoulder with glazed eyes.

"Olivia!" I snap my fingers in front of her face.

Blinking, she turns her eyes back to me. She tosses her ponytail and smirks. "Either. Both."

I clench my teeth. That bolt of jealousy is back. I think I officially hate a professional soccer player I've never met.

Chapter Seven

Olivia

Five Years Ago

I had never before hoped the way I started hoping after prom. Could Gage really have feelings for me? I'd silently pined, masking my true feelings for so long that it felt reckless to act on them now.

But I saw the way he looked at me when I came down the stairs at his house before the dance. I felt how he held me while we swayed to the music. I heard us both tiptoe and hint around what we really wanted to say.

I wanted to say "I like you." I more than *liked* Gage. I felt like I'd loved him for years, but I didn't want to come on too strong and scare him away.

"I was waiting for the right girl."

Was that me? Did he want to tell me he liked me, too? Then why didn't he?

Now, a week after prom, Gage acted the same as ever toward me in front of Annie. But when we were in class together or Annie stepped out of the room, Gage found ways to touch me and be close to me. Innocent things like putting his hand on my lower back to guide me through the hall or brushing a strand of hair out of my face.

And he watched me with those soulful, gorgeous blue eyes of his, like he was begging me to understand what he wanted to say without him actually saying it. I *thought* I was interpreting his signals correctly, but how could I be sure?

He had me so frustrated. I didn't know whether I wanted to kiss him or punch him.

On Saturday, two weeks before graduation, I was sitting in bed scrolling social media and watching stupid videos—mostly of monkeys reacting to humans showing them magic tricks—when my sister Nicole knocked on my open door.

Our family celebrated Nicole's college graduation the previous week. She lived at home while going to college locally and planned to start a master's degree program in the fall at the same university. Her hair, which I was pretty sure had been every color of the rainbow by this point, was dyed a navy-blue color.

"Hey," I greeted her.

"Hey, Gage is downstairs looking for you."

I sat up. "Gage is here? Right now?"

She chuckled. "Yeah. He's in the living room talking to Steven."

Ugh. Steven was Nicole's loser boyfriend. I really didn't understand what she saw in him.

But ... why was Gage here? He didn't text to say he was coming over.

I looked down at my outfit. I was in running shorts and an oversized T-shirt. My hair, which I needed to wash, was pulled up and wrapped in an athletic headband. I washed my face that morning but wasn't wearing any makeup.

True, Gage had seen me like this plenty of times before, but it felt different now. If he was going to look at me as a potential girlfriend—which I hoped he was—I felt like I needed to make sure my appearance wasn't a strike against me.

"Uh, tell him I'll be down in a minute."

Nicole, correctly interpreting my hesitation, smiled softly. "You look great, Liv. You always do. If he doesn't think so, he's an idiot."

I appreciated my sister's words, even agreed with them, but still ... "I'll just be a second."

I kept the running shorts but switched out the oversized T-shirt for something more fitted. I took out my headband and ponytail and sprayed my hair with dry shampoo, brushing until it shined.

I didn't want to look like I was trying too hard, so for my face, I applied a layer of tinted moisturizer.

I stopped to wash my hands in the bathroom, then scurried down the stairs to the living room.

Gage stood up from the couch when he saw me. "Hey!" he said, smiling nervously. I was relieved to see him dressed casually in athletic shorts and a T-shirt.

I tucked a strand of hair behind my ear. "Hey."

"Sorry to show up without texting first, but I was wondering if you're up for a drive?"

"Sure."

When we got out to the driveway, he opened the front passenger-side door of his Jeep for me, but that was nothing new. He always tried to open doors for both me and Annie when we went places together.

As we got settled, Gage jerked a thumb toward the house. "Who was the tool?"

I groaned. "Nicole's boyfriend, Steven."

His mouth twisted into a grimace. "Huh. She could do better."

"Agreed."

Gage stuck his elbow out the open window as he steered us down the street. He cleared his throat. "Uh, anyway, I was wondering if you wanted to go out tonight."

The corners of my mouth ticked up reflexively. "Like a date?"

Gage turned to me, smirking. "Yeah, a date."

"Just me and you?" I teased.

Gage pulled to the side of the road near a park with a playground and walking trails. Shifting the Jeep into park, he turned in his seat to face me. His eyes were intense, the normally light blue a deeper shade than I'd ever noticed in them before.

"Yeah. Just me and you." The meaning he injected into those words sent shivers down my back.

I smiled widely. "I would love to."

The afternoon of graduation, my family dropped me off on the "visitor" side of Burger Stadium before parking and finding their seats. Burger Stadium was part of a centralized athletic center in south Austin. Because the schools in Austin didn't each have their own football fields or basketball arenas, the sports teams from multiple high schools shared several large complexes. Burger was the largest, and also where I played my home soccer games throughout high school. It felt fitting to have my graduation ceremony on the same field I had spent so much of my time these last four years.

I entered the building and checked in, holding my graduation cap in my hand with my gown unzipped over my yellow ruffle dress. The PTA volunteers at the desk directed me to find my spot in the alphabetical line. I looked for Gage and Annie because the Cs wouldn't be too far from the Ds.

I spotted Gage first, standing a head taller than most everyone around him. I skipped toward him, nervous for the day and excited to see him.

Over the last couple of weeks, Gage took me on two official dates. Fun ones, too. We went go-karting on our first date, followed by burgers and ice cream.

Then the following week, we kayaked to the Congress Avenue Bridge downtown at dusk and watched the bats that lived there emerge and fly away. He even packed us a picnic with all my favorite foods. When we finished eating, we rested back on the picnic blanket to see the stars. He held my hand, and we kissed—a sweet, gentle promise of a first kiss.

We hadn't yet defined what we were doing, and I'd been holding back on talking to Annie because I didn't know what she'd think of all this. But I was giddy at the direction my relationship with Gage had taken.

When Gage saw me approaching them at Burger Stadium, his face lit up with a wide smile. He held eye contact as I moved toward him.

But Annie got to me first, tackling me in an animated hug. "Can you believe it! Graduation!" she squealed.

"I know!" I squeezed her back and grinned. "I thought this day would never come."

"I looked at the list, and I think there are only, like, ten people between us in the line. If we're lucky it could work out so that I'm sitting in the row ahead of you on the field."

"Ooh, perfect." Gage approached us and I smirked. "As long as this guy isn't sitting in front of me blocking my view with his big head."

Gage didn't laugh or even acknowledge my teasing. He slid his hand around my wrist. "I need to talk to you," he said, tugging me away from Annie and the rest of our class.

I shot a puzzled look at Annie, but she only shrugged and smiled as Gage dragged me away.

He pulled me into an alcove and kissed me, his movements confident and determined. When we broke apart, I was breathless.

"You're going to get us in trouble," I teased.

He shrugged. "What are they going to do at this point? Not let us graduate? Besides, I need to ask you something important."

"Okay." I analyzed his expression, the same determination from our kiss evident in the set of his jaw and glint in his eye.

I'd been waiting for him to make us official, for him to ask me to be his girlfriend. Maybe this was finally it!

Before he could continue, I felt something loosen around my ankle and peered down at my feet. I was wearing brand new leather lace-up sandals, and one of the straps had come loose.

"Oh, hold on a second," I told Gage and then bent down to tie my shoes again.

"Everything okay?" he asked.

I frowned up at him. "No. I thought they needed to be retied, but the strap broke." I stood up. "Let me run to the restroom real quick to fix them. Then we'll talk, okay?"

He wet his lips. "Sure. Hurry back, okay? I really want to talk to you before the ceremony starts."

I reached up and patted his cheek before giving him a peck on the lips. "We've got time. I'll be right back."

I shuffled to the ladies' room to keep my sandal from falling off. The bathroom in this part of the stadium was actually a locker room, so I found a bench to sit on while I relaced the sandal straps, so they'd tie properly again.

Behind me, near the toilet stalls, an incredulous voice rang out clear as a bell. "Are they really a thing? Gage and Delaney?"

I froze. Whoever was talking obviously didn't know I was here. I should say something to alert them of my presence, but I had a morbid desire to hear what they were going to say.

A toilet flushed as another girl laughed. "I know, right?" That sounded like Kristin Shell, one of the girls I usually ate lunch and socialized with at school. One of my "friends."

Kristin continued, "Gage is in, like, the top five of our class, and Delaney is lucky to even be graduating."

The other girl giggled, and the sound of running water echoed through the room. "I heard she had to go to summer school last year to repeat Spanish or else she would have failed out." I recognized the voice now as belonging to Jasmine Miles, another of my school "friends."

That was not even true! I did need a tutor to get through the two credits of foreign language required to graduate, but I was never really in danger of failing. I worked hard to make sure I didn't. I picked up speaking in Spanish quickly enough using an app that focused on audio lessons, but I also needed to learn to write in Spanish, which felt even more confusing than writing in English. *I passed both credits with a C, thank you very much.*

"Yeah and Gage makes, like, straight As. He's so smart."

Gage *was* smart. It was one of the things I loved most about him. He didn't know yet what kind of career he wanted, but I was sure it would be something where he used his brain to help other people.

"Maybe he's looking for a trophy wife!" They both burst into laughter. "I'd volunteer. I'm as pretty as Delaney but at least twice as smart."

I pressed my fingers to my cheeks to cool them down. My nose stung as I tried my best to hold back the tears.

If Kristin and Jasmine recognized the imbalance between Gage and me, would other people see it, too? If Gage was my boyfriend, would everyone always look at us and wonder what he saw in me? Wonder what we could possibly have in common?

I was so used to hanging out with people smarter than me—my sisters, Annie, and of course Gage—that I never stopped to consider what it might be like for Gage to be with someone as dumb as me. Would I be a liability? Hold him back?

I never wanted to do that.

The water stopped, and the hand dryer kicked on, drowning out any further conversation. They would probably be coming this way soon to go back outside to their spots in line. I jumped up and ducked behind a row of lockers. The only thing more embarrassing than overhearing that conversation would be Kristin and Jasmine knowing I overheard that conversation.

I peeked around the corner as they walked past and pushed open the door, still laughing, probably at my expense.

I straightened and bumped the back of my head softly against the side of the locker, closing my eyes.

The idea of Gage being happy with me … it was ridiculous, wasn't it? He needed an equal partner, not an obligation.

I blinked back the tears that were still trying to fall. When I cried, my eyes turned red, and there was no way to hide that I was upset. I didn't want that to happen. Gage would notice in a second. I fanned my hand in front of my eyes to dry them out.

I walked back around the corner and checked my reflection in a mirror. My eyes looked a little glassy, but not so much that it would raise any red flags. I took a deep breath and went back outside.

Gage waited outside the door, leaning against the wall with one foot propped behind him. The blue graduation gown made the color of his eyes pop. His sandy blond hair was slicked to the side, the ends curling around his ears and along the back of his neck.

He looked so good. He *was* so good. Kristin and Jasmine were right. He deserved to be with someone who could match his energy and his intelligence.

When he saw me, Gage grinned. "There you are. Did you get your shoe fixed?"

I swallowed. "Uh, yeah. Sorry. It took me a minute." I turned toward the line of graduates. "We better get back to our spots in line."

Gage captured my hand and pulled me to a stop. "Wait. I still need to talk to you."

"But they're going to walk us onto the field soon," I protested desperately.

He cocked his head. "I think we still have a minute." He paused to clear his throat and reached up to rub the back of his neck. "I ... I feel like I've been in a dream since prom, because that's the only place I ever thought I'd get to hold your hand and kiss you. The only place I ever thought you'd feel the same way I do."

Oh ... oh, no. My chest tightened as I realized where he was going with this.

"I regret that it's taken me this long to get here," he continued, grinning quickly, "and I regret that this is happening in front of the bathrooms, but not as much as I know I'd regret not seizing the moment now." He took a deep breath. "Olivia Delaney, will you be my girlfriend?"

It was everything I wanted to hear and a nightmare at the same time. I squeezed my eyes shut until spots blurred together in my field of vision. I suddenly felt all ninety-two degrees of the Texas summer heat standing there in the open-air hallway with a heavy polyester gown over my breezy dress. I needed to say something.

I opened my eyes and focused on the space over Gage's head, ready to give him any reason but the truth. "I don't think ... it's probably not a good idea. Annie might feel weird about it—"

Gage's eyebrows pulled together in confusion. "But I already talked to—"

"And we're going to different schools in the fall—"

The pressure of his hand over mine increased. "But they're not that far—"

I grasped at one more plausible excuse. "And long distance is so hard especially when we're meeting all sorts of new people. It's better if we stay friends."

He opened his mouth, then closed it again. His throat bobbed as he swallowed. "Uh, I don't understand. Olivia—"

I wriggled my hand out of his and stepped back. "So, friends, okay?"

Gage studied me, his gaze so intense that I turned my head to escape its heat.

"It'll be better this way," I said quietly.

"Okay," he finally said, his eyes clouding over. "If that's what you really want."

I nodded. "It is."

I was lying. I was a lying liar who lied.

"I better go find Annie. Get back to the line." He shook his head and turned away. He took a few steps and then called back over his shoulder, "Congratulations, Olivia," in a toneless voice.

"You, too," I whispered to his retreating form.

Good. Friends. That's how I needed it to be. But how could I go back to being friends with Gage now that I knew how his lips felt?

Chapter Eight

Olivia

The next orientation session is held in what looks to be the arts and crafts cabin. Judging by the creepy manikin torsos lying on the tables, we're going to review CPR. The camp requires staff to get certifications in CPR and first aid before starting work, but I guess they want it to be fresh in our minds.

The instructor, a serious-looking woman in khaki pants and a collared red shirt, hurries Gage and me through the door.

I look around the room and see that everyone else is already here. I glance at my watch. We're right on time.

"Since you two are the last to arrive, you'll need to work together at this table here." The instructor points at the table closest to the front of the room—and closest to her.

Gage and I exchange a look heavy with reluctance and hesitation. We chatted fine through lunch, mostly avoiding awkwardness, but can we continue the streak through partnering up for this activity? Doubtful.

The instructor, whose name badge says "Janet," claps her hands loudly. "Let's go!"

I lunge for our assigned table, Gage close behind me.

Once there, Janet hands me a sheet of paper, which I reflexively take from her. "Please read that to the class," she instructs.

Instantly, my heart pounds as my brain simultaneously short-circuits until my thoughts and movements are sluggish. I stare at the words typed on the paper, but they're blurring in and out, like my eyes are focusing and then defocusing. I try to read the first couple of lines, but the words jumble as my brain stutters through them.

All of a sudden, I'm back in fourth grade, in ninth grade, in kids' Sunday school at church, when the teacher goes around the room having each student take a turn reading part of the text out loud. I'd count how many classmates were ahead of me to see which paragraph would be mine, and then read it to myself over and over, looking for any words that might trip me up, until it was my turn.

I open my mouth to speak, but my throat is dry, and my tongue is like sandpaper. Even if I could talk, I'm not sure what I would say.

"I'll read it." Gage jumps forward, prying the paper out of my clenched fingers.

I sink back and lean against the wall as he reels off some stats about drowning, choking, and asthma attacks among children in Texas. I take a deep breath, and my head clears. Eventually my heart rate gets back to normal.

Being asked to read on the spot out loud to a room full of strangers is a top three nightmare scenario for me, right behind missing a critical goal in an important game and, well, unexpectedly coming face-to-face with Gage Carter. *Today is really not my day.* Good thing I'm not playing soccer later.

Gage finishes reading and passes the paper back to the instructor. She reminds the class of the basic steps of CPR, and with the attention off us, I catch Gage's eye and mouth "Thank you." He tilts his head in acknowledgment.

Before long, Janet directs us to practice CPR on the manikins. She starts her observations on the other end of the classroom, walking slowly from table to table and jumping in with corrections as needed.

I gesture to the dummy. "You want to go first?"

Gage eyes the bald head and half torso on the table in front of us. "Shouldn't we give him a name and backstory first? I mean, what's my motivation here?" He grins.

"I don't think that's necessary." After my mini freak-out over reading the paper, I don't want to give anyone more reason to think I'm not smart or serious enough to be here.

"Let's see. How about Stan da Manikin?" He snaps his fingers. "No, I know! Manikin Skywalker."

I bite back a smile. "He definitely has the body for it, but I'm not sure we're certified to treat lava burns."

Gage snorts. "Come on, Olivia. If ever any of the kids gets the high ground over another, we need to know how to handle it."

I shake my head, but I can't keep a wide smile from taking over my face. Same old Gage. Too much charisma for his own good.

"I've always loved your smile," Gage lets slip.

My smile drops, and I whip my head around to look at him. His pale-blue eyes widen as if he didn't mean to admit that. He looks entirely too serious and entirely too delicious, with messy strands of his sandy blond hair sticking out from under his backward baseball cap, to be saying things like that.

"Gage," I warn.

He shrugs, then turns his attention back to Manikin Skywalker. "Sorry," he murmurs.

"Let's focus on reviewing CPR."

Janet bustles over to us at that moment. "How's it going over here?" she asks.

Oh, you know, awkward, painful, bewildering. "Fine," I answer.

We stay on task the rest of the class, hesitantly working around each other while avoiding unnecessary conversation or touching.

💗 💗 💗

When the session is over, we have a break before dinner, so I duck out of the room before Gage can try to make more awkward conversation.

I walk to the main office and drive my car to the cabin that will be my home for the next three months. I open the trunk of the car and lug my duffel bag and rolling suitcase up the stairs of the front stoop and through the screen door. I dump my bags in the entryway and look around.

I'm not a cabin counselor, so rather than staying with a group of kids, my small cabin houses me and one other staff member. Each side of the cabin has a bunk bed and a small dresser. There's no closet, but when I open the door on the back wall, I find a bathroom with a toilet, a pedestal sink, and a tiny shower stall hidden behind a dull green plastic curtain.

I haven't met my roommate yet, but her side of the cabin tells me a little about her personality. A gorgeous blue-and-yellow quilt adorns the bottom bed of the bunk, with the top acting as a storage unit crammed with two large purple suitcases and a set of blank, shrink-wrapped painting canvases. On top of the dresser is an assortment of colorful paint containers, a mason jar with a dozen or so wooden paintbrush handles sticking out of it, and a sparkly pink shower caddy filled with bottles.

I move my luggage to my side of the cabin and start unpacking. The screen door creaks open and slams shut. I look up to see a Black woman with mahogany skin, light brown eyes, and dark hair slicked back into a ponytail. Her bright orange patterned tunic is tucked into cut-off denim shorts. I remember seeing this woman in the orientation classes today, usually partnered up with a slim guy with dark brown hair and board shorts.

"Hi!" I greet her brightly.

"Hey! You must be Delaney. I'm Nina." She eyes me, as if sizing me up.

I take a step toward her and extend my hand. "Yeah. Nice to meet you, Nina."

"Sorry I didn't introduce myself earlier today during the orientation sessions." Nina raises her eyebrows. "It looked like you already made a friend, and I didn't want to interrupt."

My cheeks heat. "Oh, no. That's just Gage. We know each other from back home."

She crosses her arms. "That's what Brynn said."

I shift my gaze behind her searching for a subject change. I gesture to the art supplies. "Are you an artist?"

Her face brightens. "Yes! During the school year, I'm an elementary school art teacher in San Antonio with an Etsy shop on the side. I'm the craft counselor here. My second summer. It's such a fun summer job."

"Oh, cool. It's my first time here, or any camp that's not centered around soccer." I shrug.

Nina chuckles. "Fair warning, my boyfriend works here, too, so you won't see me around much on weekends. They won't let us share a cabin because we're not married, even though we live together at home." She rolls her eyes. "Rocky's the camp lifeguard. He's bunking with Jake, the nature counselor."

Between arriving late at camp and being a little preoccupied that Gage is here, I haven't been great about introducing myself to my coworkers today. I met Brynn, of course, and now Nina, but I barely noticed the other staff members in the orientation sessions today. "I guess I missed all the introductions yesterday, huh?"

She waves away my concern. "You'll meet everyone tonight. After dinner, Linda has an ice-breaker activity planned." Nina walks toward the bathroom as she continues talking to me over her shoulder. "You should move your car, though, if you're all unloaded. If you keep following this dirt road past the lake, you'll find the staff parking lot near Linda's cottage."

"Thanks." I wave to Nina and grab my keys. I'm not sure what to think about my roommate. She seems nice but also like she's not really looking to be friends. I'm sure we'll get along in the cabin, but I probably need to look elsewhere to find a buddy for the summer. That will be my focus tonight at dinner and at the activity afterward. I'll put Gage out of my mind and make friends. Fun, cool Delaney has always been good at that.

Chapter Nine

Gage

At dinner, Olivia's back to sitting as far away from me as possible. I didn't mean to make things weird by complimenting her smile during the CPR training. It slipped out. To be fair, I have a hard time concentrating when Olivia smiles at me.

So now, she's down at one end of the table, surrounded by several of the other female counselors whose names I can't remember, and I'm on the other end of the table. Matt, the counselor from the cabin next to mine, sits across from me.

Brynn approaches and takes the seat next to me, setting her plate of meatloaf and mashed potatoes on the table.

"Hey, Gage!" she chirps as she settles onto the bench well within my personal bubble.

"Hey, Brynn," I greet her, quickly scooching over to put a few more inches of space between us. "Have you met Matt?"

Like Olivia and me, Matt is also new on staff this year. We seem to be in the minority. Camp Prairie Star has a lot of returning counselors, many who started working here during college and now are on their fourth or fifth summers. Some of them even attended camp here when they were kids. Matt is younger than me, still in college, so maybe this will be his first of many summers at Camp Prairie Star.

It will be my one and only, I already know. By next summer, my life will be fully occupied by my doctorate program. I knew coming in that this is my only chance to experience a summer at Camp Prairie Star and hopefully connect with where I come from in the process.

Matt and Brynn finish their introductions, and meanwhile, Brynn has somehow closed the gap between us again. Our thighs are almost touching already when she leans closer and puts a hand on my arm.

"So, Gage, what's up with you and the new girl?" Brynn asks.

I lean away, but I'm already at the end of the bench so I can't scoot any farther over. "We told you already, she's friends with my sister."

Brynn hums. "She made it sound like it was a bit more than that."

I freeze. *Really?* "What, uh ... what did she say?"

She shrugs. "Something like y'all almost dated once?"

Even though "almost dated" is a fitting description for what happened between us in high school, it also feels like a vast understatement. I'm equal parts disappointed and intrigued. I'm intrigued that Olivia would admit even that much to a total stranger. I'm disappointed that "almost dated" might actually be how she categorizes our past together.

I still have so many unanswered questions. How was our time together not as earth-shattering for her as it was for me? What happened at graduation that made her stomp the brakes? Her excuses—not wanting to deal with a long-distance relationship, not wanting to upset Annie, that she thought we were better as friends—were weak, especially since we *stopped* being friends after that, and the two of us not being friends is actually what upset Annie.

I realize Brynn is still waiting for my response. "Oh ... uh, yeah, something like that."

Matt lets out a low whistle. "You hooked up with her?" he asks, jutting his thumb toward Olivia's end of the table. "Congrats, man. She's hot."

And this is how rumors get started. I hold up my hand. "No, nuh-uh. First of all, we're talking about high school. This was, like, five years ago. And we didn't 'hook up.' We were just..."

I'm not sure how to finish that sentence. Just finally, finally creeping toward admitting our feelings for each other? Just flirting like crazy for weeks after going to prom together as "friends"? Just sharing the most incredible kisses I've ever experienced?

"We just went to prom together," I finish lamely. "As friends."

Brynn tilts her head. "Delaney said something about pining."

My ears burn. *Olivia told Brynn that I'd been pining for her?*

Before I can respond, feedback screeches through the room as Linda taps on the microphone to check whether it's on.

"Hello? Hello?" She blows into it and looks up at us. "Is it working?"

"Yes!" a handful of staffers chorus out loudly.

"Oh, good! As you finish eating, please make your way out to the fire circle. I've got a great icebreaker planned to help all of us get to know each other better."

I slide off the bench to clean up my food—and to escape this conversation. Still, Brynn sticks close to me as I scrape my plate and deposit it in a bin of warm, soapy water along with my silverware.

She's right at my elbow as I walk out of the mess hall toward the fire circle. "So, you're *not* interested in Delaney?"

I stop walking and look down into Brynn's face. "No, I'm not interested in Delaney."

I justify the lie by rationalizing that I find *Olivia* a heck of a lot more interesting than *Delaney*. Olivia is the girl I've known since I was twelve and the one I fell for back in high school. The hope that Olivia is still Olivia underneath all that Delaney is what keeps me too interested for my own good.

Brynn smiles brightly and hooks her arm through mine as we start walking again, following the crowd to the fire circle. I don't shake her off, even though I want to.

I look for Olivia as we arrive and see her in a patch of trees on the periphery of the circle, gathering sticks. Two other counselors are laying bundles of kindling in the fire pit on top of four large logs. The assistant director, Linda's son Troy, squirts some lighter fluid onto the pile, strikes a match, and tosses it in. Within minutes a fire is blazing.

Olivia approaches Linda with an armful of sticks. I'm too far away to hear what they're saying, but Linda motions toward the fire pit, and Olivia adds her kindling to the pile.

My eyes follow Olivia as she takes a seat near the same group of women she ate dinner with. She glances at me once but quickly turns back toward the front as Linda calls us to attention.

"For tonight's icebreaker, I'm going to ask a question, and each of you will get a chance to answer as we go around the group. But only the person holding the sharing stick can talk."

Sharing stick? Are they for real with this?

Linda turns and bends down, searching the ground behind the log benches. Her mouth pinches, and she says something to Troy, who frowns and drops to his knees, his eyes on the leaves and dirt around him.

The counselors murmur to each other until Linda straightens and calls, "Has anyone seen the sharing stick?"

We all check around our feet and behind us, but I don't see anything resembling a sharing stick. "What does it look like?" I ask.

Linda purses her lips. "It's a skinny stick about a foot long. On the top are leather tassels." She goes on to describe something that sounds very much like a regular stick, but with flair.

Olivia glances back at me again, but this time, she's grimacing.

Before I realize I'm moving, I slide onto the bench next to her.

"What's wrong?" I whisper.

She turns her head and startles. "Where did you come from?"

Everyone else still has their eyes pointed at the ground, searching for the stick.

"What's wrong?" I ask again.

Olivia scrunches up her nose. "The sharing stick," she mutters under her breath.

I try to make sense of those three words in conjunction with her uneasiness. "You're concerned that the sharing stick is lost?" I ask, trying to puzzle out why this would bother her.

"No!" she whispers. "I know where the sharing stick is."

I glance around near her feet but don't see anything. "Where?"

Without turning her head, she shifts her eyes toward the fire, then back to me. Her exaggerated movements are funny, despite her obvious discomfort, and it's all I can do to hold back my laughter. Then I realize what she's trying to tell me.

"Olivia. Did you throw the sharing stick in the fire?" I hiss out, not wanting anyone to overhear. But I can't stop the loud snicker that comes out of my mouth.

"I didn't mean to!" Olivia murmurs, the corners of her mouth quirking up. "I thought it was a regular stick!"

"A regular stick with tassels on it?"

The smallest nervous giggle escapes her lips. "I did think that was a little weird—"

Silent laughter shakes my shoulders as I try to catch my breath. "What do I do?"

I wipe the tears from my eyes and look at her. "You have to tell them."

Olivia frowns. She nods decisively and stands up, clearing her throat.

"Um, Linda?"

The camp director straightens from where she's literally digging a hole in the dirt in her search for the sharing stick. Does she think someone buried it?

"Did you find it?" Linda demands.

"No, not exactly. But I do know where the sharing stick is."

"You do? Where?"

Olivia winces. "In the fire. It must have gotten mixed in with my bundle of kindling."

Linda chuckles. "What?"

Olivia's mouth is set in a line, and she squeezes her eyes shut. "Unfortunately, I'm serious. The sharing stick is in the fire."

Linda's face goes slack. I can tell she's trying to maintain composure. "You're saying that the Camp Prairie Star official sharing stick, that has been a part of camp tradition for thirty years, is burning up as we speak?"

Olivia shrugs. "Or already ashes. Wood that old would probably burn quickly."

I choke back a laugh.

Linda takes a step away from Olivia. She opens her mouth and closes it again without saying anything.

Olivia rushes to add, "But hey, it's okay, I'm sure we can find another stick to be the new sharing stick. I can start looking now!"

Linda sinks down onto the log bench. By now, the other counselors are whispering to each other, passing the news that Olivia tossed the sharing stick into the fire from person to person until everyone is staring at her with heated expressions.

"She burned the sharing stick?" someone whispers.

"I can't believe her! Doesn't she have any respect for tradition?" says someone else.

"My dad used that same sharing stick when *he* came to camp here," comes another lament.

A quick study of Olivia's expression tells me that while she feels bad about accidentally destroying the sharing stick, she's also bewildered by how seriously everyone is taking it.

Olivia's mouth is appropriately turned down and her hands clasped apologetically in front of her, and no one who doesn't know her well would be able to see the glint of amusement in her eyes. It's as if they're screaming "Are you people for real? It's only a stick!"

I sigh and step in. I clap my hands loudly to get everyone's attention. "Hey, everybody, I know this is a tragedy. RIP sharing stick. But we can't let it spoil the whole evening! That is not the Camp Prairie Star way!"

This gets a few murmurs of agreement from the crowd, so I keep going. "What we need to do now is *honor* the sharing stick by sitting around this bonfire and sharing the heck out of our feelings." I pump my fist in the air to punctuate my suggestion.

The other counselors love this. I even get a smattering of applause.

Linda rises purposefully from the log bench. "Gage is right!" she exclaims, her voice still a little wobbly with emotion. "This is a dark day in Camp Prairie Star history, but the sharing must go on!"

Everyone cheers and gathers back around the fire pit. They all find seats but give Olivia a wide berth, eyeing her with suspicion.

Holding back laughter, I cross the proverbial picket line and sit with Olivia. She grabs my arm. "What the actual—" she swears in a low voice next to my ear. "Gage, is this a cult? Are we in a cult?"

I laugh as quietly as possible. I don't want to be ostracized like Olivia, after all. "I think we're safe," I whisper back to her.

Chapter Ten

Olivia

What have I gotten myself into? These people are absolutely bonkers.

Do I feel bad for throwing their special stick into the fire with the other kindling? Of course I do. But I don't think we need to have a funeral for the darn thing.

Linda decides that in lieu of the sharing stick, we can hold hands in a circle and lift our joined hands when it's our turn to share.

It's as if we don't need a sharing stick at all! Imagine that! This whole day has got my patience level at full snark.

A woman I haven't met yet is on one side of me. I hold out my hand to her, and she takes it, albeit with great reluctance. I manage to hold back an eye roll.

Gage is on my other side. When he slips his hand into mine, every nerve ending in my body goes on high alert. His rough palm sliding against mine and his thumb slotted into the space between my thumb and fingers are enough to make me shiver. I glance at him, but he gives no indication that the contact has the same kind of effect on him.

"Remember that the idea with this icebreaker is to be vulnerable, to share something important about yourself, so that we can build trust as a group," Linda tells us. "The question we're each going to answer tonight is 'what is your biggest fear?'"

I groan to myself. I would rather throw *myself* in the fire pit than share vulnerable feelings even with my closest friends and family. There's no way I want to share my biggest fear with a group of strangers who all apparently hate me.

"Let's start with our new staff members," Linda continues. "We only have three this year. Matt, why don't you go first?"

Matt, who's standing on the opposite side of the circle between Brynn and Nina, is a muscular guy with brown hair and average height. "Um," he hedges. "I don't know. Maybe snakes?"

We all wait for him to say more, but when he doesn't, Linda goes on. "Okay, thank you, Matt. Delaney? What about you?" Her tone has an edge to it when she says my name, but I can tell she's working hard to let the whole sharing-stick incident go.

It probably doesn't help things when I grin and answer, "You know, my biggest fear is probably destroying a sacred talisman on my first day of work, leading to all my new coworkers hating me."

I laugh to let them know I'm joking. Still smiling, I dart my eyes around the circle, only to be met with a lot of glares. On my right, I hear Gage groan softly.

"Too soon?" I whisper to him out of the corner of my mouth.

Gage sighs but doesn't answer me, so I elbow him in the side until I see him bite back a smile.

"I see," Linda says. "Gage, how about you?"

I turn my attention to Gage, my hand still firmly encased in his.

"Uh," Gage hesitates a moment before answering, meeting my eyes briefly before focusing on the fire as he speaks. "I guess it would be never knowing who I really am."

Whoa. Did he give a real answer?

Linda beams at him, then calls on the next staff member to share.

Gage still isn't looking at me, but I feel compelled to support him somehow after that confession. I shift my hand in his so that our fingers are interlaced, and I squeeze.

He looks at me in surprise, and I smile. It's not like I'm proposing here, just comforting my best friend's brother.

He squeezes my hand back, holding the pressure steady throughout the rest of the activity.

When Linda calls the session to a close and dismisses us, I try to catch up with Nina or Brynn to do some damage control, but they disappear pretty quickly.

So instead, I approach a group of counselors talking and laughing near the fire.

"Hey!" I wave. "I haven't met everyone yet. I'm Delaney."

Their chatter stops and they stare at me, animosity written all over their faces. "We know," one of the women says, her arms crossed over her chest.

My smile falters, but I freeze it in place. "You're Sara, right? And Malik and Gabi and Beth?" I try to remember from the icebreaker activity, but I'm not very good with names.

"Bethany," the woman in the back with light brown hair corrects.

"Oh, right. Bethany. Sorry about that."

Sara, who seems like the ringleader of this little group, turns away and starts walking. Over her shoulder she says, "We've actually got plans right now."

The other three counselors follow her.

"Oh, right. Of course. See you tomorrow, then!" I call.

Gage comes up behind me chuckling. "I'm guessing that didn't go as well as you'd hoped?"

I turn toward him. "What is wrong with these people?" I gripe. "It's a stupid stick!"

"A stupid stick with *tassels* on it. You're forgetting the tassels."

As we talk, we leave the fire pit area and start walking toward the cabins.

I scoff and shake my head. "Oh yeah, my mistake. The tassels really add that air of mysticism to it for sure."

Gage laughs. "They'll get over it."

I bump him with my shoulder. "Sure they will, Mr. 'RIP Sharing Stick'. What the heck was that?"

Gage smirks. "It *is* the sharing stick. Decades of camp tradition. That's a pretty big deal."

I groan in frustration. "How do you even know?"

Gage scuffs his feet and puts his hands in his pockets. "My mom went here when she was a kid."

I lift my eyebrows. "Dawn did?"

"Uh, no. I meant Maggie, actually."

Maggie is Annie and Gage's birth mom. Their parents adopted them as infants, but Maggie has always been a part of their lives. They even spent a month or more with her most summers growing up. Her adoption is not something Annie wants to talk about often, so Gage bringing it up surprises me.

The pieces click into place. "Does this have something to do with what you shared at the fire circle?"

Gage rubs the back of his neck. "Kind of. Maggie was talking about how it's a tradition in her family for kids to come to camp here. Her ten-year-old son Duncan will be here for a week in July."

I nod my head. Duncan and Callie are Gage and Annie's brother and sister—the kids Maggie had after she got married about thirteen years ago, before I knew them.

"So anyway," Gage continues, "I thought I'd come check it out, you know? Participate in the family tradition."

"That's really cool, Gage."

We approach a wooden dock that juts out into the lake. Gage gestures to it, an unspoken question in his expression. I nod, and we walk to the edge of the dock and sit, our feet dangling over the edge above the water.

"How old is your little sister?" I ask.

"Callie's eight."

"She's not coming to camp this summer?" Eight is the minimum age to be a camper at Camp Prairie Star.

"No. Maggie feels like she's still too young. This is Duncan's first year even."

I swing my legs slowly, the edge of the dock digging into my thigh. "I've never met them. Duncan and Callie."

Or Maggie either, for that matter. Whenever Annie sees Maggie, she usually goes to their house in Fort Worth. I think Maggie must have come to our high school and college graduations, but I don't remember meeting her. Those days were such a blur, and I was celebrating with my own family.

I know Annie and Gage's parents, Dawn and Ted, well of course. We were always at each other's houses in middle and high school.

"I know."

Reticence is not usually Gage's style, at least it wasn't back when we were kids. Maybe that's changed in the last five years, but I doubt it. I think about how he worded his greatest fear during the activity: "never knowing who I really am." Does he feel like he doesn't know who he is because he was adopted? It's not something that ever seems to bother Annie.

I study Gage's face in profile. Despite the darkness, I'm close enough to see that the corners of his lips are turned down. He looks so serious, so unlike the Gage I remember.

Maybe he senses me watching him, because he lies back on the dock and focuses his attention on the night sky.

I lie down next to him, careful to settle far enough away that we don't accidentally touch. I chuckle to myself. This is not where I expected to be, or who I expected to be with, when I got in my car to drive to camp this morning.

We lie in companionable silence, looking at the stars, listening to the cicadas chirping in the trees.

Gage shared a piece of his real struggles with me tonight. That was brave, considering how we left off after high school and that we've hardly spoken since. We were so close once, all three of us. There wasn't anything we didn't know about each other. Well, except for my feelings for Gage. I kept those a secret from both my best friends, for obvious reasons. Maybe he kept a secret or two from me, too.

I feel like it's off-balance between us now, knowing that Gage shared something real while I've been joking around. Maybe I can be brave too.

"My biggest fear is actually being vulnerable," I say quietly into the night sky.

Gage reaches over and takes my hand, intertwining our fingers. He squeezes. I take it as a friendly gesture, the same way I intended him to take my similar gesture earlier. Entertaining anything more than that makes things too complicated.

Before long, I pull my hand from Gage's and haul myself up off the dock. "It's been a long day."

Gage hops to his feet, sliding his hands into his pockets. "Yeah."

"Good night, Gage. See you tomorrow."

"Good night, Olivia."

Though still tentative, our truce seems promising. Maybe we *can* be friends again like Annie wants.

I let myself into the empty cabin. Nina must be off somewhere with her boyfriend. Or avoiding me.

I take a quick shower, change into pajamas, and brush my teeth. Burrowing into the blankets on the bottom bunk of my bed, I look around. I hate being alone at night. I'm not a fan of solitude in general, but at night the quiet is overwhelming.

I peel back the covers and jump out of bed to retrieve Panda from my duffel bag. Snuggling back into bed, I hide him under the blankets between my body and the wall.

Adding to my typical nighttime unease is the fact that I'm enemy number one at Camp Prairie Star. It doesn't hurt my feelings that my new coworkers aren't speaking to me—I experienced enough *Mean Girls*-style cliques in high school and college that it usually rolls off my back—but I'm not sure how long I can last without talking to *anyone*.

Except Gage, I guess. I flop my head back against the pillow. There's another problem. I don't want to get too buddy-buddy with him, but if my choices are to talk to no one or to talk to Gage, I'm going to talk to Gage. I'm not wired for seclusion.

Still feeling restless, I check my phone, prepared to scroll mindlessly through social media. I notice a text from my sister Molly, sent a couple of hours ago to our sister thread.

Molly:

> How'd your first day of camp go?

I text her back, grateful for the distraction. I also figure she might find my current predicament funny.

Olivia:

> Well I destroyed 30 years of camp tradition and I think I'm shunned now

I'm surprised when she responds right away.

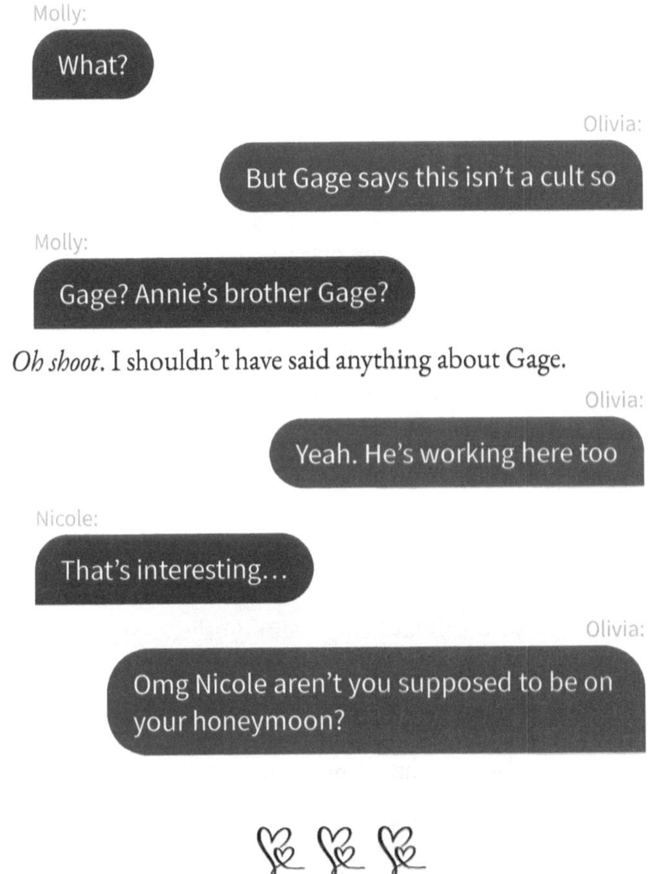

Oh shoot. I shouldn't have said anything about Gage.

The rest of the week, Gage remains the only coworker who will talk to me. Even Nina makes herself scarce. So, it's the two of us, partnering up for orientation sessions and sitting together at meals.

It's nice, actually. Not as bad as I feared. I slip back into the familiar comfort of his friendship, and it feels like how we were back before everything got complicated at prom. Hanging out with Gage satisfies my need to be with other people, and actually I have a tough time even noticing all the cold shoulders beyond our little bubble.

At least until Thursday when the junior counselors arrive.

Junior counselors are high schoolers assigned to each cabin to assist the adult counselor with their group of kids. Gage's junior counselor is a sixteen-year-old kid named Jayden, and it's Gage's job to train Jayden ahead of the first group of campers arriving on Sunday.

My job is to create the activities schedule, rotating each cabin through swimming and water sports, arts and crafts, and nature hikes throughout the week. I use the bulletin board in the main office to map out the schedule, giving each cabin a color in addition to the number Linda has already assigned them. It's easier for my brain to find the patterns that way.

As someone who thrives being around other people, working on my task alone on Thursday and Friday is unbearable. I've been waiting for the whole I-burned-your-sharing-stick fiasco to blow over on its own, but I realize I might need to help things along. I make a plan, and hope that Gage will be willing to lend a hand.

Chapter Eleven

Gage

At breakfast on Saturday morning, Olivia unceremoniously drops her tray onto the table next to mine. "*Please* come to town with me today," she begs.

"Good morning to you, too, Olivia." I smirk.

She rolls her eyes as she sits down on the bench. "Yeah, yeah. Good morning, blah blah blah. Will you come with me?"

I scrutinize her while I make her wait for my answer. She's wearing yellow yoga pants and a baggy gray hoodie. Her hair is tied up high in a sleek ponytail again. She's worn it that way all week, at least whenever I've seen her. It gives me the ridiculous urge to dig my fingers into her hair and slowly slide the elastic band out until all those golden strands fall around her face.

"Well?" Olivia prompts again, crossing her arms over her chest.

Orientation is officially over, and with campers not arriving until tomorrow, we get a day off today. Some of the staff who live in the area left last night to go home until Sunday. Others have made plans to go explore the nearby town.

I figured I'd relax around camp, maybe take a canoe out on the lake, but hanging out with Olivia sounds much more fun.

"Sure," I finally answer.

"Okay, good. Here's my plan." She lowers her voice and leans toward me. I find myself shifting closer to her, too. "We're going to decorate a new sharing stick and give it to Linda to, like, make amends. So, we need to buy supplies."

I laugh. "Wait a minute, what do you mean 'we'? I didn't incinerate the sharing stick. I don't need to make amends."

She gives me a sharp look, and I know she's trying to seem stern, but she's too cute to pull it off, at least to me. "*But* if you help me get back into the camp's good graces, you won't have to keep hanging out with me all the time."

That sounds like an incentive to *not* help her. Hanging out with Olivia has been fun. It feels a little like old times. Almost as confusing as old times too, with my body reacting to her in ways I haven't felt since I was a teenager.

I can't admit any of that, of course, so I laugh. "Sounds good."

"Meet me in the staff parking lot at 01800 hours," she says quietly, like we're spies with a secret mission.

I shake my head. "01800 hours doesn't mean anything. 1800 hours would be 6 p.m." I look at my watch. "Do you want me to meet you at 9?"

She nods, her face serious. "Should we synchronize our watches?"

I laugh again. "I don't think that's necessary." I unfold myself from the bench and stand with my tray. "I'll see you then."

I head back to my cabin to take a shower and change my clothes before I meet Olivia. I've been wearing gym shorts or board shorts all week—we're at camp after all—but if I'm going to spend the day with Olivia, I feel like I want to clean up a little. I don't have my nicest clothes with me, of course, and dressing up too much would look strange, but I can at least wear chino shorts with my T-shirt instead of basketball shorts. I leave my beloved Longhorns hat behind and actually comb my shaggy hair. I even put a little mousse in it.

I start walking toward the staff parking lot a little early, figuring I'll need to wait for Olivia. But she's already there, leaning against her old sedan and twirling her key ring around her finger.

When she notices me walking toward her, she stops twirling, as if flustered, and the key falls onto the gravel parking lot.

I smile to myself. Clearly the chinos and mousse were a good idea.

Olivia bends down to pick up the key, wiping it against her pants to clean off the gravel dust. She looks down at her outfit. She's still in the same yellow pants but has removed her hoodie now that the day is warming up. Her top is a cropped black T-shirt that shows off a slice of her stomach above the high waist of her yoga pants.

She looks pointedly at my outfit. "I didn't realize we were dressing up."

I grin. "I didn't realize shorts and a clean T-shirt mean I'm dressed up."

"Whatever. We're just going to Walmart, right?" She tilts her head, and the hair at the end of her ponytail slides off her shoulder. "Let's go."

She's in the car before I can even open the passenger-side door. I'm only halfway into my seat when Olivia starts the engine. Immediately, a deep voice comes through the speakers. "Chapter four," it says.

Olivia yelps and fumbles for her phone, turning the audiobook off before the narrator says anything else. Her face is red from her cheeks all the way to the tips of her ears. She stares at her phone screen, not making eye contact as I settle into the passenger seat and buckle my seatbelt.

I didn't look at the media screen on the front dash in time to see the title of whatever she's listening to, but I can guess based on her reaction.

I smirk at her. "What was that?"

"Nothing," she says quickly. "An audiobook I was listening to."

I raise one eyebrow. "A smutty audiobook?" I tease.

Olivia's forehead wrinkles for a split second, so fast I almost miss it. Then she's all smiles, like a switch has flipped somewhere on her face. She tosses her head, swishing her ponytail from side to side.

"Wouldn't you like to know," she answers with a flirty giggle.

So, *not* a smutty audiobook, then. But she wants me to think it is, and I would have if I didn't know her so well, even after all these years.

It's embarrassing, and honestly concerning, how easily I've fallen back into reading Olivia's every expression. After spending most of high school cataloging and interpreting each look, noting every emotion, even the ones she tried to hide, I became an expert in Olivia.

She's changed, of course, in the five years since then. Her hair is longer and lighter, her face more angular. She's sunken deeper into the persona she cultivated in high school, the one I associate with the name she prefers—Delaney: athletic, shallow party girl who takes nothing seriously unless she's on the pitch. Too cool to care—about her grades, about her future outside of soccer, or about the herd of guys she strung along.

I always knew better. The front she put up at school faded away when she was at our house hanging out with Annie and, by default, me. I may have been one of the many guys at school in love with Olivia Delaney, but I had a sense of satisfaction knowing I was the *only* guy at school who knew who she really was behind the facade.

Not anymore, though. Her facial expressions and body language may have stayed the same, or close enough that I can still decode them, but I'm not her safe space like I once was. I can tell she's hiding something with that audiobook, but five years ago I would have known what, because she would have told me, and we'd probably be listening to it together.

I steer us back to safe conversation as we drive to town. "How are your parents doing? Are they enjoying being empty nesters?"

Her cheeks blaze again. "They're doing great, but I'm still at the nest, so it's not quite empty yet."

Okay, maybe that topic of conversation isn't as safe as I thought. "After the summer, I'm moving back in with my parents, too," I tell her.

She glances at me quickly before turning her eyes back to the road. "Really? Why?"

"The school I'm going to this fall is actually right on the outskirts of our neighborhood. It didn't make sense to get my own place and pay rent when they already have space for me so close to school."

She bobs her head up and down. "It *is* a cost savings."

We fall into an awkward silence, which is unusual for us. Even this week, with all the weirdness of our past haunting us, conversation has come easily. I don't know if it's the close quarters of being in the car together or what.

I *am* acutely aware that I'm sitting less than two feet away from Olivia, and it feels strangely intimate. Maybe it's because the smell of her shampoo—a mixture of rosemary and mint—is so strong I can imagine what it would be like to bury my face in her hair, to brush my lips across the skin on her neck, to gaze deeply into her blazing green eyes—

"Stop staring at me," Olivia orders.

I abruptly turn my head away, looking out the passenger-side window instead. "Sorry," I mutter. "I wasn't staring at you. I was zoned out."

Olivia smirks knowingly. "Uh-huh."

Soon the pastures outside my window shift into gas stations and restaurants as we drive into town. Olivia pulls into a spot in the shopping center parking lot, and we head into the store.

She makes a beeline for the craft section—four whole aisles of various paints, beads, fabric, buttons, ribbons, and glue. I have no idea where to start.

"So what's the plan?" I ask Olivia.

"Okay, so I already found a good stick. It's about a foot long with plenty of room for decoration. We need supplies. I was thinking bedazzled, maybe with some cute ribbons?" She puts her hand on her chin as she assesses the options in front of us.

Forty minutes later, I'm carrying a basket stuffed with rhinestones, ribbons in Camp Prairie Star colors, paints and paintbrushes, and a hot glue gun. She has a vision, she says.

"Why did you need me here, again?" I ask, though I'm not at all disappointed to be spending time with Olivia.

She levels a glare. "Your stellar company, of course," she deadpans.

I laugh. "Glad I could help."

As we walk toward the front of the store to check out, we pass the women's clothing section. Right out front along the aisle are a collection of colorful muumuus and bathrobes. I stop in my tracks and step toward the display, setting the basket down at my feet.

I pull out a silky orange-and-yellow nightgown with an obnoxious pineapple pattern in the largest size available.

"Gage," Olivia hisses, but I'm already tugging the garment on over my clothes.

I smooth the draping fabric around my hips and then rotate slowly for my audience. "Well, what do you think?"

Olivia has her hands pressed against the sides of her face, her shoulders shaking with silent laughter. She opens her mouth, and a gasping breath comes out. "Oh my gosh, Gage!"

I feign a frown as I look down at myself. "Do I need a bigger size?"

She shakes her head. "No," she answers in between giggles. "It's perfect. Like it was made for you."

I beam. "So, I should get it?"

"Definitely." She steps closer, reaching for the muumuus hanging on the rack. "But if you get one, I'll feel left out if I can't buy one, too."

"Ah, of course, madam." I sort through the various colors and designs. "Let's see…" I unhook a hanger from the rod and hold it in front of Olivia. "*This* one would look divine on you."

It has a V-neck and a dark green background with a loud, neon floral print. "Really brings out your eyes." I'm joking around, but when I shift my gaze from the nightgown to her face, her eyes *do* have me in a trance.

I realize how close we're standing to each other, the garment and a couple of inches between us. Olivia stands frozen, her wide eyes locked on mine. My fingers, holding the hanger near her face so the shoulders of the dress line up with her shoulders, brush softly against her cheek of their own volition. It would be so easy to lean in, angle my head, and kiss her, especially when the look on her face says she wouldn't stop me.

My foggy brain clears enough to remember our surroundings. I can't kiss Olivia for the first time after five years standing in a Walmart wearing a muumuu. That's not the memory I want.

I force myself to step back, my breath ragged. I slide the hanger back on the rack. "We should probably get going."

Olivia shakes her head, as if waking up after a dream. "Yeah."

I strip the muumuu off and hang it up before grabbing Olivia's basket of supplies. I force a languid smile and extend my hand to guide Olivia ahead. "After you."

Chapter Twelve

Olivia

"How about ice cream?" Gage asks after we shove the shopping bags in the trunk. He points toward a little shop across the street.

I sigh. "That sounds amazing, but I spent a small fortune on craft supplies so ..."

He chuckles. "My treat."

I tilt my chin toward him and grin. "And *this* is why I needed you here."

This feels better. The banter and joking around with each other is much safer than whatever that moment was back in the store. Attraction was never the problem between me and Gage. Camaraderie wasn't either. The problem was ... well, me.

That attraction was crackling again as we stood too close in the muumuu section of Walmart. As his fingers grazed my cheek.

He stepped away first, but I was still mesmerized, especially when the front of his shirt stuck to the nightgown as he removed it, lifting to reveal the abs I punched all those years ago. Except not the same abs at all. Fourteen-year-old Gage was strong for his age, but he was still a kid. The stomach I stole a glance at today was all man. Chiseled muscles underneath a sprinkling of blond hair so light I wouldn't have noticed it at all if I wasn't looking so closely.

My stomach flutters now thinking about it.

"Let's go!" Gage calls out. He's already halfway across the parking lot. I jog to catch up with him, and we cross the street together.

The ice cream shop is one of those old-fashioned parlors lined with glass cases featuring huge tubs of ice cream in a dizzying array of flavors.

But I already know exactly what I want.

"Let me guess," Gage teases as we peer into the freezer cases, "you're going to order chocolate peanut butter in a waffle cone?"

Okay, so my ice cream preferences haven't changed since high school. Why mess with success?

I laugh and tap my nose. "And for you..." I pause as if I need to really think it over. "Blue raspberry in a cake cone."

Gage smiles. "Guilty."

He orders our cones and pays at the register. We wait for the worker to scoop our ice cream.

I lean back against the freezer case and eye Gage. "You haven't found a flavor you like better in the last five years?"

"Well," he allows, "I have branched out. I don't always get blue raspberry anymore. It's still usually a fruit ice cream, though. You haven't either?"

I grin. "You can't get much better than perfection."

His expression turns suddenly serious as he studies me. "No. You can't."

My heart rate picks up when I clock his double meaning. The shop employee hands me my cone, so I take it and beat a hasty retreat to the white wrought iron tables on the other side of the room.

"So," Gage asks as he joins me at the table, "other than Camp Prairie Star, what have you been doing for work since graduation?"

I feel my body stiffen involuntarily but try to hide it by flashing him a teasing smile. "Oh, a little of this and a little of that."

He tilts his head. "Like what?"

Internally, I groan. I don't really want to get into it. It's embarrassing, especially after learning that he's been working at his dad's office for the last year and plans to go to graduate school this fall.

Resigned, I answer his question while avoiding his eyes. "Mostly coaching soccer skills classes for little kids. I also pick up shifts reffing for youth soccer leagues."

"Sounds fun. Do you like it?"

"Yeah, actually I do. It's fun to watch the kids' confidence grow as they learn new skills." My posture relaxes as I think about the group of kids I coached in the spring. I'm even smiling. "The hours are all over the place and the pay is lousy, though. I'm still looking for a more permanent career direction for my life."

My barriers go right back up. Admitting how lost I am to Gage, who has his life totally together, is embarrassing. It's evidence of why we would never work together.

"What did you major in?" he asks.

"Exercise science," I admit. "I was thinking more about passing classes than job prospects when I picked it. I've realized since then that a lot of the careers for exercise science majors require more school, which I'm not willing to do."

I grimace. The idea of *more* school, when I feel like I barely survived the schooling I've had makes me feel a little panicked. Exercise science was a safe major choice for me because it focused on how the body moves—which has always come naturally to me—and required less reading and fewer papers than most other majors. We had a lot of labs and hands-on work, which I enjoyed.

"What about something like personal training?" Gage suggests.

My shoulders lift. "Maybe." I've considered that road before, but I'm not sure how much I'd like working one-on-one with clients all the time. I do better with a larger audience. But I've had enough of talking about my lack of direction in life. I steer the conversation toward Gage instead. "What does someone planning to be a pediatric occupational therapist major in?"

Gage considers a beat before answering. "There's a range of possibilities. A lot do exercise science, actually. But my degree is in psychology. I took a psych course as part of my gen ed requirements and loved it. I declared my major, and it was only later that I decided to go into OT. But it's a natural fit. Many of the kids I'll eventually work with will have functional challenges that stem from differences in their brains. It'll be helpful that I have an understanding of the mind and how it affects behavior."

Man, he's really got it together. My parents and sisters keep telling me that lots of people need time to figure out their next move after college, but *they* didn't. Gage doesn't. Maybe everyone in my life is better at this whole adulting thing than I am.

Not that Gage is *in* my life, necessarily, but we're trying to be friends again. I flash back to that moment in the bathroom at graduation when I realized how out of my league Gage really was. He still is. I'm glad that kiss in the store didn't happen. While I can handle being friends—as long as I keep my physical distance and control myself—trying for anything more is as problematic now as it was in high school.

I need to keep reminding my body and my heart that we're not going there.

When we get back to camp, Gage and I spend the rest of the afternoon working on my masterpiece. True to her word, Nina is not often around, so it's Gage and I sitting on the wood plank floor of my cabin getting glitter everywhere.

For step one, I paint the stick a deep green color. Once the paint dries, I wrap the stick in purple ribbon, so it spirals around from the bottom to the top, leaving parts of the now-green stick exposed. I add a dab of hot glue every inch or so to hold the ribbon in place. Then, I add rhinestones here and there so the new sharing stick will sparkle in the firelight. Finally, I add a handful of green and purple ribbon to both ends in place of the lost tassels.

While I work, Gage helps where he can—holding the ribbon steady as I glue, cutting where I tell him to—but mostly he sits with his back against the bedpost, his long legs stretched out in front of him on the floor, and watches me.

At one point, I suggest he might have something better to do. He shrugs and says, "Not really."

We play music through his phone and break open a family-sized bag of white cheddar popcorn to snack on while we work.

It's nice. Really nice. I'd forgotten how much fun I used to have doing nothing with Gage. Hanging out. And if I secretly admire the taut definition of the calf muscles in his leg and the sexy tousled look his hair gets when he runs his hands through it, no one's the wiser.

Once the new sharing stick is done and dry, I hold it up. "What do you think?"

Gage puts out his hand, and I give him the stick. He makes a show of studying it from every angle and tossing it back and forth between his hands as if testing how easy it will be to pass around a circle of campers.

"I think..." He pauses dramatically, but it works, and I feel the tension rising as I wait for him to continue. "I think that decades from now, Camp Prairie Star campers and staff alike will still celebrate the day you burned that ugly old sharing stick, because it was the day you made way for this *beautiful, bedazzled, beloved, beyond* compare new sharing stick."

He's being so over the top, but it *works* for me. Warmth pulses in my chest at his praise, expanding out until I feel it in every inch of my body, including my cheeks, which I'm sure are flushed pink.

I wave off his compliments with faux modesty. "Oh, it's just something I threw together last minute."

He laughs, and I revel in it. I forgot how much I love the sound of his laughter. His voice is rich and deep, confident and carefree. I feel like I could pull the sound around my shoulders like a blanket and burrow down.

"Do you want to go find Linda in the front office and give it to her now?" Gage asks.

Now, I laugh. "I know it's been a few years since we hung out, but do you know me at all?"

He runs his hand through his hair, a half smile on his lips. "You're going to make a big spectacle of giving it to her in front of everyone at dinner, aren't you?"

I bat my eyelashes slowly and grin. "How else will they all know it's okay to forgive me?"

When we walk into the mess hall a few minutes late that evening, I find Linda and head straight toward her. Gage breaks away toward the tables.

I stop. "Aren't you coming with me?"

He grins and shakes his head. "I'm going to find a good seat and enjoy the show." He salutes. "Knock 'em dead, Olivia."

He sits on the bench at a table near where Linda is standing to oversee the meal. Gage crosses one leg over the other, props his elbows on his leg, and rests his chin in his hands.

Putting what I hope is my most repentant expression on my face, I approach Linda.

I lay a hand gently against her arm to get her attention. "Linda, hey," I say softly. She turns to look at me, and I drop my eyes as if I don't dare meet her gaze. "I want to say again how sorry I am about what happened earlier this week. Clearly I have a lot to learn about Camp Prairie Star tradition."

"Oh, Delaney, it's fine. I won't pretend we're not all devastated with the loss, but what's done is done." She nods her head resolutely.

Wow, okay. For that, I decide to double down on my little performance.

I speak louder when I respond. "Even so, I want to make amends. I know nothing will bring the sharing stick back or ever make up for its loss, but ..."

A few of the other staff members are openly watching our exchange now, which is exactly what I want to happen.

I pull the new blinged-out stick from behind my back. I extend both my arms and hold the stick out to her, balanced on my palms. I almost want to get down on one knee and bow my head like I'm presenting her with the sword that took down her mortal enemy to really milk the moment, but I'm afraid that it would be taking things a touch too far.

"I made a new sharing stick. I know it doesn't have the history of the old one, but maybe it'll do?"

Linda brings her hand to her chest, her eyes wide as she takes in the new stick in all its glory. "Well! Delaney, this is ... this is beautiful!"

"Thank you," I say humbly. "I tried to do it justice."

More staff members are looking on now, some standing up from the table so they can see better.

I catch sight of Gage, still sitting on the bench with his legs crossed. He has a fist against his lips, his face red, and his eyes watering from the effort of holding back his laughter.

It was a mistake to look at him. I've been playing this totally straight until now, but one look at his face and I'm swallowing my own laughter. *Don't laugh. Don't laugh. Don't laugh.*

As Linda takes the sharing stick from my hands and holds it up to the light to inspect it, a giggle threatens to escape. I bring my hand up to cover my mouth and play it off as a cough.

Still holding the sharing stick in one hand, Linda rushes to the front of the room and picks up the microphone, fumbling to turn it on. When she does, she taps it, sending feedback throughout the mess hall.

"Everyone! May I have your attention, please. Our own Olivia Delaney has crafted a new Camp Prairie Star sharing stick! It's even decorated in camp colors, which, of course, are the colors of the beautiful prairie blazing star flower common in this region." She extends her arm above her head, holding the stick high for all to see.

I clamp my lips together to keep from laughing as my coworkers move closer to Linda, clamoring for a better look. Oh man, this went even better than planned, except that I'm seriously about to lose it.

Don't laugh. Don't laugh. Don't laugh. I repeat the mantra as I focus my eyes on the floor.

Someone tugs on my arm, and I look up to see Gage pulling me toward the door. Once we're outside and the door slams shut behind us, I fall into one of the rocking chairs on the porch and burst into an uncontrollable fit of laughter.

Still holding my arm, Gage crouches on the ground in front of the rocking chair, doubled over and howling.

"Oh my gosh!" I say between giggles. "You got me out of there just in time. I don't know how much longer I would have lasted."

Gage wipes his eyes. "I know. I could tell."

I freeze. "They can't see us out the window, can they?"

We both lean to the right and turn our heads to look through the window. Everyone is still crowded around Linda, the stick being passed from person to person.

This sets off a whole new round of laughter, and I quickly straighten so I'm out of view again.

Gage joins in, giving me a puzzled look. "Why are we laughing now?" he asks, trying to catch his breath.

I snort. "I don't know!"

But it feels good, so I keep laughing with Gage until my stomach muscles are sore and the skin on my arm is tingling where Gage's hand remains steady.

Chapter Thirteen

Olivia

The campers start arriving at noon on Sunday. Unlike the cabin counselors who have to help all the kids in their cabin get situated, my main job today is to provide the campers with an overview of activities during the welcome meeting.

I also have a meeting with the rest of the activities team to share out the schedule for the week. My roommate, Nina, is the craft counselor, Jake is the nature counselor, and Nina's boyfriend, Rocky, is the lifeguard. Each cabin of kids will have swimming time, supervised by Rocky and me, every day, as well as rotating options for hikes, crafts, and boating.

I drop the color-coded schedule off with each of the cabin counselors as part of my morning responsibilities. I linger a little at Gage's cabin, checking things out. I haven't seen inside one of the kids' cabins yet.

It's a nice set up. There are seven sets of bunk beds, meaning each cabin can fit twelve kids and two counselors—though Gage tells me they try to keep it to eight campers—and a gang-style bathroom with three showers and three toilet stalls.

I can tell Gage is busy, but after spending so much time with him this past week, it feels natural to have him close by. I end up lingering under the guise of helping him by making sure the bathroom has enough soap and toilet paper and checking the mattresses on each bunk.

But, when he's distracted, I surreptitiously check out his personal space. He's set up on the top bunk, with his junior counselor, Jayden, on the bottom. Gage's bed is neatly made, with the edges of his blue sheets and lightweight blanket tucked under the mattress. His pillow still has a visible imprint from his head, and I have to fight the impulse to crawl into his bunk and lay my head in the divot.

He has a few pictures taped to the wall next to his bunk. There's one of him and Annie at his college graduation, his smile wide and his fist above Annie's head, threatening her with a noogie. Another one of his parents, sitting on the front-porch swing of their house in Austin. One of a pretty brunette woman and a tall man with dark hair, two kids in front of them. This must be Maggie and her family.

The last picture is Gage surrounded by a group of friends. I look at each face but don't recognize a single one. It's a weird realization that I don't know his friends anymore. I don't really know what he's been up to the last five years or what his life is like. He was such a big part of mine for so long, and I literally walked away.

"Find anything interesting?" Gage's voice teases from behind me, startling me from my thoughts.

I turn and hop down from where I've been standing on the edge of Jayden's bunk, embarrassed to be caught. "Just looking at the pictures."

He leans against the wall, arms folded and a cocky smile on his face. "Okay."

I take a step toward him and push on his chest. "Oh, whatever. I have to say, though, I'm impressed your stuff is so neat."

Gage pats the side of the mattress. "Hospital corners. It's an occupational hazard of having a doctor for a mom."

"Remember this isn't a military camp. Your kids don't have to make their beds every morning."

He raises his eyebrows. "Uh, of course they do."

"Right, okay. So you're going to be the counselor nobody likes. Got it."

Gage takes a step closer to me, a devilish look on his face. "No. Everyone will love me. I'm irresistible."

A truer statement has never been spoken. I'm 90 percent sure that the slang term *rizz* was created especially to describe Gage Carter's special brand of charisma. Everything about him, from his eyes to his caretaking instincts to his magnetic personality, draws me in.

But he can't know that.

"You wish." I scoff and brush past him toward the door. "I have more schedules to deliver." I lift a hand as I leave the cabin, not bothering to turn around. "Catch you later!"

I hear him chuckling as the door shuts behind me.

❦ ❦ ❦

I think I underestimated the level of chaos that exists when one hundred excited eight-to-fourteen-year-olds are all together in a room.

This mess hall is *loud*. Fortunately, this is where Linda's inability to use a microphone comes in handy. As usual, when she picks it up, the screech echoes through the room, and it signals the kids to be quiet.

"Welcome to Camp Prairie Star!" Linda whoops.

The returning staff and campers respond to her greeting by stomping their feet and shouting. The newbies soon catch on, and it's absolute pandemonium.

Troy—the assistant director and Linda's son—lets out an ear-splitting whistle, and the crowd quiets again.

"We're excited for a great week of fun, friendship, and challenging ourselves to reach higher. You've already met your counselors and cabinmates. They're your group for the week as you go through the various activities we have in store for you. Olivia, come on up and tell us more."

I do a double take when I realize she called me Olivia. I shake it off and walk up front, taking the microphone from Linda.

I go through my whole spiel about the activity schedule and all the fun things we have planned. Then I hand the microphone back to Linda and step out of the way again.

Nina nudges me. "I love the color codes on the schedule you made," she whispers. "It's so nice when something boring can become beautiful."

The compliment hits me right in the feels. "Thanks," I murmur, warmth spreading through my chest.

As I look out at the group, my eyes find Gage without even meaning to. He meets my gaze and mouths "Good job," flashing me a thumbs-up. I know he's referring to my stint at the microphone—there's no way he heard Nina's comment—but his praise stacks right on top of hers to fortify my bruised confidence.

See, now, something that simple from Gage shouldn't light up my insides like a floodlight. I have to get these reactions under control if I'm going to work with Gage and be friends with him this summer.

After the welcome meeting with the campers, I need a breather before dinner and the opening campfire. I walk out onto the main dock, this one larger than the dock by the swimming area where Gage and I looked at the stars that first night. When I'm all the way at the end, I inhale the fresh air and take in the beautiful lake view in front of me.

It's interesting how genetics work, even within families. My sisters both loved school—at least the academic parts, if not always the social—and went on to get graduate degrees and work in academic jobs.

I couldn't be more different.

Though I hated it, I did okay in school, especially once my dyslexia was identified and I started receiving support and accommodations. I did okay enough to go on to graduate college. But I would never get a master's or doctorate like my sisters.

Their jobs involve working inside a library or a lab, cooped up all day. I don't know how they do it. Outdoors is where I feel most alive, most like myself. If my body isn't moving, I get restless. If I don't start my morning with a run, everything feels off the rest of the day.

It's probably why I'm so unsettled today. I overslept and nearly missed breakfast, so instead of starting my morning with movement, I started my morning a little stressed out. I can probably get in a quick run in between dinner and the opening campfire tonight, and then I'm sure I'll feel better.

I'll feel less like I'm falling back under Gage's spell, and more like I can exercise some self-control and keep us in the friendship zone.

Leaving the serenity of the dock, I duck into the boathouse on my way past, triple checking that everything looks in order for the campers tomorrow.

The boathouse is a wooden structure built onto the main dock. It's not much larger than a walk-in closet but works to hold the life jackets and paddles campers need to take the boats on the water. The canoes and kayaks themselves are lined up on the shore on either side of the dock.

My phone vibrates, and I glance at the screen to see Annie video calling me.

"Hey!" I answer, holding my phone in front of me as I walk back to my cabin. On the screen, Annie stands in her bedroom, discarded clothes visible in the background piled on her bed. "What's going on?"

"I have a date tonight, and I need your opinion on outfits."

"Ooh, a date! Who's the guy?" Focusing on my best friend's love life for a few minutes sounds like a great distraction.

Annie and her long-term boyfriend broke up in February. I wasn't a big fan of Spencer, but it's shaken Annie's confidence enough that she's dated very little since. I'm glad she's going on a date, and that she seems excited about it.

Even over the phone, I see Annie's blush. "Someone I met at the office. Tanner."

I frown. "Coworker or client?"

Annie is the office manager at a midsize law firm that specializes in divorces, though ironically her real passion is writing romance novels. If her date is a client, it most likely means he's soon-to-be or recently divorced.

"Neither. We had to hire a cybersecurity company to come in and evaluate our online security for the website and intranet. Tanner was one of the consultants."

A breathe a sigh of relief. "Oh, that's great. Cybersecurity consultant sounds like a cool job."

Annie props a hand on her hip. "Delaney," she says in a warning voice.

"What?" I smirk at her. One of my running jokes about Spencer is that he has the most boring job on the planet. He's an actuary and was always talking about "loss reserving" and "stochastic modeling."

Actually, I'm sure risk assessment can be a very interesting job; it was the man himself who was duller than a drawer of manila file folders.

"Spencer was not boring. He was reliable and steady."

I reach my cabin and push open the creaky screen door. "He wasn't right for you. A guy doesn't have to be boring to be reliable."

Annie, with her hand still on her hip, narrows her eyes. "Oh and you know this from all your successful long-term relationships?"

Okay, fair. But still, rude to bring it up. The truth is I've never liked a guy enough to have a serious relationship with him. Well, other than Gage, that is. I always kind of told myself that I'd take a relationship seriously when I found a guy I liked more than Gage. It hasn't happened.

I groan. "Let me see the outfits. After that crack, you'll be lucky if I don't pick the ugliest one."

♥ ♥ ♥

The first week of camp speeds by. Weirdly, the kids and even other staff keep calling me Olivia, even though I definitely introduce myself as Delaney. I correct each person the first few times, but it becomes so frequent that I start letting it go. I don't know where they're getting it from.

Monday is all about helping the kids get comfortable with being at camp. I walk each group through how to safely use the boats and help Rocky squirt a half-vinegar, half–rubbing alcohol solution from a baby bottle into the kids' ears to prevent swimmer's ear when they get out of the lake.

Tuesday, I make my rounds to check on Nina in the craft cabin in between water sports groups. She has a group of eight-year-old girls making friendship bracelets with tiny rubber bands and beads in a rainbow of colors.

Wednesday is "wacky Wednesday," and the kids and staff are encouraged to wear our craziest outfit combinations as we eat breakfast for dinner and make up new, chaotic rules for the games we play.

Thursday is color wars day. The campers are divided into two teams: purple and green. They compete in a series of challenges, earning points for their team to see who the final winner will be. There's tug-of-war and water Olympics, which I'm in charge of and includes a fire brigade relay and water balloon toss. In the afternoon, there's a massive game of capture the flag that includes the cabin counselors, where the winning team has a chance to double their point total from the morning's events.

Friday is the final day of camp, culminating in Skit Night, where the campers' families arrive for a bonfire and show. The kids sing camp songs and perform the skits they've written about their week at camp while stuffing themselves with s'mores. Skit Night wraps up around six, and the kids check out and leave with their families to go home.

And through it all, I really only see Gage in passing, like when he brings his campers to the lake for swimming or boating.

At first, it's a relief. I'm grateful for the space so I can get my head straight and go through all the reasons Gage and I being together is a bad idea. Reasons that are really hard to remember when I'm with him.

But after a few days, I begin living for the glimpses of him I get across the mess hall. When I know it's time for his campers to have free swim in the lake or go out in the canoes, I notice I'm on edge, jittery until I see him marching toward me, black Longhorns cap on backward as he leads the way for his kids.

When he greets me with that sunshiny smile, I like to imagine there's a little something extra in his expression reserved for me. And when his hand brushes mine softly, maybe it's intentional and sends the same shiver across his skin as it does mine. Like he's also spent the day looking forward to this small interaction. Like it's the highlight of his day, like it is for me.

Chapter Fourteen

Olivia

Finally home from the honeymoon and back to our regular schedules

Aww, I hope you had fun!

We had so much fun! I can't believe I'm MARRIED!

[gif of excited girl]

How's camp going Liv?

Molly:
Yeah, any updates on the Gage situation?

Nicole:
There's a situation??

Molly:
Well just that he's there working with her

Nicole:
You know, she totally had a thing for him back in high school

Molly:
Really? Oooh

Molly:
If you need any help navigating the whole falling for your coworker thing, let us know. Nicole and I are experts [wink emoji]

Olivia:
I hate you both so much

Nicole:
No you don't

Molly:
You love us

After the near-constant activity and noise around camp all week—and I hear *everything* that's going on with the other staff as they rotate in and out of the lake area each day—the quiet on Friday night after the campers leave is palpable.

Other than cleaning up our areas and making sure we're ready for the next group of kids, the counselors are all off now until Sunday morning.

Many of the counselors, including the juniors, waste no time getting out of Dodge for a few days. The staff parking lot is conspicuously emptier by eight that night.

The camp cooks—a super sweet couple named Rob and Stephanie who are around the same age as my parents—will set out grab-and-go type foods at mealtimes through the weekend for staff who choose to stay on property.

While I might head to Austin on a Saturday later this summer to hang out with Annie, I don't see any real reason not to stick around at camp. I can hike and relax without burning through gas in my car, and because Nina has already warned me that she won't be around on weekends, I know I'll have the cabin to myself.

Of course, I wonder whether Gage is staying at camp this weekend, though I'm not quite brave enough—or foolish enough—to seek him out at his cabin to ask. I may go check the parking lot for his Jeep, though.

When I get back to my cabin after straightening up the boathouse, the man himself is sitting on the stoop.

I stop in my tracks, my heart slamming rhythmically against my rib cage. "Hi."

It's like I summoned him magically through my wishful thinking.

Gage stands and dusts off the seat of his shorts. "Hey." He smiles crookedly. "I feel like I haven't seen you all week."

I grin. "The campers kept you pretty busy, huh?"

"Yeah, definitely. So, when I noticed your car in the staff parking lot, I thought I'd check in with you about your plans for the weekend."

"Oh." I shrug. "Don't really have any. I'm going to hang around the camp and relax. What about you?"

He runs his tongue over his lips, my eyes following the movement. "Well, I was wondering if you wanted to hang out a little. There's a short hike Jake told me about that sounds fun. And you know you should always hike with a buddy for safety reasons, so."

His bumbling invitation makes my stomach swoop. "You planning to get injured on this little hike?" I tease.

"Olivia," he says with the perfect solemn intonation, "hiking injuries are never planned and rarely expected."

"In that case, how could I risk you dying alone in the Texas wilderness?"

"Annie would be pretty mad at you," he says, straight-faced.

I shake my head, a small smile creeping across my lips. "Can't have that."

"Nope," he says, popping the P at the end of the word.

"I'm in."

His face lights up. "Cool. I'll meet you at the mess hall at eight tomorrow morning? We can grab some breakfast and then go."

"Yeah," I agree. "Now, if you'll excuse me, I'm going to go in my cabin to shower and collapse in my bunk to try to recover from this week."

He chuckles. "Same, honestly."

I poke his arm, widening my eyes comically. "You're *also* going to come into my cabin to shower and collapse in my bunk?"

Gage clicks his tongue. "If wishing made it so."

His lips curve up into a deliciously wicked smile that makes my face heat, and my legs go a little wobbly.

How easily he can still make me swoon is worrisome, but my heart hasn't felt so alive in years.

"Good night, Gage," I say pointedly.

"Night, Olivia."

After breakfast Saturday morning, Gage leads me to a little trailhead off to the right of the lake. It's a flat four-mile loop that follows the path of a small creek near the camp.

Gage looks all kinds of attractive. His navy-blue walking shorts hit him at mid-thigh, exposing the way his quads flex and stretch with each step. He's wearing a beige cotton T-shirt that stretches across his chest and clings to the curves of his biceps. His signature black baseball hat sits backward on top of his head, like normal. The only complaint I have is that his dark, sporty sunglasses cover up his brilliant blue eyes.

Like me, he carries a water bottle, though his hangs from a strap he throws over his shoulder like a purse, and I have mine tucked away in a backpack big enough to hold a few essentials.

The morning air is cool and dry, and sunshine filters through the leaves around us as we walk. I close my eyes to bask in the warmth on my face and the satisfying burning sensation in my leg muscles.

We don't talk, but it's an amicable silence as we trek down the path, the trickle of water running over rocks in the creek the loudest sound.

At the halfway point, we stop for a brief rest.

"This is nice," Gage says, breaking the quiet.

"Yeah." I smile at him. "I'll be honest, I didn't know you were capable of going that long without talking."

"Oh, ha ha," he mutters. "I can be quiet when I want to be."

"I'm sure you can, but I've never witnessed it for myself." I smirk. "It was impressive."

He raises his eyebrows, a smile playing at the corners of his lips. "Is that how you want to be?"

"What if it is?" I challenge, propping my hand on my hip and lifting my chin.

This banter, the friendly debate and competition between Gage and me feels so familiar and natural. It's easy to sink into the moment and leave my brain on autopilot.

"Well, then," he starts, stepping close to me, "I think..." He wraps his arm around my waist and effortlessly lifts me. I squeal and kick my feet to try to force him to put me down.

"...we need to cool you off," he finishes as he gently drops me into the creek. It's only ankle high, but I end up sitting in the shallow water with my hands braced behind me and my knees folded up near my chest.

The water is *cold*, and it's seeping through my thin running shorts, chilling the skin underneath.

I glare up at Gage. "You're in big trouble now."

He pouts his lips. "I'm sorry, Olivia. I shouldn't have dumped you in the creek, no matter how funny it was."

He sticks out his hand in an offer to help me up. I take it, immediately yanking him toward me with as much force as I can. I don't know how he's not expecting it, but he's not, so he topples forward and lands in the water next to me.

His mouth hangs open, but if he's surprised, it's his own fault.

"I can't believe you fell for that! It's literally the oldest trick in the book. Super cliché."

He laughs, and the sound echoes through the trees around us, floating up into the Texas summer sky.

We finish our hike in damp clothes, which actually feels nice once the sun starts beating down on us.

Back at camp, we each break off to our own cabins to shower and change into dry clothes. We meet up again at the mess hall for lunch. A few of the other counselors—including Brynn and Matt, and some others I haven't spent much time with yet—have also stayed at camp this weekend.

We all eat together, and then Brynn suggests playing a game. We find a deck of giant Uno cards and play game after game until the other counselors all step away one by one. By the last game, it's Gage and me in a bitter fight to the death, neither of us holding back on the action cards.

Finally, I'm down to one card, a red five. Gage plays a wild card, and I hold my breath waiting for him to decide which color to call. I have a one in four chance here; either I'll win with my next turn, or I'll have to take my chances with the draw pile.

After what feels like forever, Gage says, "The new color is ... red."

"Ha!" I shout, slapping my card onto the discard pile.

Gage hangs his head and groans. "I *had* to pick red." He lifts his head. "Do you want to play again?"

"Nah, I'd rather make sure I go out on top," I tell him with a grin.

Still, neither of us make a move to leave. I don't want to play another game of Uno, but I also don't want to stop being with Gage.

So, I ask him a question about his experiences in college and playing baseball, and we sit at the table in the mess hall talking for at least another hour.

Before we know it, Rob and Stephanie are setting food out for dinner, and a few of the counselors we were playing with earlier wander back in.

"Have you two been in here the whole time?" asks a confused Brynn.

Gage and I exchange a look and shrug. "I guess so," I say.

Brynn tilts her head, staring at me. Most likely she's trying to reconcile what I've told her about not being interested in Gage and all the time we're spending together today.

I'm not sure I can explain it either.

I should stay away from Gage and continue to fight this desire for him that has lain dormant in my heart for so long now. But it's reawakening, as dangerous as it was in high school.

Other than us both being five years older, nothing else has changed. He's still a brainy go-getter on his way to amazing achievements, and I'm still me, struggling to find anything I'm good at off the soccer field. If anything, the imbalance between us is even more stark now, and I'm still nowhere near good enough to date Gage Carter.

Maybe it's selfishness that keeps me hanging around. Maybe it's that when I'm with him, I remember all the best parts of myself. Maybe it's *him*, his magnetic charisma that pulls me in and holds me in place.

Whatever the reason, instead of doing the right thing and retreating to my cabin alone after dinner, I ask Gage if he'd like to canoe with me at the lake.

He agrees with no hesitation.

Chapter Fifteen
Olivia

O nce we're in the center of the lake, we stop paddling and let the canoe drift. Gage lays his paddle across the sides of the boat, holding it in the center like the lap bar on a roller coaster.

We relax in the canoe as the sun starts to set; the sky shifts from blue to pink and red and orange, silhouetting the trees until they appear black against the colorful sky. The air already feels cooler as the sun sinks low.

I think back on the first week of camp—the activities I led, how much fun everyone had, and the kids I met.

"You know what's weird?" I ask.

"What?"

"Almost everyone this week called me Olivia instead of Delaney."

Gage looks away. "Huh. I guess I'm a trendsetter."

Before that super suspicious reaction, I figured Linda maybe got confused about which name I use and it caught on. Now, I'm questioning whether Gage had anything to do with it.

"Why do you look guilty?"

"Do I?" He shifts in his seat, keeping his eyes on the sunset over the trees.

"Should you?"

"Umm."

"Gage," I say sternly. "Look at me."

He finally meets my gaze again. I give him my best no-nonsense look. He matches my expression for a beat but can't stop the grin from spreading over his lips.

"You did something!" I accuse.

He shrugs. "Not really. All I really did was mention you a lot in conversation with the other staff and overemphasize your name. Your actual name."

"Gage!" I groan. "There's a reason I prefer to be called Delaney."

"Ah. Well, then please share. What's the reason?"

I hesitate. The real reason is that I didn't want to be "Stupid Olivia" anymore. I decided to reinvent myself heading into high school. No one would notice my shortcomings in the classroom if I dominated on the soccer pitch and my popularity made everyone want to be my friend. So I became cool, fun Delaney. But it still wasn't enough.

He reads my reluctance to share as reticence. "You've got nothing, do you? And 'Olivia' suits you. I never understood why you wanted to change something that was already perfect."

I scoff. "Nothing about me is perfect." I pause, deciding to share part of the truth. "You want to know why? Fine. Heading into high school, I wanted to differentiate myself. From my sisters, who the teachers all remembered and then expected me to be just like, and also from who I was before. I wanted to be … fun."

Gage tilts his head, as if trying to figure me out. "You've always been fun. You still are. I had an amazing time with you today."

"It was a good day," I agree.

He doesn't need to know how I'm filing away each and every moment from this day together to pull out and relive after this summer is over and we go back to living our separate lives again.

We row back to shore in the postsunset twilight and pull the canoe up the bank and out of the water. I leave Gage on the shore as I put the life vests and oars back in the boathouse.

When I return, he's sitting in the grass with his eyes trained on the sky.

"What are you doing?" I ask.

"Stargazing," he answers, then pulls on my hand until I'm sitting down next to him. "Join me."

I turn my head up to look at the stars, painfully aware that he's still holding my hand. The night is quiet; the only sounds are the buzz of the cicadas and the soft lapping of the lake water on the shore.

Without thinking, I lean against Gage's side, tilting my head until it rests on his shoulder. His body stills, as if he's afraid moving might break the spell.

Slowly, he brings his face down and kisses the top of my head with agonizing softness. Then he stops, but when I don't push him away, he moves on to my forehead. His lips linger against my skin, and I close my eyes, drinking in the sensation.

I switch my brain back to autopilot. Playing in the creek, tussling together over cards, relaxing into conversation on the lake; everything about today with Gage has lulled me into my feelings and away from the very good reasons I have for leaving him alone.

I tilt my face toward him, giving him better access, and he kisses down one side of my face—to my eyebrow, my cheek, my jawline, my chin—and then back up the other side. His mouth is warm when he parts his lips and presses an open-mouthed kiss to my temple.

His nearness and his touch are so exhilaratingly loud and bright in the dark quiet that they leave no space for my doubts. So, I push the doubts aside.

I shiver, and he wraps an arm around my shoulder, pulling me close. The shift puts my mouth mere inches from his, so close I can feel his breath on my lips as he breathes in and out. Time stops, and we're suspended in this moment, hearts pounding and breaths ragged, for too long.

He doesn't come closer, doesn't make a move, and my frustration ratchets up with each second that passes. I reach out and clutch the fabric of his T-shirt in my fist, hoping to jolt him into closing the gap between his lips and mine.

"Olivia," he breathes out. "If you want this—"

"I want it," I murmur.

"It's your move."

I don't second-guess. It's like the thread holding me back has unraveled bit by bit and now it snaps, and I'm falling into him. My lips are on his in an instant, desperate and needy. He returns the same energy, moving his mouth over mine with a frenzy that leaves me gasping for air.

We can't get close enough. He pulls me onto his lap, and I use the new angle to deepen the kiss. With one hand still gripping his shirt, I slide the other to the back of his neck and drag my fingers through his hair.

He has one of his arms braced behind my back while the other cups the side of my head. When his mouth detaches from mine, I whimper, then gasp as he drags his lips down the side of my neck to my shoulder.

A deep, low-pitched "hoo-hoo, hoo-hoo" from the nearby trees startles us away from each other.

Gage chuckles, smoothing a hand over the wrinkles in his shirt from where I was gripping it. "An owl, I think."

I nod, though I'm not sure he can see me. It's gotten dark quickly.

With the loss of his proximity, my brain switches back on, and the doubts crowd back in.

I check my smartwatch to distract myself from the impulse to reach for him again. Wow, it's late. So maybe it hasn't gotten dark quickly; we've been out here a while.

The realization sets my nervous system into panic-mode. Questions shoot through my mind so quickly I don't have time to consider answers to any of them. *Was this a fluke? What is Gage thinking? What did this mean to him? How can we move forward as friends after this?*

I clear my throat, forcing myself to channel the detachedness of my cool, unbothered Delaney persona. "We should probably get to our cabins so we can get some sleep before the new group of campers arrive tomorrow."

Gage is quiet. The owl hoots again, and a breeze blows over my bare arms, causing me to shiver.

"Yeah," he says finally, his voice subdued. "Let me walk you back."

At my cabin door, he leans forward and brushes a strand of hair off my face. I watch him, searching his face for any indication of what he's thinking, how he's feeling. But he's impassive.

For him, that kiss must have been a bit of closure on our halted relationship five years ago. For me, it was a compulsion, something that I couldn't have stopped if I wanted to, despite my better judgment and my desire to do the right thing.

As if confirming my thoughts, he brushes a dispassionate kiss to my cheek before stepping back. "Good night, Olivia."

"Night," I echo.

Once inside, I lean my back against the closed door and squeeze my eyes shut with enough force that red spots ignite behind my lids.

Hot shame rolls down my back like beads of sweat during a grueling soccer practice. Kissing Gage was reckless, but leading him on would be unforgivable.

When we talk about this tomorrow—and knowing Gage, I'm certain we will—I need to set expectations. Throw up boundaries and restrictions. Make it clear I know where I should stand with him.

I know I'm not a good long-term match for him, but after those explosive kisses, I need more.

Maybe there's a way to kiss him for now without tying him down. Maybe we can lean into our physical chemistry without getting his heart involved.

I groan and run my hand down my face. Maybe when I kissed Gage, I made this summer a whole lot more complicated.

"What have I done?" I whisper into the dim cabin.

Chapter Sixteen

Gage

I kissed Olivia Delaney. The realization runs through my head like a refrain as I walk back to my empty cabin.

It's hard to believe. If someone had told me a month ago that not only would I see and talk to Olivia again, but I'd *kiss* her again, I'd have laughed in their face. I'd closed that chapter of my heart, even if I hadn't left it behind completely.

At the same time, the fact that Olivia and I kissed tonight is somehow the most natural thing in the world. It was inevitable, really. From the moment we locked eyes in the office on her first day at camp, we've been careening toward this very thing.

That whole first week of orientation when Olivia was essentially forced to hang out with me, because I was the only person who would talk to her, we fell easily back into friendship. That first weekend when we went into town together, we started crossing the line, flirting, and hinting at an attraction that must still be there for both of us.

Then this past week, being dropped back into a routine that didn't include spending time with Olivia every day, I felt ready to crawl out of my own skin. Those brief moments when I brought my campers to swim or boat were the focal point of my days only because I got to see her.

Sometimes after dropping them off, I had to leave to check in with Linda or prepare for another activity, but when I could, I stayed. I would watch her organizing the groups and instructing the kids and interacting—talking and laughing with a smile on her face. The joy she brings to her job. The competence. I could watch her all day.

Which all meant that I was desperate to spend time with her this weekend. I sought her out on Friday night, hoping against all hope that she would be staying at camp. That she would grant me a little bit of her time today. Instead, she gave me nearly all of it, and greedily, I gobbled it up. I still want more.

But I don't know where her head is. I don't know how she feels about me or our kiss or what it means for her and me as an "us."

I'd do anything to keep her from walking away from me again. Anything to keep her in my life this time around.

And that's terrifying because I still don't know why she walked away the first time. I don't know why she turned me down on graduation day, and I don't know why she ghosted me after.

Clearly I need answers. I go to bed resolved to have the conversation with her in the morning, even if it's hard.

Sunday morning, I sit in one of the rocking chairs in front of the mess hall and wait for Olivia. I thought about waiting outside her cabin, but I don't want to look overly eager. Even though my instincts are telling me to grab her and hold on, my self-preservation cautions that I should tread carefully.

Finally, after what feels like hours but is likely less than ten minutes, I see her coming up the path toward me. I stand, and when she sees me, she gives me a tentative smile.

I let her come to me most of the way before I cover those last few steps that bring us toe to toe. I hand her the mug of coffee I poured for her in the mess hall before I started my vigil on the porch.

"Thank you," she says, taking the mug.

"You're welcome."

The air between us is fraught with awkward tension. I shuffle my feet. I want to tell her everything about how much that kiss meant to me and the way it reawakened all the feelings I had for her back in high school and more.

But instead, I wait, wanting her to speak first, needing to know what she's thinking before I make a fool out of myself again.

"About last night—" she starts, and I can tell by the regret in her eyes that I won't like what she has to say.

I quickly interrupt her. "I know. I shouldn't have kissed you. I'm sorry. I think I got swept up in the moment."

Relief crosses her face, and my heart sinks.

"So, I was actually thinking ... Well, what I'm trying to say ..." She blushes. "It's clear we're attracted to each other, right?" She looks at me for confirmation.

I bob my head vigorously up and down. "Yes, definitely," I agree.

"So, what if..." she continues. My heart speeds up, a hope I haven't felt since high school lifting me. "Well, what if we kept doing this? Kissing? Like ... like ... like a summer fling?"

"A summer fling," I echo hollowly. As quickly as it came in, the hope leaks out of my body. "What would that mean," I say carefully, "for you?"

"Well, like, we enjoy a physical relationship this summer." My eyebrows rise. "PG-13," she clarifies quickly. "We're both here, we both want it, and neither of us want anything serious, right?"

Wrong, I think. *Absolutely wrong. Could not be more wrong.*

I lift one shoulder. "I guess?"

The truth is I've wanted Olivia for so long that I'll take whatever she's offering. Happily. And maybe by the end of the summer, she'll feel differently about a real relationship.

I put away my questions about our past, so I can focus on my new mission here and now.

"So, are you in? Summer fling?"

I grin at her, hoping she can't detect the ambivalent feelings under the surface. "Yeah," I agree. "I'm in."

I really hope I don't regret it.

This week, I have a very active group of nine ten-year-old boys. One of the boys from last week, Martin, is back again, but everyone else is new.

I learn quickly that a boy named Gabriel is determined to set himself apart as the funny kid. He has plans for jokes and pranks and isn't satisfied unless he's making someone laugh. I'll admit, he *is* pretty funny, but the more I let it show that I'm actually enjoying his antics, the more carried away he gets. It's hard maintaining a stern face when I'm dying laughing inside.

Of course, his energy is contagious, and pretty soon I have nine boys running around trying to prank, wedgie, and horseplay with each other and with me.

I decide to help my campers channel all that spirit into some safe and sanctioned hijinks that also have the benefit of letting me spend time with Olivia. Sort of.

The boys help me plan our attack. First, we stockpile our arsenal of squirt guns, water bombs, and water blasters. We discussed it and agreed not to use water balloons because of the mess and the danger to the wildlife. None of us want to spend an hour afterward picking colorful pieces of latex off the ground.

Next, we choose our targets. The ten-year-old girls are an obvious choice, and it works out that we don't have any activities scheduled during their free-swim time. Plus, I notice that some of my boys seem to be terrified of the girls, so hopefully this will help break the ice a little too.

The boys ask me why we would start a water fight when the girls are already in their bathing suits and swimming. "Wouldn't it be funnier to get their dry clothes all wet?"

I explain that we want this to be fun for everyone, and the girls might not appreciate us soaking them in their regular clothes. Also, we have to attack while the girls are at the lake so that I can see Olivia, though I don't share that part with my kids.

I also remind them that the lifeguard has a very important job to do and is off-limits.

Then, we suit up. Literally, I have all the boys put their swimsuits on, but they also want battle paint. We borrow some washable paints from Nina in the craft cabin and soon the campers are decorating their own and each other's faces—dark lines across their cheekbones, blue (because boys rule, naturally) dots across their noses. One kid even does the whole *Braveheart* look, which surprises me because aren't these kids a little young to know *Braveheart*? That movie came out almost ten years before I was born, even.

Finally, we're ready to attack. There's not much cover between our cabin and the lake, but we do the best we can hiding behind buildings and a few scrawny trees. We approach as the girls are lined up on the dock getting a safety reminder from the lifeguard, Rocky. Their backs are to us, so they don't see us approach.

It's an ambush.

I silently motion the boys to stop walking. Then I hold up my hand, putting one finger down at a time for a silent countdown. *5... 4... 3... 2... 1!*

With roars and shouts, we run toward the dock, squirting our guns, and launching water at the girls when we get close enough.

The girls turn their heads when they hear the commotion and start screaming, some of them jumping into the lake to avoid the attack.

I'm armed with a Super Soaker that holds thirty ounces of water, giving me plenty of ammunition to annihilate my opponent. Of course, I have a specific opponent in mind.

I see Olivia standing at the end of the dock, trying to avoid the water war going on in front of her. There's no way I can get to her without her seeing me, but she also has nowhere to go.

And she knows it. She stands with her hands on her hips trying to hide her smile as I get closer and closer, blasting her with the Super Soaker with every step.

"Gage," she warns. "Don't you dare! I should have known it was your little hooligans leading this attack."

Her white T-shirt is drenched to the point I can see the black one-piece swimsuit she wears underneath. Her hair, in its high ponytail, is plastered against her neck.

Without losing momentum, I drop the squirt gun and grab Olivia around the waist before launching us both into the lake. I hold her tight as we fall and splash through the surface of the water.

She grips my arms as we come up again, both treading water to stay afloat. Taking advantage of the situation, I skate my hand up her side and around her back. Her breath catches, and she tilts her chin up to look at me full in the face.

Drops of water roll from her hairline down her face. I follow a bead as it slides down her forehead, between her eyes, off the tip of her nose, and drips right onto her lips.

I glance around us. Pulling Olivia behind one of the wooden dock pilings, I press her back against it and besiege her mouth with mine. She retaliates with equal force, hooking her legs around my waist and drawing me closer.

It's a stolen moment, but I pull away before anything gets out of hand.

Olivia grins at me, and we both swim toward the shore.

When she gets out, I tear my eyes away from the shorts sticking against her skin long enough to notice a streak of green slime across the back of her T-shirt. It must have smudged onto her from the piling.

She turns her head and catches me staring. "What?" she demands.

I smirk. "Nothing, babe." After all, this *is* a war.

I look around to see my boys are as sopping wet as the girls, and the weapons are pretty evenly distributed between the two groups now too.

Everyone is laughing and having fun. I think we can call the battle a stalemate.

Chapter Seventeen

Olivia

I am now in a situationship of sorts with Gage Carter, the boy—now man—I've been on-again, off-again in love with since I was thirteen.

In a way, this plan is brilliant. I have lots of experience with situationships and brief flings that don't go beyond a few dates. I've been the queen of "date 'em and dump 'em" for years, but using that same strategy with the one man I actually want is a dangerous game.

One thing I know for sure is that I don't want Annie to find out. Based on that phone conversation when I first got to camp, if she thought there was even a smidgen of a chance that Gage and I could be something serious long-term, she'd be over the moon. I don't want to get her hopes up.

Lying in my bunk, I gasp and pull out my phone to text Gage.

Olivia:

you haven't said anything to Annie about us, have you?

He replies right away.

Gage:

Not yet

I breathe a sigh of relief.

Olivia:

let's not

The dots indicating Gage is typing appear and disappear several times before his reply comes in.

Gage:

Annie is my best friend

Olivia:

excuse me?

Gage:

[eye roll emoji] Let me rephrase. Annie is *my* best friend, but I'm not *her* best friend. That honor goes to you, of course

Olivia:

damn straight

Gage:

Not telling her will be hard. I tell her every-thing

Olivia:

I get that. I do too. but you know how she is. She'll want this to be something it's not

Olivia:

she's not here. We won't see her. She doesn't have to know

The dots appear and disappear again.

Gage:

I guess so

Olivia:

it's probably best if no one knows

Gage:

No one? Like sneak around?

I bite my lip, considering.

Olivia:

how about no one from back home?

Gage:

If that's what you want

💕 💕 💕

One week goes by, then two, then three, all following the same routine but with different groups of kids.

Nina is a decent roommate when she's here, but usually she's out somewhere with Rocky. Because neither of them are cabin counselors, they have some free time in the evenings, like me. But she keeps her things neat and is quiet when she sneaks in after I'm asleep. On Friday nights, she and Rocky head home as soon as they can and don't return until Sunday morning.

In my position, I interact with pretty much everyone every day. The counselors bring their kids to the lake for free swim and water sports time. I check in with the activity counselors and coordinate with Linda and Troy. I even usually see Hannah, the camp nurse, when I pick up the bottle of swimmer's ear solution from her each morning.

All of that means that if something happens at Camp Prairie Star, I usually know about it. I hear—and unintentionally see—all the best gossip, and I know that Gage and I are a hot topic among the other counselors.

Even so, during the week while Gage is busy with his campers, our fling is more like longing looks across the crowded mess hall. A few times a week, he comes to find me in the boathouse while his kids are crafting with Nina or hiking with Jake. He pulls me into the corner and kisses me senseless and then takes off again, leaving me spinning.

But from Friday night after the campers leave until Sunday when the new group arrives, we spend every waking minute together. Canoeing or swimming or driving into town or hanging out in one of the cabins.

And we kiss. Long, slow kisses and frenzied, desperate ones. I've never before been kissed like Gage Carter kisses me. It's like I'm his sole focus, and his only mission is to make me forget anything but him.

Now, we're halfway through June and finishing up the fifth week with campers, and my sixth week here total. It's a scorcher of a week, too. A heat wave has been lingering in the area, with temperatures reaching one hundred degrees some days.

My phone rings when I'm almost to the mess hall for dinner after another Friday Skit Night. Actually rings. Like, with a phone call. I check the screen. It's my sister Molly.

I answer, and since it's a video call, her face appears on the screen.

"I'm bored!" she whines.

I chuckle. "So have your husband entertain you. I'm about to eat dinner."

"I can't. He's in Alaska on a work trip."

"Ah. Sorry." I sit down in one of the rocking chairs outside the mess hall.

Molly's eyebrows pinch together. "Seriously, I don't know how I did this every day."

"Did what? Came home to an empty apartment?"

"Yes! It's so lonely." She pouts her lips.

I lean back in the chair and push off the ground with my toe to start rocking back and forth. "Didn't you basically work, like, all the time to escape that exact thing?"

"Ugh, yes."

I squint. "You need a hobby."

"I could start one, but then I'd abandon it when Jonathan gets back." She smirks. "My hobby with *him* is—"

I make a face. "Eww, Molly. I don't need the details."

Molly laughs. "I was going to say Scrabble. But hey, we're newly-weds—what do you expect?"

"Newlyweds. You've been married for six months. How long does that distinction last anyway?"

Her expression turns dreamy. "Hopefully forever." She sighs.

Aww. I really hope so too. I love seeing Molly like this.

"So, anyway. Hobbies," I say. "Oh! Do you remember that one summer when I was, like, five and you decided to take up juggling?"

"Yes!" Molly squeals. "I thought it looked fun, so I spent my entire saved allowance on a juggling kit. Six balls, four pins, and a how-to DVD."

"How long did that last?"

"Oh, I gave it my all for about a week, and then I moved on ... to unicycle riding, I think?"

"Apparently you were in your clown era," I deadpan.

We're both still laughing when I see Gage come up behind me through the phone. Before I can say anything, he smacks a kiss on my forehead.

"Gage," I say meaningfully. "I'm on a video call with my sister."

He looks at the screen, then looks at me, smirking. "Oops," he says. "Hey!" He waves toward the phone.

"I'll meet you inside okay?" I nudge him away, and he heads into the mess hall.

When I look back at the phone, Molly's eyes are wide, a knowing smile on her face. "Was that Gage? Annie's brother Gage?"

I nod reluctantly.

"Wow, I haven't seen him since he was, like, fourteen. He sure has grown up." She pumps her eyebrows.

"Molly! Oh eww!" Though she's not wrong.

"I'm just saying," she laughs. "Are you guys together?"

"Oh, um, not really. It's a summer fling."

Molly clucks her tongue. "I didn't know that summer flings"—she holds her fingers up in quotation marks as she says the phrase—"include forehead kisses. Seems a little tender for a no-strings-attached situation."

"No," I protest. "Forehead kisses can totally be part of a fling. The main thing is that there's an expiration date. This thing is done when camp's done."

Molly's brow furrows. "Are you sure that's a good idea? He's your best friend's brother. What if you get attached?"

Little does she know I've *been* attached, and no, I'm not sure this is a good idea. "It'll be fine, Mol."

"Okay. I don't want you to get hurt."

I appreciate Molly's concern, and I don't want her to worry, but I already know for certain I'm going to get hurt. I've accepted it. Because being with Gage now, however temporary, is well worth it.

"Hey, by the way," she adds, "did you finish that audiobook? The one I recommended?"

She's talking about the book I finished about the history and ecology of the Great Lakes. "Yeah, it was really good. Got any other recommendations?"

"Sure. I'll text them to you."

"Cool. I've got to listen to the one about the history of the Chicago World's Fair next before my loan is up in Libby, but I could do with some more science this summer."

"Sounds good." She smiles. "Thanks for providing some entertainment. I'll let you go eat dinner now." She winks. "And see your man."

I shake my head. "Bye, Molly."

We hang up, and I march into the mess hall. I walk right up to Gage, who's sitting in our usual spot at the end of the table on the far end of the room.

"What the heck, Gage?" I hiss at him. "You outed us to my sister."

He grimaces. "Sorry. I think the heat is getting to me."

I relax my shoulders. "Same, honestly." I take a seat next to him and reach for the other half of his sandwich. "It's fine. It's not like Molly talks to Annie."

She'll definitely tell Nicole, though, and they'll both tell their husbands. I make a mental note to text Molly later to make sure she doesn't say anything to our parents. I don't think she would, but she's bored, so who knows?

"What a relief," Gage says in a sarcastic tone.

I ignore his jab and change the subject. "Is it supposed to cool off anytime soon?"

"Maybe next week." He shrugs. "But I'm not holding my breath."

"Ugh, this is crazy!" I whine, fanning myself with my hand even though the mess hall is air conditioned. "It's only June. It's not supposed to be this hot, yet."

"That's a Texas summer for ya."

I'm feeling unreasonably cranky all of a sudden. I know Gage is counting on spending time together tonight, but I'm hot and tired. "Hey, I'm going to take a cool shower and go to bed early tonight. Is that okay?"

"You're bailing on me?" he teases, then runs a hand through his hair. "It's probably for the best. The heat is making me kind of grumpy, and I don't want to take it out on you. We're still hanging out tomorrow, though, right?"

"Yes. Inside preferably." I fan myself with my hand again.

"No problem. I'll think of things we can do inside. As long as I get to spend time with you, that's all I ask. After all, I only get the weekends as it is. I'm not giving up any of my Saturdays with you."

I can think of plenty of things we can do inside tomorrow. Things that involve a lot of kissing. But I'm also not going to complain about quiet time with him spent talking or playing games. I think about my conversation with Molly. I know that Gage and I are blurring the lines between "fling" and "real relationship," but I'm going to maintain my delusion that as long as there's an end date established on this ... whatever it is we're doing, none of it is real, and he won't get attached.

Chapter Eighteen

Olivia

I feel better after a cool shower and a good night's sleep in the air conditioning. I hope Gage does, too.

He's already at the mess hall when I arrive to grab some breakfast and coffee. It's still hot enough to fry an egg on the sidewalk outside. The brief walk from my cabin has me sweating.

"Good morning." Gage greets me with a kiss on the forehead.

As usual on Saturdays, there are a handful of other camp staff hanging around, but everyone mostly keeps to themselves.

"Morning," I respond. "Are you feeling less grumpy today?"

"I am. It's amazing how tired chasing a group of ten-year-old boys around all week can make a person."

"Yeah, I bet."

"What about you? Ready to spend the day in the AC with me?"

I'm always ready and eager to spend any day with Gage, but I exaggerate a groan. "If I have to." I grin while I tease him.

He nods seriously. "You do. It's a contractual obligation."

I laugh. "What contract? I didn't sign any contract."

"Well, we'll have to fix that. I'll have my lawyer draw something up."

I roll my eyes. *His lawyer.* I pat his chest, noting, as always, how firm it is under my hand. "You do that, champ."

Gage grins. "I have a surprise for you."

"Ooh, what is it?"

"Eat your breakfast." He chuckles. "And then you'll see."

After breakfast, Gage walks me toward his cabin. At the doorway, he covers my eyes with his hand. "Keep 'em closed until I say *open,*" he tells me.

I keep my eyes open and try to see through the cracks in his fingers as he opens the cabin door and leads me inside. Even still, I can't see much.

"Okay, open!" I quickly close my eyes while Gage moves his hand. I make a show of opening my eyes and blinking.

On one side of the aisle between the bunk beds, Gage has hung up a white sheet. It's stretched taut and tied off at the corners like a movie screen.

Across from the sheet, a small projector sits on the bare mattress of the bottom bunk of one of the beds. The top bunk of that same bed is decked out with pillows propped against the wall and blankets lining the mattress.

I clap my hands. "Movie day?" I ask eagerly.

"Yep!" He gestures to a tray of goodies sitting on one of the other bunks. "With snacks, of course. I even have some Dr Pepper, though it's not cold."

I eye the tray and see that it's stocked with my favorites, along with some fruity gummy candies for him. He has chocolate–peanut butter pretzels, cheddar–sour cream potato chips, Milk Duds, honey-roasted peanuts, and a bag of caramel popcorn.

"This is so fun!" I exclaim. "Where did you get the projector?"

"Linda had it in one of the storage closets. They pull it out to play movies in the mess hall when the weather's too bad for the kids to be outside. But it only takes DVDs, and the selection was not the best."

I hold out my hand. "Well, let's see."

He laughs. "Not yet. First, take off your shoes and climb up to your balcony seats. Get comfortable."

I do as I'm told and relax into the blankets and pillows on the top bunk.

"Okay," Gage announces. "Our movie choices are pretty much every Pixar movie made in the nineties, *The Parent Trap*, but it's the original Hayley Mills version not the Lindsay Lohan one, and my personal favorite: *Heavyweights*."

I wrinkle my nose, trying to remember if I've ever heard of *Heavyweights*. I come up blank.

"Okay, I'll bite. What's *Heavyweights*?"

Gage's face splits into a grin. "Only a cinematic masterpiece of the mid-90s about boys at a weight-loss summer camp. Ben Stiller plays the super intense camp owner who kills the Blob! The Blob, Olivia!"

"I've never heard of it. Ben Stiller's in it?" I purse my lips. "And weight-loss camp for kids? Really? What is wrong with people?"

Gage shrugs. "It was the nineties. Body positivity wasn't really a thing. The culture was all about being super skinny and dieting."

I cock my head and raise one eyebrow.

Gage holds up his hands. "Okay, I feel like I'm not selling this movie, but I promise it's really funny. You have to look past some of the more problematic plot points."

"Where did you hear about this movie again?"

He looks away. "I watched it at Maggie's house. She loved it when she was a kid."

Oh. No wonder he wants to watch it, especially here at the summer camp Maggie attended as a kid.

I consider for a minute, adjusting the pillow behind me. "Do they ... do they make fun of the kids?" I ask warily. I can't imagine Gage finding that sort of thing funny, but I have to check before I blindly agree to watch it.

"No," Gage says quickly. "Well, the villains of the movie do, but it's portrayed as mean, which it is, instead of funny or acceptable."

I relent. "Okay, let's watch *Heavyweights.*"

Gage pumps his fist. "Yes! You won't regret it, trust me."

And he's right, the movie is great, with Ben Stiller playing a hilariously unhinged camp director and coach. The kids are cute, and the underlying message is one of self-acceptance and friendship.

As the credits roll, I snuggle deeper into Gage's side. "It was good," I admit.

"Told you so," he murmurs, kissing my neck in that delectable way I love.

"But now"—I playfully wiggle away from him—"it's obviously time for a *Toy Story* marathon."

He grunts and pulls me back to his side with a wink. "Intermission first."

We spend the rest of the day cuddling and kissing while kids' movies play in the background. When we're hungry, we snack on the treats from the tray, but by dinner time, it's clear we both need to eat something more substantial.

So, we walk to the mess hall for sustenance, braving the suffocating air that lingers even though it's well into evening time.

When we finish eating, Gage leans in close to me. "I have one more surprise for you today," he whispers in my ear. "Meet me by the little dock at 8:30. Wear a swimsuit."

"Why?" I turn and look up at him.

His eyes sparkle. "You'll see."

Chapter Nineteen

Gage

As requested, Olivia is waiting for me by the dock after sunset. She's wearing a sporty two-piece swimsuit with running shorts over it and holding a towel.

She sees me approaching and calls out, "What's this all about?"

I wait until I'm only a couple of feet away, then I grin. "Night swim."

The smile that lights up her face is immediate. "Ooh, fun!"

I take her hand and start pulling her toward the dock. "I'd like it to be acknowledged for the record that, despite my baser instincts, I did ask you to wear a swimsuit tonight."

"Very gentlemanly of you."

"If, however," I continue, "you prefer *not* to wear it, I'm totally game." I turn my head and smile at her wolfishly.

She laughs. "Swimsuits are a must."

I heave an exaggerated sigh. "Fine."

"That was a good try, though." She pats my shoulder.

She drops her towel onto the dock and shimmies out of her shorts and sandals. I realize I'm watching her too intently, my mind and eyes wandering where they shouldn't, so I clear my throat and focus on my own preparations.

I pull off my shirt and am pleased to find Olivia staring at my bare chest. I flex a little to show off.

She blinks out of her daze and moves toward the side of the dock by the cordoned-off swimming area. I follow. We peer over the edge at the water below, almost black in the low twilight.

"Do you think it's cold?" Olivia whispers.

I chuckle. "I mean, I'm hoping so. Cooling off is kind of the point."

She stares down at the water. "It looks so dark."

I nudge her with my elbow. "Come on. You're not scared, are you?"

"Of course not," Olivia says quickly, glaring at me.

"Then jump in."

"I'm about to."

"Okay, go ahead." I nudge her again.

She elbows me back. "You haven't jumped yet either."

"Fine. At the same time?" She nods, and I take her hand, intertwining our fingers. "One ... two ... three..."

We jump together. The water is refreshingly cool, but fortunately not freezing.

Olivia laughs when she surfaces. "It feels so nice!"

I shake my head rapidly like a dog, sending droplets of water from my hair flying everywhere.

Olivia shrieks and dunks under the water, popping up again a little farther out.

Even though I'm closer to shore than she is, I yell out, "Race you to the swim raft!"

Without waiting for her response, I start pumping my arms and kicking toward the small wooden platform fifty feet from shore. It floats on the outskirts of the swimming area, anchored to the lake floor underneath by ropes.

I hear Olivia splashing behind me as she tries to catch up. Suddenly I feel her fingers wrap around my ankle as she tries to yank me back. Her jerking is not very effective, though, and definitely doesn't stop my forward movement.

She moves her hand a little higher, and a sharp snap of pain has me bending in two as she charges ahead of me. *She pulled my leg hair!*

I recover quickly and start swimming again, but it's too late.

Olivia reaches the raft before me, crowing triumphantly. "I beat you!"

I arrive at the raft and rest my elbows and forearms on the platform. "Only because you cheated."

Olivia smirks. "I didn't cheat! That's called resourcefulness."

"Seemed an awful lot like cheating," I mutter.

She reaches over and tickles my chin with her fingers. "Aw, don't be mad."

She runs her knuckles up and down the scruff on my cheeks, looking damn near perfect, mostly submerged in the water with moonlight shining around her. How could I be mad?

I flash her a smile. "I don't get mad, babe. I get even."

She snorts. "Ooh, I'm so scared."

"Okay, fine. But when you least expect it, I'll strike."

She laughs softly, folding her arms on the top of the platform and resting her head against them. I lean my head in, too, and we hang there facing each other like that in silence for a few minutes, kicking our legs gently to stay afloat.

Olivia speaks first. "I realized you never answered my question about why you're working here this summer. I know you said that Maggie went to camp here, but you were probably making more money working at your dad's office."

I don't respond right away. Instead, I weigh my need to protect my heart against my intense desire to share everything with Olivia. I want so badly to have as strong an emotional connection as we do a physical one. Despite agreeing to this whole "summer fling" thing, I want so much more of Olivia than her kisses, amazing as they are.

But she's hurt me before, and it took me a really long time to get over her desertion.

I'm close enough to Olivia that even in the dark, I can see her pinch her eyes closed. "Never mind," she backtracks. "You don't have to answer that."

But if she wants me to, I will. She could ask me for so much more than this, and I would give it to her happily. She could ask for everything, if only she wanted it from me.

I clear my throat. "No, it's fine. Um, working at Camp Prairie Star has nothing to do with the money for me. I wanted to be in this place. Maggie did come here when she was a kid. It's kind of a tradition in her family. They've been going to camp here for generations."

Olivia nods. "You want to feel like you're part of that tradition."

I bobble my head. "Yes, but there's more to it than that. You know, right, that Maggie got pregnant with us when she was fifteen and she was sixteen when we were born?" I look at her for confirmation.

"Mm-hmm. Annie told me."

"Well, her last summer at camp was the summer before she started high school. She was fourteen. She told me and Annie that this place, Camp Prairie Star, was the last place she remembers still feeling like a kid, feeling like the world was open to her with endless possibilities and promise. She had to grow up quickly after that."

Olivia reaches one of her hands over to cover mine. "She was so young."

I swallow a lump in my throat. "She was, which is why I understand logically why she felt giving us up was her best option. But ..." I trail off, trying to gather my thoughts and the best way to express them.

Another part of my hesitation is that the only other person I've ever shared these thoughts with is my therapist, Dr. Francine. I tried to talk to Annie, but it was a conversation she didn't want to have. I feel awkward and ungrateful at the thought of talking to my parents about it.

Olivia shifts closer to me, aligning our bodies as we hang on the raft side by side. Her hip fits perfectly in the space above mine.

It would be a relief to air my conflicting emotions about my adoption to Olivia, for someone else in my life to see that part of me. At the same time, trusting her with my deepest feelings is terrifying, especially because she's left me before.

I blow out a breath of air and take a leap of faith. "But I can't stop obsessing about the unfairness of it all. It's not right that she had to hand her newborn babies off to a stranger. It's not fair that Annie and I … that I had to be separated from the mother that grew me and nurtured me before I was even born."

Olivia's forehead wrinkles. "You were only a few days old, though. You can't possibly remember."

I shift slightly away. "No, I don't remember, exactly. But I still feel it, and that feeling's always been in me. A feeling like … it's hard to explain, but a feeling like I was left to fend for myself, that the one person who was supposed to be there to protect me was gone. If *she* could disappear, what would stop everybody else from doing the same?"

Olivia's quiet for a few moments, processing. "I didn't know you felt that way about your adoption," she says finally. "Annie's never mentioned that it bothers her."

I shrug. "I don't think it does. But that doesn't mean it can't bother me," I say gently.

"No, of course. Sorry." She rests her chin on top of my bare shoulder.

"And while I've always had that feeling of something not being right inside me, I didn't actually know how to put words to it until recently. I took a developmental psychology class in college where we talked about attachment theory and how abandonment and grief can impact secure attachments between parents and children. It all felt so ... familiar."

"So, what about your parents? Dawn and Ted, I mean. You don't feel like you ... like you 'attached' to them?"

"No, I do. I love my mom and dad. They're the best. But I also felt like I was always trying to prove to them that I was worth keeping. Not consciously, but I did well in school because that made my mom proud, and I worked hard at baseball because that made my dad proud. They never suggested that I needed to earn my keep or anything, but that feeling inside me was driving me."

Olivia's quiet again. "You're really self-aware about all of this," she says softly.

I chuckle mirthlessly. "That took time. There's a term used in the adult adoptee community: coming out of the fog. It means you're ready to acknowledge and start to deal with your negative emotions around your adoption instead of repressing them. Once I came out of the fog with the help of that psychology class, I felt really confused and kind of angry. I started seeing a therapist who was familiar with and competent in adoption issues. She's helped me talk through a lot of this stuff."

"I had no idea, but Gage ... I'm proud of you. I wish I would have been there to support you through all that."

I don't know why she says that, because we both know she wasn't there because she cut me out of her life, abandoned me after high school. What I don't tell her is that her leaving me is what made that niggling feeling inside me grow and fester so that when I read the part in my developmental psychology textbook about attachment theory, it resonated. That feeling that told me that relationships are not permanent, and the people I love would leave me, got louder because of her.

Of course, she was a teenager and couldn't possibly understand the implications of her actions back then. I didn't even know at the time why I reacted the way I did.

I toss my head to clear my thoughts. Although all too often it doesn't *feel* like it, high school graduation and the way that Olivia and I parted ways all those years ago are all in the past.

Right now, in the present, I'm with Olivia, and I can pretend that she'll never leave me again so I can enjoy this time with her.

Speaking of which, I dip my head to place a lingering kiss on Olivia's forehead. "Thanks," I tell her.

She tilts her chin up to give me better access to her lips, but instead, I kiss her temple and then her cheekbone right under her eye. From there, I taste her skin down her jawline and onto her neck.

She shifts even closer and kicks her feet in the water for the momentum to wriggle her body up, so our faces are inches apart.

With a smirk, I kiss her neck again, and she whimpers, clearly wanting my lips on hers.

So, I bring my mouth close enough that I'm hovering next to her lips. And then even closer.

At the last second, instead of kissing her, I push myself away from the raft and start swimming back to shore.

I laugh as her frustrated grumble follows me across the water.

"Are you freaking kidding me?" she shouts after me.

I turn my head enough to call back, "That's what you get for cheating in the race!"

"Gage!" she roars, and I hear the splash of her chasing me down.

That's where I want us to be, honestly—her chasing me for a change. Because while my little trick is revenge for her pulling my leg hair earlier, it's also maybe a little bit for abandoning me all those years ago, too.

Chapter Twenty

Gage

Another week of camp with another group of wild, hilarious ten-year-olds passes. We're about halfway through the summer already, and though those first couple of weeks seemed slow paced, the time is flying past now. I'd like it to slow down again because I need this time with Olivia to last as long as possible.

This weekend, Matt invited me to drive to New Braunfels with him and a group of several other counselors to spend Saturday at Schlitterbahn Waterpark, stay overnight, and come back to camp Sunday morning before the new batch of campers arrive.

Saturdays are my days with Olivia, and I'm not about to give up even a single one, so I extended the invitation to her and hoped she'd agree to come.

She didn't need a lot of convincing. Olivia loves water parks. We used to go to Schlitterbahn all the time growing up—it's only about an hour from where we live in Austin—and in high school, Olivia, Annie, and I spent a lot of time there during summer breaks.

We head out early on Saturday morning, hoping to get to the park around nine. The drive is about two and a half hours from Camp Prairie Star. We take Brynn's crossover SUV, the group winnowed down to Matt, Brynn, Olivia, and me after a couple more coworkers ditched last minute.

Brynn's driving, with Matt beside her in the front seat. Olivia and I are in the back, and, according to Matt, are way too animated for this early in the morning.

"It's annoying," I insist again to Olivia, "how in soccer games you never really know when it's going to end because the timer counts up instead of down."

"You know when it ends! Each half is forty-five minutes. When the clock gets to forty-five—"

I interrupt, "It could still be another ten to fifteen minutes of this stoppage time. Nobody knows!"

She laughs. "Yes, the referees know."

"But they don't share that information. There's no timer of the stoppage time that adds it up throughout the game for the spectators to see."

"At least we have timers. In baseball, y'all don't time anything. That's why the games are so damn long!"

"We do now! There's the pitch clock," I say smugly.

She lifts her sunglasses onto the top of her head to make sure I can see the incredulity in her eyes. "You actually like the pitch clock?"

"Yeah, I do."

She shakes her head. "I'm surprised, especially with your stance on the designated hitter."

Whoa, whoa, whoa. She's bringing the DH into this? "Okay, that's a whole other thing—"

"Here he goes—"

"Back in the day—"

"Oh lord, when he starts with 'back in the day'—"

"—every baseball player had to be good at their position *and* at bat, even pitchers."

"Wow, I really got you going now, didn't I?"

"Don't talk to me about the designated hitter, Olivia. You know better."

She pats my thigh. "I do. I do know better."

We grin at each other, and I'm tempted to kiss her right here in the back seat of Brynn's car.

Matt turns around. "You two have the weirdest dynamic. If you're not making out, you're arguing."

"We don't argue," I protest.

"We debate," Olivia finishes.

"Well, whatever you call it, can you keep it down please? I'm trying to nap before we get there."

"Sorry," Olivia whispers.

She lays her head on my shoulder and shuts her eyes.

I smooth a hand over her shoulder. "You going to rest, too?"

She yawns. "Maybe a little."

Putting my mouth close to her ear, I tease her. "What, did you stay up too late last night or something? What were you doing?"

She smiles, her eyes still closed. "Like you don't know what I was doing."

I chuckle. Making out with me, that's what she was doing.

Once Skit Night finished and all the campers and their families went home, I took Olivia into town for dinner. It was raining when we got back to camp, so we curled up in my bed and watched a movie on my phone—no fancy sheet screen and projector this time. The screen was small, meaning we had to crowd each other a little bit, and even then, I don't think I could tell you much about the plot of that movie. Though that's probably more to do with the fact that I was paying more attention to Olivia than to it.

In a low voice, my mouth still next to her ear, I say, "You could remind me."

She opens her eyes, a wicked glint in them that makes me think she'll do just that, even with Matt and Brynn a few feet away in the front seat. I can't seem to make myself care about their presence either.

I lean in as Olivia's phone starts ringing, my sister's name flashing on the screen.

Olivia pulls away from me and sits up. "I better get this."

She accepts the call. "Hi! What's going on?" Olivia says into the phone. She listens. I can hear Annie's voice, but not what she's saying.

"Same old, same old here," Olivia responds. "How about you? Oh! You never told me how that date went with the IT guy a couple of weeks ago."

Hold on. Annie didn't tell me about any date with an IT guy. I tap my hand against Olivia's thigh to get her attention. She looks up at me. "What guy?" I mouth.

She waves me off and focuses back on her conversation with Annie. She squeals. "He didn't!"

I tap her again. "What did he do?" I whisper.

She glares at me. "No, no. I'm on the way to Schlitterbahn with a few of the other counselors." I try to get her attention again to tell her to *shut up*, but she ignores me.

I hear Annie's voice pitch louder on the other end of the phone. Olivia freezes and looks up at me, her eyes wide. "Oh, uh, yeah." She rubs her forehead. "I guess Gage is one of the other counselors going. He told you about that, huh?"

I groan.

"Yeah, it's a bunch of us, so..." She listens, then smirks at me. "Yes, I'll make sure he wears sunscreen."

"Unbelievable," I mutter.

"You know, he hasn't been hanging out with me very much..." I scowl at her. She's going to get me in trouble with my sister, making me sound like I'm not keeping my promise to try to be friends this summer.

"Uh, yeah, he's in the same car as me. Yep. Oh, you want to talk to him? Yep. Give me one second."

Olivia mutes the call and hands me the phone. "Play it cool," she warns me.

I take the phone from her and unmute the call. "Hey, Nini."

My sister's voice comes through the phone. "Gage, tell me you haven't been ignoring Delaney."

I give Olivia a dirty look. "No, I haven't been ignoring her." I smile smugly. "If anything, I think *she's* been ignoring *me*."

Olivia smacks my arm. "Ow!" I say involuntarily.

"Are you okay?" Annie asks on the other end of the line.

"Yeah, fine. Sorry about that."

"Listen, do me a favor and make sure Delaney has fun today please."

I grin. "Oh, you want me to make sure she has *fun* today?" I waggle my eyebrows, which makes Olivia stifle a laugh. "I can probably handle that."

I can make sure Olivia has all sorts of fun at the water park today, though I'm not planning on telling Annie the details.

"Okay, thanks. Love you, Gage. Can you give me back to Delaney now?"

"Yeah, here she is. Love you, too." I hand the phone back to Olivia.

The girls chat for a few more minutes. When Olivia hangs up, I ask her, "What was that about Annie dating some IT guy?"

"Oh, a date she went on a few weeks back. She says they're not going out again."

"I still don't know why she and Spencer had to break up. I liked Spencer."

"You liked Spencer? Why?" She stares at me incredulously. "He was so boring."

"Yeah, that's why I liked him."

Olivia scoffs. "No. Don't do that caveman thing. It's not attractive. Your sister can decide for herself who she dates."

I raise my eyebrows. "So, I guess she doesn't need *your* help either?"

"That's different. Best friends are supposed to give dating advice."

I scoff. "Oh really? So, should I call *my* best friend back and get her opinion on my romantic situation this summer?"

Olivia glares at me. "Stop. You know why we aren't telling her."

But I don't really. I know the reasons Olivia told me why she doesn't want to tell Annie. Those reasons don't make sense to me.

Annie *wants* Olivia and me to get along; whether that's as friends or more, I don't think she minds. Unless Olivia is anticipating some disastrous ending to our "fling" once the summer ends, I don't really get the secrecy.

My goal is to prove to Olivia that we're so much more than a summer fling so that when camp ends, our relationship doesn't. Already, the way we are together and how she acts toward me suggest that this is much more of a boyfriend-girlfriend thing than only a physical situationship.

But I don't want to pick a fight this morning. I push down my annoyance, and the fear behind it, and close my eyes. I rest my head on top of hers and snooze the rest of the way to the water park.

Schlitterbahn is busy, as is to be expected on a Saturday in the peak of the summer season. We bought our tickets online earlier in the week, but we still have to wait in line at the entrance to the park. Once we're in, we head straight to the lockers and rent a large one to share.

We strip out of our cover-ups and pile everything in the locker. Olivia wears the same swimsuit she had on for our night swim last weekend. It's a red two-piece with a top similar to a sports bra but cut low in the front. The bottoms are high-waisted, hitting right above her belly button. All along the edges of both pieces is a white trim that accentuates the golden glow of her skin.

Olivia pulls a tube of sunscreen from her bag and quickly applies it to her exposed skin, rubbing the lotion all along her arms, legs, stomach, and chest. The tips of my fingers tingle with the desire to touch her like that.

"I can get your back," I offer.

She hands me the sunscreen. "Sure. Thanks."

I squeeze lotion into my hand, then tuck the container under my arm to scrape my hands together, spreading sunscreen on each one. Slowly, I press my hands against Olivia's back and gently coat her skin with the lotion. I get the stretch of skin between her swimsuit top and bottoms and work my way up to her shoulders, sliding my fingers under the straps of her swimsuit.

"Gage?" Olivia turns her head to look at me, still holding her ponytail out of my way.

"Yeah," I respond, my voice rough.

"I think you got it." She grins, and I drop my hands sheepishly.

"Don't want you getting burned," I defend.

"I appreciate that." She smirks. "Let's do you now."

She takes the sunscreen from me and squirts a small amount onto her fingers. "Come here," she instructs. "Crouch down."

I stand in front of her and bend my knees so I'm closer to her height. She uses her fingertips to softly brush sunscreen across my cheeks and forehead, down around my chin, and even the shells of my ears.

She watches her fingers while she works, while I watch her eyes. The pretty green color, the depth, the concentration—I could get lost right here and wouldn't want a map to find my way out.

With a final pat to my cheek, she meets my gaze. The air between us is heated, and not from the Texas humidity.

"I promised Annie I'd make sure you wore sunscreen," she reminds me in a soft voice.

I start to answer when Brynn groans loudly. "Come on, you two! We get it, you're into each other. Put on the dang sunscreen, and let's get in the water."

Olivia blinks, her cheeks turning red. "Sorry, not sorry," she teases, smirking in Brynn's direction.

She passes the sunscreen back to me. "I think you can take it from here."

I chuckle and finish applying the lotion, though I notice Olivia watching longingly as I spread it over my chest and ab muscles. When she meets my eye, I wink at her.

"Let's hit the Raging River first," Brynn suggests.

"What's that?" asks Matt, the only one in our group who hasn't been to Schlitterbahn before.

I slap him on the shoulder. "Come on, my friend. Let me introduce you."

Chapter Twenty-One

Olivia

From the lockers, we go straight to the Raging River, which is one of Schlitterbahn's classic rides—a whitewater rapids–style adventure that's a mix between a waterslide and a lazy river. It takes thirty minutes from start to finish, alternating between fast-moving rapids and more leisurely floating. It's fun, for sure, but part of my enjoyment of it is the nostalgia factor.

Summers coming here with my sisters or with Annie and Gage are in the front of my memories as we float along. When we pass underneath the entrance building, we reach our hands up and pull ourselves forward on the low-lying ceiling of the tunnel, laughing when Matt calls this part of the ride a "claustrophobic person's nightmare."

The park is busy, so we get jammed up a few times in the slower moving parts of the river. At the end of the tube chute, we're emptied into the Comal River—a real river that borders the park.

Next, we ride a couple of the water coasters before moving on to tube slides. The lines throughout the park are long, and we're all too broke to buy Fast Lane wristbands to skip the waits.

Gage is at peak flirty at the water park today, and I am here for it. His hand is always on my arm or my shoulder or wrapped around my waist. He holds my hand as we walk around. He keeps sneaking looks at me in my swimsuit and winking at me when he catches me checking him out.

The energy must be contagious, because as the day progresses, I notice Matt and Brynn flirting more and more, too. They're not together, as far as I know, and I try to keep a pretty close eye on the Camp Prairie Star gossip.

Maybe once Brynn realized that Gage is, in fact, off-limits, she set her sights on Matt. He's a nice guy, maybe a couple of years younger than me, and he's definitely attractive. He's no Gage, of course, but Brynn could do much worse.

For lunch, we eat barbecue inside the park and then hang out in the Lagoon pool for a while as we digest.

Resting my head back against the pool's edge, I close my eyes. I haven't been able to stop thinking about what Gage shared about his adoption last weekend. Gage always seemed so happy growing up, so carefree. And I guess nothing he said last weekend indicates that wasn't the case, but I didn't know about everything else going on under the surface.

When he was talking about his adoption, his voice sounded so sad, and I've never heard Annie talk about it that way. As far as I can tell, Annie loves her parents, she loves Maggie and Maggie's family, and she's a little self-conscious about having such a complicated family, but she's never hinted that she felt disconnected or unattached from either side.

Though of course Gage and Annie are different people, even if they're twins. They don't need to feel the same way about their adoption. It's ironic that Gage, with his go-with-the-flow attitude, is the one hung up on it instead of Annie, who overthinks everything.

I told Gage that I wish I could have been there for him while he was sifting through all these feelings in college, and it's true. I know it's my fault that I wasn't there for him. I know that I not only rejected him as my boyfriend but also ghosted him as a friend.

I spent so much time worrying about protecting myself, that I didn't fully consider how much I was hurting Gage. I figured I'd be easy for him to get over, that I wasn't especially important to him to begin with.

This summer, I'm beginning to see how wrong that assumption was.

I'm also wondering if I'm making the same incorrect assumption now, and if so, where does that leave Gage when camp ends?

Someone presses into my side, and I open my eyes to see Gage sidled up next to me in the pool.

He points a finger at me. "You have a tattoo!" he accuses.

I lift my foot out of the water, the monogram-style tattoo inked there clearly visible. "What tipped you off?"

"I just … how didn't I notice it before now? When did you get it?" He looks flustered, like he doesn't like that there are things about me he doesn't know. I can relate.

"My sisters took me to get it after I turned 18." That would have been a couple of months after graduation, after I started avoiding Gage. "We all got them to match."

He squints through the water. "What is it?"

Squaring my hands on the wall behind me, I push myself up until I'm sitting at the edge of the pool. I lift my foot again, and this time Gage catches it in his hands to examine it.

He traces the letters with his finger. "M. N. O." He bites his lip as his chin lifts toward the sky. "Molly. Nicole. Olivia," he finally guesses.

"Mm-hmm."

He squeezes my foot. "I never realized your names were in order like that. Did your parents do that on purpose?"

I consider the question. "Not at first, I don't think. They named Molly and Nicole and then when I came along, they realized they could continue the pattern. They only really considered names starting with O for me."

"What were the runners-up?" Gage hasn't let go of my foot. Instead, he's using his thumbs to massage my arches, his hands sliding along my wet skin.

It's making it hard for me to focus on his question. "Um, they said once that if I was a boy, I would have been named Owen. They've also mentioned Ophelia."

Gage cringes. "If you were named Ophelia, I would have been more supportive about the switch to Delaney."

I shove his shoulder. "Rude. Ophelia is a beautiful name."

He nods. "It is, but it's not *you*." I wave him away, but he continues. "Have you ever looked up what the name Olivia means?"

"Sure." I shrug, but I don't really remember the meaning.

"It means peace. That's what I feel around you. Peace."

My field of vision narrows, and everything around us in the crowded pool area disappears. A wave of assorted emotions roll over me—gratitude, insecurity, awe, doubt. A sensation prickles behind my eyes, and I slide back into the pool and under the water to hide.

Why is Gage so good to me? He makes it really hard not to fall for him.

The poignant moment threatens to overwhelm me, so I push it away.

When I pop back up out of the water, I say, "Enough of this lazing around—let's race."

Gage quirks his eyebrows up. "What did you have in mind?"

"Two words: Downhill Racer." The Downhill Racers are head-first mat slides that sit side by side, perfect for some friendly competition. I point to myself and then at Gage. "Head-to-head. Me and you."

Gage smirks. "It's on." He sets one palm on the side of the pool and launches himself up and out, somehow landing on his feet on the pool deck.

He looks back—undoubtedly to catch my reaction—and when he sees my wide eyes, he winks. He flexes his biceps. "It's all in the arms," he says cockily.

As ridiculous as he's being, I'm grateful for the shift in tone. Confident, arrogant Gage is much easier to deal with than sweet, sensitive Gage.

I scramble out of the pool behind him, the bottoms of my feet stinging as they hit the hot deck.

Gage finds Matt and Brynn in the crowded pool to let them know where we're going. They decide to hang here a while longer, and, because our phones are in the locker, we pick a time and place to meet back up later.

"Looks like it's just the two of us," Gage says as we walk away.

I punch a fist into my hand. "Yep. And you're going down."

He smirks. "I am. I'm going *down* the slide faster than you."

I groan.

We continue the banter all the way to the Downhill Racer slides near the park entrance, our smack talk becoming even more lame as we go.

We each grab a blue foam mat and carry them toward the stairs. The mat isn't heavy, but it's bulky and keeps bumping my legs as I walk.

Gage holds out his hand. "Give it here."

I turn the mat away from him. "It's okay. I've got it."

Then the bottom of the mat hits the ground right as I take a step, and I'm tripping forward. Gage grabs me around the waist and sets me on my feet.

"Thanks," I mumble. I'm not sure if my face is hot with embarrassment or because I'm standing directly in the sun. We'll say it's the sun.

Without saying a word, Gage holds out his hand again. I give him my mat, paired with a scowl. He smirks and gestures for me to walk ahead of him as we start climbing the stairs to the top of the slides. We make it halfway up before we're at the end of the line. Fortunately, because there are four slides—two sets of two—the line moves quickly.

When it's our turn, Gage hands me my mat, and I set it in the water on the innermost slide. I grip the handles, leaning over the mat but not yet lying on it.

On his side, Gage remains standing, holding his mat by the handles. He's hoping for more momentum by starting from a stand.

The lifeguard gestures to let us know it's safe for us to go, so Gage counts us down. "Three. Two. One!"

I dive forward to propel my mat down the slide, turning my head to see how close I am to Gage. I can't tell with the wind and water blowing past my face. I glide over one drop, then the second, and soon I splash into the runout at the bottom. When I slow to a stop and stand up, Gage is already out of the water, smirking as he leans against the handrail of the steps to exit the ride.

"Best two out of three!" I call.

We can't keep our mats—there's a small line of people waiting to take them from us—so we give them up and get in line again.

After a short wait for mats, we go back up the stairs. This time I try a standing start, but my foot slips as I push off the ground and I end up starting at least a body length behind Gage. Needless to say, he beats me to the bottom.

He waits for me on the steps of the exit pool again, smirking.

"It's because you weigh more than me," I huff.

Gage holds up a finger. "Last one."

When it's our turn again, I push off the ground to launch myself and my mat down the slide. I lean my body forward and try to keep my legs straight and tight. I lower my head, which I hope will reduce drag, but which also means I can't keep tabs on where Gage is.

As soon as I stop at the bottom, I jump up. Gage is standing up at the same time.

"Who won?" I shout over to him.

He shrugs. "I don't know. A tie?"

"No way." I slosh through the ankle-deep water to the exit steps, dragging my mat behind me.

Gage meets me on the wooden deck at the top of the exit steps and takes the mat from my hands.

"Not a tie," I insist as we walk toward the line of people waiting for mats.

"Fine. You, then." His voice pitches higher, bright amusement evident in his tone.

I narrow my eyes. "Are you saying that because you actually think I won or because you're humoring me?"

Gage hands our mats to the next two people in line, and we move to the side, toward the cabanas.

"Have you always been so competitive?" he teases.

I think back to the weekends we spent climbing trees in the woods behind my house. Gage and I challenged each other to climb higher and higher while Annie watched nervously on the ground. Or the summer afternoons spent by the Carters' pool, when Annie judged who had the biggest splash when we cannonballed into the water or the smallest splash when we tried pencil jumps.

"You know I have."

He stops walking and pulls me to the side of the walkway, almost into the landscaping. "Yeah," he agrees in a low voice. "And I love it. It's hot."

I tilt my chin up and kiss him, opening my lips right away to feel his tongue glide against mine as smooth as the mat against the waterslide.

He groans when I pull away, resting his forehead against mine. "You're the best kisser, that's for sure."

I think I can agree to a tie on that one.

Chapter Twenty-Two

Gage

We retrieve our things from the locker before we leave the park, and I note a missed call from my dad. He followed up with a text asking me to give him a call when I can, though he says it's not urgent.

We hit a drive-through for dinner and then find the hotel and check in—Matt and I are sharing one room, with the ladies in another. I go upstairs long enough to drop my duffel bag off in my room and say good night to Olivia outside of her room, and then I go back downstairs, find a chair near the pool to sit, and call my dad back.

The line rings a couple of times before he picks up.

"Hey, son," he says.

"Hey, Dad. What's up?" I lean back in the pool lounger and bend an arm behind my head.

"Your mom asked me to call you about the Fourth of July party. Are you planning to come home for it?"

I scratch my head. Every year for as long as I can remember, my parents host a huge party for the Fourth of July. They invite neighbors, friends, coworkers, anyone and everyone who shows even the smallest interest in joining us. We set everything up in the backyard by the pool and keep the gates open to encourage people to wander in and out. They cook brisket and ribs with potato salad, jalapeno poppers, cornbread, beans, and more on the side. For dessert, my mom bakes Texas sheet cake and serves it with cold vanilla ice cream. It's one of the best days of the summer.

"Time is meaningless at camp," I joke. "When's the Fourth of July again?"

He chuckles. "Well, you see, it's on the fourth day of the month of July."

"Ha ha. Thanks, Dad. That's helpful."

He laughs again. "It's in a couple weeks. It's a Saturday this year, so I think that's between sessions at camp right? A day off for you?"

My Olivia day. I'd love to go home to see my parents and Annie, but I've avoided it because I don't want to lose any time with Olivia. And because we're keeping our fling or whatever a secret from our families and friends at home, we'd be strictly "friends only" back in Austin, I'm sure.

But I would hate to miss the big party. Maybe Olivia would come with me, if I asked her.

"Yeah, I'm free on Saturdays. I'll be there. I'll drive over on Saturday morning and stay over that night, if that's okay."

"Of course it's okay. This is your home. We can't wait to see you, son."

I miss them, too. I've lived with or close to my parents my whole life. Even for college, I stuck close to home, attending UT right there in town, even though I lived in the dorms because room and board were included in my baseball scholarship.

I was devastated when both Annie and Olivia decided to go school three hours away in Houston. I like having the people I love right by my side at all times. Other than summer trips to Maggie's house in Fort Worth when we were kids, and now this summer working at camp, I've kept close to my parents, and to Austin.

"Oh!" my dad says. "I almost forgot. Annie mentioned that Delaney is working at the camp there with you, too. Bring her along for the party, if she's free. Her parents are coming, and we'd all love to see her."

I smile to myself. Convincing Olivia to come with me just got easier. I know I won't be able to touch her or kiss her while we're with our families, but at least I won't have to totally miss out on one of my Saturdays with her.

I get back to the room twenty minutes later, exhausted from being in the sun all day and ready to crawl into bed. I scan my key card and open the door when the digital lock turns green, but it gets caught on the swing bar.

"Matt!" I call through the small opening. "It's me. Can you let me in, please?"

It takes a few minutes, but Matt finally appears at the door, disengaging the swing bar. He blocks me from entering and comes out into the hallway, closing the door behind him and shoving my duffel bag into my arms.

"Hey," he says furtively. He's changed out of his swimsuit into athletic shorts, but he's not wearing a shirt. His hair is disheveled, and his face looks a little red, maybe from too much sun at the water park today.

"Uh ... what's going on? I'd like to go into our room and get some sleep."

"Yeah ... you can't do that."

I clench and unclench my fists. "Why the hell not?"

Matt glances up and down the hallway before he points a thumb at the door behind him. "I've got Brynn in there," he whispers furiously.

I scrub my hand across my eyes. It's been a long day—fun, but very tiring. I want to go to sleep.

When I don't respond, Matt leans in. "You know, like to spend the night?"

"Yeah, Matt. I got that. Where am I supposed to sleep?"

He shrugs. "If Brynn's with me, that leaves an open spot in *your* lady's room." He wiggles his eyebrows. "Maybe we'll both get lucky tonight."

I groan, feeling anything but *lucky* in this situation. Olivia wouldn't like Matt's idea at all; it goes way beyond the PG-13 fling she envisioned.

Sharing a room—and a bed—with Olivia, though.... Well, let's just say that if I thought she'd go for it, I'd be knocking on her door already.

As much as we've been connecting—and kissing—these last few weeks, and as much as we had an amazing time together today, Olivia does better with space. She reacts best when I let her come to me in a no-pressure situation.

Showing up at her hotel room door and asking to stay the night is exactly the kind of thing that will put her on the defensive and make her close back up.

"I don't think that's a good idea," I finally say.

"What's the big deal? You guys are dating, aren't you?"

"Yeah, but not sharing-a-hotel-room-level dating. And I'm pretty sure Olivia would have a problem with you even saying 'dating.'"

Matt stares at me. "Come on," he says. "You guys are clearly into each other."

"It's more complicated than that," I explain. "I don't know, man. I don't think that conversation's going to go well."

Matt shrugs. "I feel for you, but not my problem."

And then he's gone and the door slams closed in my face.

Seriously?

I heave a deep breath trying to release my exasperation with it. Then I walk down the hall and knock softly on Olivia's hotel room door.

She opens the door in a huge T-shirt that grazes her thighs, her legs bare underneath. I snap my eyes up quickly. Her face looks freshly scrubbed, her cheeks pink from all the sun we got today. Her eyes widen when she sees me.

"Gage?" she says. "What are you doing?"

"Umm," I stutter.

"I thought maybe it was Brynn, and she lost her key. Have you seen her?"

I shift my duffel bag on my shoulder and hold my hands out, palms up. "Sort of?" I answer.

She tilts her head, waiting for me to explain. I take a deep breath, and then it all comes out in a rush. "MattandBrynnare-hookingupinmyroomcanIsleephere?"

Olivia narrows her eyes. "What?" she asks.

I sigh and repeat myself more slowly this time. "Matt and Brynn are hooking up in my room. Can I sleep here?"

The panic in her eyes is evident. Her "cool girl" mask has slipped, and the look on her face is pure pre–high school Olivia. Uncertainty mixed with determination—all emotion with none of that detached Delaney facade that's been her default for years. My heart twinges. There's no way I don't fall for this Olivia. Real Olivia.

She's reacting about how I expected, proof that she's nowhere near ready to be as vulnerable with me as this situation might require. She's not acting defensive, though. At least, not yet.

"I mean, is there a couch or something I can crash on?"

Finally, she blinks, tosses her head, and turns to evaluate the hotel room behind her. "A couple of armchairs," she says. "And one bed."

"Oh."

We stand in the doorway staring at each other. "Okay," I finally say. "I'll go see if the hotel has an extra room available."

I start to turn, but Olivia sighs and grabs my arm. "Wait. Just … just come in," she says. "We'll figure it out."

I can't help but grin as I close the door behind me. Unfortunately, she sees it. Her hands fly to her hips.

"What?" she asks.

I quickly school my features. "Nothing," I say.

She narrows her eyes and makes a humming sound in her throat. "The bed's a king, so there should be plenty of space for both of us. I was finishing up in the bathroom. When I'm done, you can have it." She glances at me, waiting for my reaction. I keep my face impassive.

"Sounds good," I say. Inside, I'm giddy. Yeah, I'm still annoyed with Matt for kicking me out of my own hotel room, but if it means sharing a bed with Olivia, I may actually owe that guy a thank-you card. She could put a wall of pillows between us on that bed, and I guarantee she'd still be the best roommate I've ever had.

She pops back out of the bathroom, where she's put leggings on underneath her baggy T-shirt. Her hands are on her hips again.

And the ponytail is gone, her hair now flowing like a soft river across her shoulders and down her back. The way it frames her face makes the angles of her jaw softer. I have the almost uncontrollable impulse to bury my hands in that hair and feel the silky strands glide through my fingers. I know I'm staring, but Olivia doesn't seem to notice.

"Tell me the truth," she says. "Is this some sort of a plan that you guys put together? Are you hoping to...." She trails off, wanting me to fill in the blanks on my own, which I do.

"No," I say quickly. "I swear." I draw an X over my heart with my pointer finger.

She glares at me, assessing my truthfulness. Despite the fact that I really do only have honorable intentions, I sweat a little under her gaze. I mean it's not like I haven't thought about it. A lot. But I'm not stupid, and I know *that* kind of fling isn't what either of us wants.

"Okay, good," she finally says. "Because that's not the kind of thing I would do with someone who's just a summer fling."

Even though I literally had the same thought, I bristle at her wording. I can't help but push back. "You're still clinging to the whole 'summer fling' thing, huh?"

She blinks at me. "Of course. That was our agreement."

I lift a hand to her cheek, running my thumb across the collection of freckles that dot her skin. I move my hand up and back, my fingers parting and then disappearing into the strands of her hair. I close my eyes at the feel of it, even better than I expected. Her hair is still wet in some places, and the damp spots chill my hand as I wrap Olivia's hair around my palm.

I open my eyes and immediately lock them with hers. The gold flecks in her green eyes glow in contrast with the low light that surrounds us. Her pupils dilate, and she leans toward me the tiniest bit. Her neck and cheeks flush pink, and I'm slammed with the intense impulse to erase all the distance between us, both physical and emotional. I pull her body into mine easily. The emotional chasm will be more difficult to bridge.

"We're more than a fling," I whisper into the shell of her ear, my voice husky and cracking.

Instantly, Olivia shuts down, like a switch has been flipped. It's actually pretty impressive to watch. The emotion—desire, longing, affection—drains from her eyes, leaving them hard, cold, and a little ... sad. Her hands drop to her sides. I untangle my hand from her hair, and she steps back, restoring the distance between us.

"That was the deal," she says flatly. "If you want out..."

I hold back a groan. I want to shout. I want to shake her. I want to push her down onto the bed and kiss her until she can't remember her name, let alone why she insists on holding me at arm's length. I don't do any of those things.

Instead, I hold up my hands, palms facing toward her. "Hey, forget I said anything, okay? I'm going to get ready for bed."

I grab my duffel and walk into the bathroom. After I close the door behind me, I slump against it. Maybe I am stupid, because I damn well know better than to back Olivia Delaney into a corner. She always comes out swinging. At me, mostly. Or so it feels.

I take a quick shower to wash off the chlorine, river water, and sunscreen from the day. Then, as I brush my teeth, I stare at my reflection in the mirror.

Because how pathetic am I? Pining patiently for a woman who's made it very clear what she wants from me.

I don't understand the hold she has over me. *She's just a woman.* Even as the thought enters my mind, I push it away. I know it's a lie.

Olivia has never been just a woman or just a girl to me. She pushes me. Challenges me. She keeps me humble when I get too cocky. She also makes me feel like I can do anything.

When we were in high school, I was on the debate team, but my toughest arguments were always at home with my twin sister's best friend. We argued over stupid stuff like whether hot dogs are sandwiches and whether the American League or the National League is better. After one particularly fierce discussion in which I had to concede by the end that *Folklore* was an artistically more mature album than *Red*, making it objectively Taylor's best, I told her that she really needed to join me on the debate team.

She laughed and rolled her eyes. "Yeah right. I'm not smart enough for that."

I don't know why she sold herself short. She still does it. Does she think self-deprecation makes people like her more, or does she really not see how smart, strong, and capable she is even off the soccer pitch?

So yeah, she told me what she wants from me, but there's no fire in her eyes when she says it. I don't believe her. She's more than she thinks she is, and this is more than she'll admit. But I'll keep taking what I can get, hoping that one day she'll let me in.

When I'm ready, I open the bathroom door to a dark room.

I feel my way over to the bed, where my eyes have adjusted to the dark enough to see which side Olivia has claimed. She's lying on her side, facing toward the bathroom with her eyes closed. I peel back the covers on the opposite side and climb in.

I don't like how we left things before I went into the bathroom. I roll over and lie on my side, hovering above her. I gently stroke her hair.

"I'm sorry," I whisper. "I'll stick to the deal. This can be whatever you want."

I'm not even sure she can hear me. Her breathing is steady and soft; she may already be asleep. I press a kiss to the side of her head.

Quietly, to myself more so than to her, I repeat, "Whatever you want. I hope you come to find out that what you want is me."

To think I was worried about falling for her again when the truth is, I never got over her in the first place.

Chapter Twenty-Three
Olivia

I *hope you come to find out that what you want is me.*

The memory of Gage's words are a heavy brick in my stomach, causing me to pick at my breakfast the next morning. I'm not entirely sure he meant for me to hear him, but I did, before I fell asleep with his arms around me.

Oh, Gage, I think. *Wanting you is not the problem. Wanting you has never been the problem.*

The problem is that I'm playing fast and loose with both our hearts. The problem is that I should end things now before the feelings get any more real.

I'll break my own heart. That's fine. The pain will be worth it for any of Gage's time, touches, and kisses now. But if he's falling for me somehow—against his better judgment, surely—how can I hurt him when I have to walk away for his own good?

After eating—or not eating, in my case—the free breakfast at the hotel, we pile into Brynn's car to drive back to Camp Prairie Star.

Considering their rendezvous last night, I expect Brynn and Matt to be all over each other this morning, but there's even more tension between them than between me and Gage, and not the good kind of tension.

Maybe last night didn't go well? Either way, Matt folds himself into the back seat with Gage, leaving the front passenger seat for me.

Gage and I didn't have a chance to talk this morning. We overslept and then rushed to get ready to go before breakfast. Apparently, we won't have the chance to talk at all on this drive back to camp either.

Nobody talks on the drive. The entire two-and-a-half-hour trip is awkwardly silent except for Matt's light snoring from the back seat. From time to time, I glance back at Gage, but he's always facing away from me, toward the window. I can't tell if his eyes are open or closed.

I'm sure he thinks I'm mad at him, but I'm not. If I'm mad at anyone, it's at myself. Mostly I'm scared. I'm afraid I've gotten myself into something my heart won't survive, and worse, that I'll bring Gage down with me.

We finally make it back to camp, and we all grab our bags from the trunk and head in our separate directions to prepare for the campers' arrival in a couple of hours.

I start down the path to my cabin, relieved to put off any type of conversation with Gage. But it's short-lived.

"Olivia," Gage calls behind me, pulling on my hand.

I stop walking and face him.

"Are you okay? You've been really quiet this morning. Are you still mad at me from last night? I didn't have anything to do with getting kicked out of my room, I swear."

"No, I know. I'm not mad. I'm ... thinking."

Gage tilts his head. "About what?"

"About whether this"—I motion between us—"is a good idea after all."

Gage's eyes widen slightly. "Why wouldn't it be? I shouldn't have pressured you last night. This can be whatever you want it to be."

I sigh and shake my head. "I just..." I trail off, watching carefully for his reaction. "I don't want anyone to get hurt."

I don't want you to get hurt.

"Hey," he says softly, "I get that."

Then, he smirks. "But are you really saying that you want to watch all of this"—he gestures up and down his body—"this summer and not be able to touch?"

I roll my eyes, frustrated that he's not taking the conversation seriously. "Ugh, Gage, come on." Although, the man makes a good point. "We have so much history," I continue. "Can you really say you can keep feelings out of this?"

He shifts his eyes to the ground and shrugs. "I mean, yeah. You?"

My head and my heart scream *No!* It's already too late. I'm as gone for Gage as I was in high school. But if the alternative is not having him at all, am I willing to give this up and still see him every day? Especially when he insists he won't catch feelings?

"Yeah," I answer, inspecting my fingernails so I don't have to look at him while I lie.

"Okay then, problem solved." Gage nods. "I've got to go get ready for my campers to arrive, but I'll see you later, yeah?"

"Yeah, of course. See you later."

He turns around and ambles toward his cabin, while I'm left reeling from our interaction.

I rub the side of my fist against my forehead. I feel so jumbled up inside.

On the one hand, it hurts to hear Gage say that he can keep feelings out of a physical relationship with me, because *how*? But on the other hand, isn't that what I want? Isn't that what I'm insisting on?

ʕ ʕ ʕ

The chaos of another week of wrangling campers keeps me occupied long enough that my uncertainty about my fling with Gage rearranges into missing him. I see him throughout the week, of course, but as usual it's brief glimpses across the campfire or in passing while he's leading a group of rowdy ten-year-old boys.

I'm impatient to spend time with him, to relax against his chest, and joke with him. I'm greedy for the opportunity to hear more of his deepest thoughts and feelings.

Finally, it's Skit Night on Friday before the parents take their kids home. None of the groups asked me to perform with them this week—which is fine with me—so I'm sitting in the back enjoying the show.

Gage's group of boys stand to deliver their skit, the junior counselor Jayden with them. I dart my eyes around for Gage, but I don't see him. Maybe he wasn't invited to perform this week either.

The skit starts with one boy loudly reading from his notes about how there once was a camp counselor with a case of the "sadsies." When he says "sadsies" all the other kids make exaggerated pout faces and loud wailing noises.

Then Gage walks on "stage" with a similarly over-the-top pout, his puppy dog eyes wide and pitiful.

"The counselor was so sad that all the kids called him Mr. Sadsie, which made him even sadder. And nobody knew why he was sad because he wouldn't tell and maybe he didn't really remember anyway."

Again, the rest of the boys pout and wail, adding emphasis to the action like a Greek chorus.

"Then one day Mr. Sadsie decided to go on a quest to see if anyone knew why he was so sad."

Gage starts wandering among the rows of spectators, his face still reflecting that melodramatic sad expression.

"Mr. Sadsie saw lots of people and wanted to talk to them to find out why he was so sad."

Gage sits down next to various people in the audience, leaning toward them with his sad face. They laugh or smile uncomfortably until Gage moves on.

"But no one would ask him what's wrong."

Impossibly, Gage's face turns even sadder, and he hangs his head.

"He decides to try one more time."

My pulse speeds up when Gage makes a beeline for the back of the audience. He stops at the end of my row, which is mostly empty, and sits on the bench. He slides slowly down the bench until he's right next to me.

With everyone in the audience watching us to see what will happen next, he drops his head on my shoulder and sighs loudly.

Maybe I will be performing today, although I don't know what role I'm supposed to play.

Gage lifts his head again, sidles even closer to me, and then lays his head back on my shoulder. He sighs dramatically.

"Ask me what's wrong," Gage instructs quietly out of the corner of his mouth.

"Oh! Um, okay." Then loudly, I ask, "What's wrong, good sir?"

The narrator continues. "Finally, someone wants to hear about Mr. Sadsie's problems, and all of a sudden he remembers!"

"Now I remember!" Gage says emphatically. "I'm feeling so sad because I'm not really a camp counselor at all. I'm a prince, and I was supposed to marry a princess, but I can't find her anymore. Fair maiden!" He addresses me. "Will you be my princess so I can be happy again?"

Gage gives me a subtle nod, so I know how to answer. "Um, of course I will, stranger I've never met before. What could go wrong?"

The audience laughs.

"Nice ad-libbing," Gage whispers.

"That day, Mr. Sadsie became Prince Happy, and his frown turned upside down," the narrator finishes while Gage switches his expression to a wide, toothy grin.

The boys making up the chorus cheer wildly, matching Gage's ecstatic face.

"The end."

Everyone claps, and the kids take a bow before going back to their seats. Gage stays in the spot next to me, still scooted over as close to me as he can be.

"That was weird," I whisper to Gage once the next group of campers take the stage. "What was supposed to be the point of that skit?"

Gage chuckles. "No idea. It came from the brains of a bunch of ten-year-old boys. We're lucky it wasn't weirder. You should have heard all the unhinged ideas I nixed. Not to mention the fart jokes." He's quiet for a moment. "They said I was acting sad all week, and that was the inspiration for the skit."

I frown. "Were you?" I ask. "Sad all week?"

Gage slides his eyes over to look at me. "Maybe a little."

"Why?"

"I missed you." He twists his face back into the exaggerated Mr. Sadsie expression.

I chuckle. "We saw each other around. There was no need to miss me," I say, even though I felt exactly the same way, like I couldn't wait to be in the same room with him without hundreds of kids surrounding us.

This week was no different from the seven others we've spent with the campers so far this summer, as far as needing to keep our distance from each other, but it *felt* different. I felt unsettled after our falling out last weekend, not sure where we stood, even after the brief conversation we had when we got back to camp on Sunday.

"Are we hanging out again this weekend?" Gage asks, his eyes reflecting the same vague anxiety I've been feeling all week.

My eyes water, and I blink back the tears before I answer. "Yes, please."

His relief is palpable in the way he relaxes his shoulders and slides an arm around my waist. "Okay, good. I have something I need to talk to you about." I tense. "Not about anything we talked about last weekend," he says quickly. "Not really. But it is time sensitive."

I relax against him again. "It's been kind of a stressful week," I say. "Can we talk tomorrow? Maybe while canoeing?"

He kisses the top of my head. "Yeah, that sounds good. What do you want to do tonight, then?"

I tilt my face toward him and grin. "Not talk."

I need the uncomplicated surge of gratification that comes with losing myself in Gage and his kisses. I'm self-aware enough to recognize that I'm using our physical relationship as a distraction from focusing on the emotional connection, but I can't bring myself to care at the moment.

Gage returns my smile, pulling me closer to him on the bench. "As you wish, my princess."

Chapter Twenty-Four

Gage

Saturday after breakfast, Olivia and I canoe to the center of the lake. We bring a picnic lunch so we can find a nice spot on the other side of the water to eat and relax together. The air is warm today, but the heat wave of a few weeks ago has dissipated, so it's normal end-of-June heat.

I'm nervous as I consider the best way to invite Olivia to my parents' Fourth of July party. The best way being the way that gets her to say yes. I stare at the back of her head from the stern seat, shuffling potential words around in my mind as we paddle.

The rhythmic pump of my arms as I pull the oar through the water, gently on one side and then pulling it out and dipping it in on the other, calms me. The thwack of the oar as it carves through the surface, the drip of the water as it sluices down the blade, the thump of the handle against the side of the boat—these are all part of the soundtrack that slows my heart rate and quiets my racing thoughts.

We stop rowing when we reach the middle of the lake, and Olivia spins around in her seat so she's facing me. "What did you want to talk to me about?"

I blow out a breath. *Here we go.* "I talked to my dad the other day. They're getting ready for their Fourth of July party next weekend."

"Oh yeah?" Olivia smiles. "We always used to have so much fun at those."

We did. Olivia stopped coming after high school, though. Whether it was because she was busy with other things or avoiding me, I'm not sure.

"They're even more fun now that we're old enough for Dad's Patriotic Punch," I joke.

She laughs. "I did always want to try that punch, but I knew if I snuck even a sip, my mom would catch me. Or yours."

"You could try it this year," I suggest cautiously.

She tilts her head. "What do you mean?"

"I mean, I guess Annie told my parents you were working here, too, and my dad wants me to invite you to the party."

Olivia's mouth draws into a straight line, and she bites her lip. "I don't know if that's a good idea."

"Why not?"

"Just ... I don't know, Gage. It's easy here at camp, you know? No one knows us or our families or our past, and we can hang out together. But at home..." Her voice drops, and she reaches up to adjust her ponytail.

I swallow. "You don't want our families to know we're together."

"It's a summer fling, right?" She smiles ruefully and shrugs her shoulders. "No sense giving anyone the wrong idea."

I *know* the whole "summer fling" thing is her stance and has been since the beginning, but it's like a jab to the heart with a dull knife every time she says it.

"Please," I practically beg, "come with me, Olivia."

Her eyes soften, and I see her start to waver.

"You don't need to come as my date or anything," I push on. I know I'm pressing hard, but I can't stop myself. I can't give up the time I have with her. Time not only to soak her in, but also to help her see how right we are together. "Come to see Annie. Come to see your parents. I'll keep my distance if that's what you want."

"Well," she says, "we can be friends at the party. We don't need to ignore each other or anything. But, no flirting or unnecessary touching."

"So, you'll come?" I ask eagerly as the corners of my mouth lift.

She chuckles and shakes her head. "Yeah, I'll come. It'll be fun to drive over with you, and it feels like forever since I've seen Annie. Plus, I miss your parents' parties."

I want to ask her why she stopped coming, then. Why she'd been avoiding me. Why she ghosted me after graduation after she agreed to stay friends.

It's fragile, this thing between us, or at least it feels that way to me. I worry that one wrong word or one indelicate action from me could make it come crashing down like a tower of wooden blocks. And I desperately need the fortress to hold, need to keep Olivia with me.

I feign an assurance I don't feel. "Great, it's settled then. I'll let my parents know."

Olivia's eyes twinkle as she rotates to face the front again. "Let's paddle around some more before lunch," she suggests.

Before I can agree, she sinks her oar into the water and flips the blade up in my direction, sending a wave of lake water splashing onto my lap.

I yelp, barely suppressing my instinct to jump up. That would topple the whole canoe and put us both in the lake.

I shift my eyes from my wet shorts to Olivia, who's smirking.

"Did you do that on purpose?" I ask. At least I'm wearing my quick-dry shorts today.

"Would I do that to you?" She rests her chin on her shoulder and blinks at me innocently.

I snort. "Yes, absolutely. One hundred percent."

She grins. "You know me so well. But I know you, too, and I *know* you won't retaliate." Again, she bats her eyes.

"Aw, Olivia," I coo. "Maybe you don't know me as well as you think you do." With that, I dip my oar in the lake and launch a tidal wave of water onto her back.

She gasps and stands up, twisting to face me as she does. The canoe wobbles. "Sit down!" I bark. "You're going to tip the canoe."

Her expression shifts from one of shock to one of pure mischief. She smirks, looking me straight in the eye.

"You mean I *shouldn't* do this?" She shifts from one foot to the other, exaggerating the movements to tilt the boat first to the left and then to the right.

I don't want to take an unplanned dip in the lake fully clothed. We'd get wet, and our lunch would likely be ruined.

"I'm serious. Sit. Down." My tone is commanding, much more assertive than I've ever used with Olivia before. To my surprise, she listens, dropping to her seat as if her legs are spring-loaded like the screen doors on the cabins that slam against the door frame every time they shut.

Within seconds, the canoe stops swaying, and we're stable again.

My chest tingles, smug satisfaction curling the corners of my lips. Her immediate response to my words encourages me to hope that I might have power over her the same way she does over me. I'm not interested in *over*powering Olivia, but knowing how much her every whim and word control my life, it's nice to think I might have even half as much of an effect on her.

I can't hold back from murmuring, "Good girl," and though my voice is low, I know she hears me. She's facing forward again, but the tips of her ears turn an exquisite shade of pink that extends down her neck.

Olivia is unnaturally quiet as we paddle to shore and pull the canoe up on the bank.

I snag the cooler from the center of the boat and swing it by the handle in Olivia's direction. "Thanks for not drowning our lunch." I wink.

Her cheeks are still a little pink; I'm not sure if it's from the sun or our exchange. But she's still Olivia. "Thanks for not splashing me," she snaps back. "Oh wait, you did."

I set the cooler down and step closer to Olivia, wrapping one arm around her waist. Softly, I trace circles with my thumb on top of the wet spot on the back of her shirt. She shivers, and I'm once again enjoying the exhilaration of proving how much I affect her.

She tilts her chin up to look at me. "You're dangerous," she whispers, her eyes darkening.

"I would never hurt you," I respond, silently willing her to believe me.

She pushes up on her toes and wraps her hand around the back of my neck. I meet her halfway to my lips, pressing my mouth over hers. Her lips are warm from the time we spent canoeing across the lake with the sun in our faces.

Despite the sharp energy between us, the kiss is slow and tender. It's almost harder for me to handle than the hot and heavy make outs we've shared over the past month and a half. This kiss hints at *feelings*. Feelings that I've had to repress so as to not scare Olivia away. Feelings that I'm getting more and more confident she reciprocates, if only she'd admit it.

I pour my feelings into kissing her now, hoping she understands what I'm trying to communicate without words.

When I can't keep the soft pace a second longer, as soon as I feel the push to escalate my lips on hers into something faster and more frantic, I pull back. I take a couple of steadying breaths before pressing one last soft kiss onto her forehead.

"Ready for lunch?" I ask, surprised at the evenness of my voice despite how my heart's pounding.

Olivia, her eyes anchored to mine and still electrified, bites her lip. Everything about her expression tells me it's not the sandwiches she wants to devour.

Harnessing every speck of self-control I have, I manage to resist pulling her against me. I run a hand up my arm and pinch the skin near my armpit hidden beneath the sleeve. It helps redirect me.

I'm playing the long game here, wanting every signal I send to convey forever, not fling.

I take three steps back and focus my attention on the cooler of food I left sitting by the shoreline.

I turn my back to Olivia as I retrieve the cooler from the ground and a picnic blanket from the canoe. When I face her again, she sports a laid-back smile. "What did you pack for lunch?" she asks breezily.

I list the food I gathered from the mess hall as we spread out the picnic blanket. We sit in the sun so our clothes can dry while we eat.

Olivia and I so often end up soaked when we're together—water fights, water parks, accidental dips in the creek. I can only assume it's because of how desperately we need to cool down when we get within a hundred yards of each other.

We're quiet while we eat, but it's a comfortable silence. I chew my sandwich, rolling through memories of the summer so far. Even though these weekends with Olivia have been the highlight, I'm captivated with Olivia in work-mode during the week. The way she organizes the activity schedule for each cabin every week. The firm command she has when orienting each new group to the swimming hole rules or canoe safety.

"Had you done much canoeing before this summer?" I ask her. We'd kayaked together back in high school, but I don't remember canoes featuring much in her past.

She hums. "In college," she confirms. "The student rec center emphasized outdoor programs and students could rent all sorts of equipment cheaply. Canoes, but also camping gear, kayaks, paddleboards. When it wasn't soccer season, my teammates and I liked to paddle in Brays Bayou or Buffalo Bayou."

She's quiet for a few minutes, staring out at the lake. "I felt like I had to move, I had to be outside, you know? Or else I would go crazy sitting inside classrooms all day." She blinks and shifts her focus back to me, smiling wanly. "That burn in my muscles is like a kind of therapy for me."

I imagine Olivia with her friends paddling down the marshy rivers in Houston, smiling, her face turned toward the sun. The images combine with how I've seen her this summer, working with the kids. An idea strikes.

"Olivia, you should be a teacher!" I pause. "You're so good with the kids. Patient and encouraging. They all love you."

She puffs out one loud, quick laugh, then goes quiet. She can't seem to find the words to respond, leaving her mouth gaping while she blinks rapidly.

Meanwhile, the more I think about this idea, the more I like it. She already has experience through coaching and the work she's doing at Camp Prairie Star this summer. She has a college degree in exercise science, not to mention her impressive résumé as an athlete.

"A teacher?" Olivia finally sputters. "Are you crazy? I'm not smart enough to be a teacher."

I frown, and my eyebrows pull together. *Why would she say that?* "Of course you are. Listen, though. You should be a PE teacher."

Olivia sits up straighter. "Huh. A PE teacher?"

"Yeah," I say, warming up now. "It'll let you be outside and continue to work with kids, coaching them and watching their confidence grow, but in a stable job that pays ... well, not a lot probably, but at least enough for you to get your own apartment, if you want."

She narrows her eyes as she considers my words. "That's actually not a terrible idea."

I laugh. "Well, thanks very much."

"Don't you need a license or something to be a teacher?" She grimaces.

I lift a hand. "Probably? We can look up the requirements when we get back to camp."

I reach across the blanket to squeeze Olivia's hand. I know this has been weighing on her, trying to figure out what to do with her life, and more immediately, what to do after this summer job ends.

The spark in her eyes now makes me think she's considering this possibility, maybe even getting excited about it. She's buoyed by the idea, at least.

A solid, satisfied warmth settles across my chest. Maybe if Olivia can imagine a future beyond this summer for herself, she can picture me in it, too. Permanently.

Chapter Twenty-Five

Olivia

After our canoe trip and picnic, Gage and I use the computer in the front office to search up the requirements for teaching in Texas. We could use our phones—we're not so remote at the camp that we don't have a data connection—but this feels like a big internet kind of task. Even with Gage here looking over my shoulder, I'm nervous about misreading something and drawing the wrong conclusions.

When we find the information, the excitement I felt only a few moments before leaks out of me. It's complicated, and there are a lot of steps.

If, like me, someone has a bachelor's degree that's not in education, they need to apply to an educator preparation program. There's also a certification content exam I'd need to pass. Admittance to a program and passing the exam is required before I could get a probationary teaching certificate, and that's assuming there are schools willing to accept teachers with only a probationary certification.

"Well, you won't have the probationary certificate in time for this school year, but you could start working on it after the summer," Gage says optimistically.

Honestly, though, the thought of *more* classes and exams makes it hard to breathe. I envision the hoops I'll need to jump through to get accommodations for my learning disorder and the constant fight of making sure the teachers and exam administrators actually provide those accommodations. I'm exhausted thinking about it.

"Yeah, maybe," I mumble.

Where I'm sitting right now, the process feels overwhelming.

"I can help," Gage offers, and I feel even worse.

He can't help me with my teacher certification stuff after camp ends because he won't be part of my life anymore after camp ends. That boundary line between summer and after summer, also known as the dreaded post-Gage era, looms heavy in my mind.

Right now, I have a job. I have Gage. I'm happy. Why spoil that with thoughts of a jobless, Gageless future?

"Oh, well." I paste on a smile and toss my hair. "I don't have to worry about it now."

Gage persists. "No, but—"

I cut him off. "Thanks, Gage," I say dismissively, patting his arm.

He closes his mouth, understanding my message that the subject is closed.

I'd much rather dwell on the here and now, and the earlier today, when Gage was kissing me like he would never get enough.

My thoughts back up even more as I say goodbye to Gage and walk back to my cabin. I remember that I agreed to go to the Carters' Fourth of July party in Austin next weekend. It's been years, and as nervous as I am about being with Gage, and acting indifferent or even *friendly* toward him, in the midst of our families and friends, I'm also excited. My parents will be there. And Annie. The Carters have always been a second family to me, Gage the only member I've avoided over the last five years.

While I'm thinking about it, I pull out my phone to text Annie.

I chuckle but feel guilty about how unknowingly on the nose she is. When Annie asked me to come home for the party, I said I couldn't. But when Gage asked me … let's just say he has ways of persuading me that wouldn't work if his sister tried them.

The week of camp leading up to the Fourth of July is a tiring one for me. I planned special themed activities that the kids loved, but the games ended up being a pain to organize and put on.

So, when Gage and I set out for Austin and the Carters' party on Saturday, my body is drained, but my mind is spinning. My biggest worry is Annie because she knows both of us too well. She'll pick up on any little sign of attraction between us and pounce.

As Gage drives his Jeep up the rock-lined road that leads from Camp Prairie Star to the main highway, I warn him about being extra careful in front of his sister.

Without taking his eyes off the road, he says, "I still don't understand why we need to hide our relationship."

"Because we don't have a *relationship*, remember?" I shoot back.

I watch him clench his jaw, then relax it as he draws in a breath. "Right."

We're both quiet as the minutes drag by, each more uncomfortable than the last. Now, I'm not only thinking about keeping me and Gage a secret from Annie, I'm also thinking about how Gage feels about keeping the secret and about how what he feels makes me feel.

I need a distraction.

I hold up my phone. "Do you mind if we listen to my audio-book?"

It's a gamble, opening up to Gage about what I'm reading. I don't share that part of me with many people. But maybe this offer of vulnerability will reassure him of the place he has in my life, or at least my life for the summer. And maybe I'm also hoping it will lessen the guilt I feel for lying to him about how much of my life he owns, even if he doesn't know it.

Gage turns his face toward me, his eyebrows raised. "Not at all."

He sits up taller in the driver's seat and leans forward slightly as I connect my phone to the Jeep's Bluetooth.

I pull up the app on my screen and hit play.

"The answer is," a familiar upbeat voice narrates, "two dozen eggs."

Gage listens intently as the narrator continues for a few sentences. "Is that ... is that the *Jeopardy* guy? The new one?"

I bounce my knee. "Ken Jennings. Yeah." I pause the book.

The corner of his mouth tips up. "And this book is ...?"

"Alex Trebek's memoir," I mumble, chewing the skin on the side of my thumb.

Gage laughs in surprise. "Why?"

My face warms. "I like *Jeopardy*." I bristle, feeling self-conscious.

"Mm-hmm. I remember. We used to watch it together." He grins at me. "But Alex Trebek's memoir is *not* what I was expecting when you were so cagey about your audiobook earlier this summer."

I think back to that first weekend when I drove Gage into town and my audiobook began playing. I hesitate before responding. "Actually, at that point, I was listening to something Molly recommended about the history and ecology of the Great Lakes."

Gage turns his head to look at me, curiosity and surprise in his expression, before focusing back on the road.

"It won a Pulitzer," I add, clearing my throat.

Without taking his eyes off the road, he tilts his head toward me. "Was it ... was it good?"

Again, I'm ready to take offense. "Why, because how could someone like me enjoy a serious, prize-winning nonfiction book?"

Gage glances at me again, this time confusion written all over his face. "No, that's not what I meant at all. I just mean ... why would you hide that from me? Or from anyone?"

I inhale, trying to calm my nerves. I'm choosing to share this part of me with Gage. It won't help if I get defensive and jump all over him.

"I loved the book, but reading something like that doesn't really fit with my persona. People don't expect me to be deep."

Gage frowns, his posture rigid. "They should, if they've ever spent five minutes talking to you."

I sigh. "It's easier to be the fun, sporty girl. That's what I'm good at."

He rubs a hand across his chin and shakes his head. "You're good at a lot more than that."

I scoff. "Are you still talking, or can I unpause the book now?"

Gage pantomimes zipping his lips shut and gestures for me to continue.

I start the book again, and we spend the rest of our trip listening to Ken Jennings narrate Alex Trebek's personal anecdotes. We laugh at the same parts and make comments to each other.

All the while, my heart is adjusting, clicking into place, and nestling next to Gage's. My imagination is fantasizing about a future where Gage and I fit, where we listen to audiobooks together and spend the evening discussing them. Where I can keep up with him, and he has no desire to leave me behind.

It's a dangerous mindset to have right before a weekend of convincing everyone around us that I don't feel a thing.

Annie and I scream when we see each other, launching into a hug so tight, anyone would think it's been years since we'd last been together rather than two months. Gage makes a show of wincing and covering his ears, as if his hearing is in danger. Annie smacks him across the chest.

Even though it's only been a couple of hours since he dropped me off at my parents' house, my instinct is to run to him, too. It's harder than I thought it would be to control the urge to brush his hair from his face or wind my arm around his waist, the kinds of things I can do so freely at camp but that definitely don't have a place here.

I exchange hugs with Ted and Dawn, who are thrilled I came.

They ask me about my plans after the summer, and I'm careful not to look at Gage when I tell them breezily that I'm still figuring that out. I laugh as if my indecision stems from having too many options, rather than none.

As the party ramps up, it's strange to be Delaney again. I've gotten so used to everyone calling me Olivia at camp—thanks to Gage—that I almost don't recognize that "Delaney" is me. Ted's Patriotic Punch doesn't help. It is *strong*, and I'm feeling the effects after one cup. At one point, Annie repeats the name Delaney three times before I respond, concern and curiosity written on her face as I deflect with a quip about Camp Prairie Star to the small circle of people around us.

Delaney is my name here in the real world. Delaney, who is cool and unbothered, confident even when she has no plans beyond the weekend. I slip into the role on the outside, but inside I'm a mess of doubt and insecurities.

Everyone wants to know what I'm doing after my position at Camp Prairie Star ends. Everyone wants to know if I'm dating anyone special. By the time Ted launches the fireworks show, my cheeks ache from holding this phony smile in place.

Annie, thankfully, doesn't seem to notice, especially since I'm real with her about everything other than Gage when we're alone. I assure my best friend that her brother and I are friendly, that we are capable of being together in the same room again.

Meanwhile, Gage and I all but avoid each other at the party, which is probably for the best when I don't want to reveal our secret.

From across the yard, I watch Gage interact with his parents' friends. I watch the way his mouth tips up in that adorable, charismatic smile of his. The way he really listens as an elderly neighbor talks to him, and he makes her feel like she's the most important woman in the party to him at that moment.

I watch until my vision turns hazy with ... tears, I realize with surprise. I blink them back, glad Annie went inside to use the restroom and can't see me like this. She'd want to know what's going on, and I can't tell her that.

What's going on is that I'm in love with Gage. Again. Still. Always.

But now I'm in love with the man he is today. The fun, thoughtful, sweet man I'm so proud he grew up to be. And at the same time, I'm in love with every version of him I've ever known. I see them all in his eyes, all wrapped up inside his perfect heart.

Chapter Twenty-Six

Gage

As the party winds down around eleven, Olivia offers to stay to help clean up. My parents insist she should head home, so I suggest walking with her since her parents left right after the fireworks. Plus, it gives me an excuse to say good night to her properly without prying eyes nearby.

Giving her space was torture. All I wanted was to have her tucked under my arm, to kiss her openly as fireworks exploded in the sky. I wanted everyone at the party to know she's mine—not that she would admit that herself, but still.

So, when we get to her front door, I kiss her like I've wanted to all day. I back her up against the wall and devour her mouth with mine.

At first, Olivia pushes me away. "My parents," she whispers.

I stroke her cheek with the side of my hand. "I'm sure they're asleep."

She looks unconvinced, but when I kiss a trail up her neck and nibble her earlobe, she buries her doubts. I nudge her chin with my nose and catch her lips again.

She giggles and pulls away. "It feels weird."

"Gee, thanks," I deadpan.

She hits her hand lightly across my chest. "No, I mean kissing you here. In front of my parents' house. Not at camp."

I press my lips to her neck. "Do you want me to stop?" I murmur.

"No."

I smile against her skin, feeling the pulse of her heartbeat in her throat.

"But you don't think it's weird?" she presses.

"No. I'm happy kissing you anywhere."

When I get back to my parents' house, I help clean up—bagging trash and folding up chairs and tables for my dad to return to the rental company tomorrow.

Annie helps, too. She's staying here tonight since her apartment is downtown and the area will take a while to clear out from the big fireworks show the city holds over Lady Bird Lake.

When my dad ducks inside to ask my mom where she wants the lanterns, Annie corners me.

"You two are dating, aren't you?" She sets her hands on her hips and shoots me a look that's part excitement and part hurt.

"What?" I say quickly, not because I didn't hear her question, but because I need more time to figure out how to answer it.

"You and Delaney," she clarifies. "You're dating."

She doesn't frame it as a question this time. She's certain. Still, I try to dodge the implication.

"What makes you say that?" I ask.

Annie cocks her head and narrows her eyes as if to say "Seriously?"

"You couldn't take your eyes off each other all night. Even when you were conspicuously on opposite sides of the yard, you both always knew where the other was. You, in particular, were looking at her like you used to in high school, with those big heart eyes like an emoji."

Was I really that obvious? I sigh, knowing I can't lie to my sister. We're clearly busted.

"I wouldn't say *dating* exactly." I grimace.

"What would you say?"

I frown. "Olivia would say 'summer fling.'"

Annie stares at me. "Summer fling?" she repeats. "That's the stupidest thing I ever heard."

I shrug. "I don't disagree."

Annie looks thoughtful. Dad comes back outside, and Annie whispers, "Meet me at the treehouse after the parents go to bed."

I scoff but nod in agreement. Our dad built the treehouse in the oak tree by the back fence of the yard when Annie and I were six. It was always our own hideaway where we'd go to talk to each other about anything and everything. I remember many nights when one of us would whisper, "Treehouse" to the other before bed, and we'd sneak out of the house and talk late into the night without our parents knowing.

I'm not even sure it can still hold our weight, but Annie is a sucker for nostalgia.

An hour later, I climb the rope ladder to the treehouse, where Annie is already waiting for me.

I scrunch against one wall of the treehouse, my knees to my chest and my neck at an angle to keep from bumping my head on the ceiling. Annie sits by the opposite wall with her legs crossed and a blanket around her shoulders. She's not struggling to fit into this little space like I am, though she is nearly a foot shorter than me.

Didn't this treehouse use to be bigger?

"Spill," Annie commands, without preamble.

So, I do. I tell her about the sharing stick and the muumuus, the hike and canoeing, the movie day and Schlitterbahn. I don't go into detail about the kissing, but Annie is pretty good at reading between the lines.

"Wow." Annie breathes out when I finish. "Do you love her?"

She watches me carefully. The glow from her phone screen is the only light we have between us.

I nod slowly, owning up to it. "I always have," I add softly.

"Does she love you?"

I chuckle sardonically. "That's the million-dollar question. I'd like to think so. I mean, she acts like she does, but if pressed, I'm pretty sure she'd deny it."

"But why?"

"I don't know. I still don't even know what happened between us at graduation."

"You haven't asked her?" Annie's eyes widen.

I shake my head. "It's all so tentative. I don't want to do anything that will scare her off or make her ghost me again."

It sounds pathetic, what I'm willing to put up with to have Olivia around at all.

Annie tilts her head, regarding me. "That doesn't sound like a very healthy relationship, Gage."

I puff out a breath. "I know."

"So, what *is* your plan?"

I shrug. "Convince her to let this be a real relationship before the summer ends?"

"How?" she asks, crossing her arms in front of her.

I consider her question, but the truth is, I don't have a very good answer. "With my charming smile and abs of steel?"

Annie looks at me with squinted eyes. "I think you're going to need more than that."

I throw my arms up, nearly smacking them against the ceiling of the treehouse. "Well, *you're* her best friend. Help me!"

She shakes her head. "You know I love you, Gage. And Delaney. But the two of you need to figure this out for yourselves." She hesitates.

"What?" I ask.

Annie holds eye contact. "Just ... just be prepared if it turns out her feelings aren't as deep as yours. Be careful."

I exhale a breath. *Not exactly the encouragement I was hoping for.*

"I'll try," I say. "Don't say anything to Olivia, please. She can't know that you know."

Annie scrunches her nose. "I'll do my best."

Back at camp for week nine, I have my biggest group of kids yet. All twelve of the bunks in my cabin are occupied, so Jayden and I have our hands full.

Jayden's been a great junior counselor this summer. He gets impatient with the campers, especially when they're hyper, but he has a talent for crowd control and thinking of fun ideas for games and skits. He goes home to Houston most weekends, giving me the cabin all to myself, which is another point in his favor.

I hardly have a moment to think, let alone see Olivia, all week. On Friday evening, when the skits are all finally over and every one of my campers are packed up into their parents' cars and heading home, I can finally turn my thoughts to what's next. Namely, my weekend with Olivia and my nervousness about my little brother coming to camp next week. He'll be in my cabin.

I still get this weird, kind of uneasy feeling in my stomach whenever I call Duncan my brother or Callie my sister or even Maggie my mom. Almost like I'm not sure I'm allowed to use those terms.

Even though by any definition Duncan is surely my brother. We're genetically related and we have the same mom, even if we weren't raised by the same people or in the same household. And

I'm not sure who I think is authorized to give me that permission. Maggie's fine with it and so is my mom.

Our family situation is messier and more complicated than a lot of people are comfortable discussing, even if I wanted to share all the personal details with a stranger.

Or then there are some people who find out I'm adopted and think that entitles them to know everything about my story because it's different and they're curious. No matter how polite I am when I decline to share, they still walk away looking offended, like they have a right to hear about my life, and I'm rude to deny them.

But either way, Duncan is my brother. Annie and I both fell in love with him instantly when we held him for the first time in the hospital when we were thirteen. The same for Callie two years later.

Duncan is kind of a quiet, shy kid. He reminds me a lot of Annie at that age, actually. Maggie asked Linda, the camp director, for him to be assigned to my cabin. She thinks it will help him adjust to camp more easily.

I meet Olivia in the mess hall for a simple dinner and remind her that Duncan will be at camp on Sunday. Plus, Maggie and her family booked a hotel in the town nearby for Saturday night so they can take me to dinner before Duncan's week at Camp Prairie Star begins.

"Oh, yeah!" Olivia says, sitting on the bench across from me and stabbing a forkful of taco salad. "Are you excited to see everyone?"

I give her a half shrug as I push my food around on the plate more than eat it. "Yes, but also kind of nervous?"

She puts her fork down and leans over the table to get closer to me. "Why? What's up?"

I shrug again. "I don't know. I mean, I came here this summer to try to feel closer to my roots because of Maggie's family's legacy, you know? But I don't feel like I've really done that."

"No?" Olivia tilts her head.

"I've been a little distracted," I remind her, my eyebrows raised.

Her cheeks turn pink. "Because of me?" she squeaks. "I'm sorry, Gage! I didn't mean to distract you from your goals this summer." She angles her head down, looking at the table instead of me.

I reach across and nudge her chin up with my hand. "Hey," I murmur when her eyes meet mine, "I'm not complaining. The summer has been amazing so far."

"It has," she agrees with a smile that flips my stomach. "How about if I plan an activity for us tomorrow?" She falters. "Unless you'd rather have some alone time to process before your dinner with Maggie."

I finger a strand of hair that's escaped from her ponytail and tuck it behind her ear. "I'd rather be with you. What kind of activity do you have in mind?"

She bites her lip. "It's a surprise. Meet me here for breakfast at eight—realistically, maybe 8:30—and we'll go from there."

I grin at her. "Can't wait."

Chapter Twenty-Seven

Gage

I'm awake by six on Saturday morning, so I try to alleviate my nervous energy with a run. I've been so busy this summer at camp that I've traded my runs and sessions in the weight room for chasing campers around on nature hikes. I'm staying active, but in a different way than my body's used to.

The burn in my legs and lungs feels good, and I find that I'm calmer when I'm done. I shower and get dressed with time to spare before meeting Olivia for breakfast.

When I see her, she smiles sleepily behind her coffee mug. "You look chipper this morning."

I grin and sit on the bench next to her. "Chipper?"

"Yeah, you know, animated, bright, alert?" She nudges me with her shoulder.

Chuckling, I nudge her back. "I know what it means. It's just not a term I hear people say often."

"Do you want to do the activity I planned, or not?" Olivia huffs, feigning annoyance.

"I definitely do. I swear I'll be good and keep the teasing to a minimum." I hold up three fingers side by side. "Scout's honor."

She smirks and shakes her head. "You're not a scout."

I put on my most earnest expression. "For you, I could be," I tell her with a straight face.

"Shut up!" Olivia laughs and shoves my chest. "Finish eating so we can go."

Twenty minutes later, Olivia practically drags me across camp to the craft cabin.

"Are we doing crafts?" I ask. Not my strong suit, but we'll make it fun.

"Sort of." Her eyes twinkle as she holds back a smile. "Nina gave me permission to use some of the craft materials for a special project."

Olivia leads me by the hand through the door of the craft cabin, the screen door screeching and slamming in the way I've gotten used to this summer. She gestures to a table piled with zip-top sandwich bags each filled with a different color. I squint to look more closely. Little rubber bands that remind me of the ones the orthodontist used to put on my teeth.

My forehead furrows. "We're going to ... adjust our braces?"

Olivia giggles and squeezes my hand. "No! We're going to make friendship bracelets. For each other."

My eyes snap to hers, and though she holds the contact, uncertainty flashes across her face. She swallows and presses her lips together in a tight smile.

Am I reading too much into this? Exchanging jewelry—even camp-craft bracelets made out of rubber bands—feels romantic, like a promise. Like a commitment we'll still see each other after the summer ends.

I play it cool, though. Olivia spooks easily.

I stretch my lips into an easy grin. "Taylor Swift style?"

Her shoulders relax, as if she's been holding them taut and has now finally released the tension in her muscles. She breathes out a shaky laugh. "Similar, but we're going to use rubber bands instead of jewelry elastic. We can still use beads though."

I let go of her hand to rub mine together. "Let's do it!"

She beams, bolstered by my enthusiasm. "Have you ever made a loom bracelet before?" she asks.

I purse my lips, tilting my head at her.

She laughs. "Well, I don't know! You could have been up to anything the last five years."

"I have not been making bracelets out of rubber bands," I tell her.

Olivia gestures for me to sit down at the table. When I do, she sits next to me and picks through the pile of baggies until she finds what she wants.

"We're going to make double-band fishtail-patterned bracelets," she explains. "You choose two or three colors, depending on how you want the final design to look."

She opens a bag of light blue rubber bands and another bag of a bold yellow color. She holds up two fingers and stretches a blue band between them, with a twist in the middle. Then she adds a yellow band, with no twist. She adds a third band, no twist, and then flips the first blue band up somehow so that it bunches in the middle of the other two.

I squint my eyes. "Wait, wait. What did you do?"

Olivia smirks and slides the rubber bands off her fingers. "I'll show you on your fingers. What colors do you want?"

I consider. "Are these my for-real colors, or to practice?"

She shrugs. "It could be your final bracelet if it goes well."

"Okay, then. Give me a minute."

I shift the baggies around on the table to examine my options, and there are a lot of options. Some of the rubber bands are neon, some pastel, and some even have designs on them with multiple colors on one band.

I stop short when I see a baggie filled with the perfect rubber bands. Before I reach for it, though, I shoot a glance at Olivia, who's watching me.

I divert my hand to a bag of purple bands and then add in a bag of white ones. "This is going to be my practice bracelet," I tell Olivia. "The real one is going to be a surprise."

She chuckles. "Okay, weirdo." She adjusts my hand so that two of my fingers are pointing up.

She walks through the instructions for starting a bracelet again, this time using my fingers to demonstrate. She leans in close to manipulate the small rubber bands—so close that her shoulder rests against my chest and her hair brushes against my nose. I inhale quietly and am rewarded with the sharp, minty smell of her shampoo.

"Got it?" Olivia asks, turning her head toward me so that our faces are inches apart.

Oh, right. I was supposed to be paying attention to the bracelet-making instructions. "Umm. Maybe you could show me one more time?"

She sighs, her breath tickling my lips. *If I slant forward a bit...*

"Gage!" Olivia laughs, angling farther away. "Focus."

"I am focusing," I mutter as I bring my hand up to her ponytail and run my fingers through her hair.

She scowls, narrowing her eyes and jutting her bottom lip toward me. "I mean on the bracelet."

I zero in on her lips. "Mm-hmm," I say, before closing the distance between us. She's not frowning anymore as I kiss her in that languid, gentle way I've discovered she loves.

Of all the things I've learned about Olivia this summer, after knowing her so intently in our growing-up years, I value knowing these privileged details about her the most. I want to know everything about the way her hands wander while she kisses me, from my shoulders to my back and up to my neck and face. Everything about the soft, uncontrolled sounds she makes when my hand is in her hair. Everything about how her eyelashes flutter as she closes her eyes and loses herself to me.

We eventually get back on task making the bracelets, and I stay turned away from Olivia so the design I picked for hers will be a surprise.

We work in cozy parallel, on separate projects but together in the space we're taking up and the air we're breathing. When I finally get serious, the bracelet is easy to make, even when I add in beads for extra flair.

It doesn't take long before we're ready to unveil our creations. Olivia goes first. She pulls the bracelet from behind her back.

"The blue is for your eyes, obviously," Olivia explains as she points out the features she's included, "and the yellow reminds me of your sunshiny personality. You always make my day brighter, and the way you're lighting up my life this summer is something I'll always be grateful for."

Her eyes sparkle, but the blush on her cheeks tells me it's an effort for her to be this vulnerable with me. My heart stretches and crackles in my chest. This woman. Doesn't she know that I'd rather spend every day reliving my worst-ever at bat than leave her?

No, she doesn't, a voice in my head whispers, *because you're afraid telling her will push her away.*

"And I added your name, of course," she finishes, indicating the white alphabet beads with black lettering that spell out *Gage*.

I smirk at the irony and give her a one-armed hug, careful to keep her bracelet hidden behind my back. "Thank you, babe. I love it."

I hold out my wrist, and she immediately fastens the bracelet around it. "Look at that: a perfect fit." I grin at her.

Olivia bounces in her seat. "My turn!" she chirps, leaning forward to try to peek behind me.

"Drumroll, please," I tease. She giggles, and I wait. I clear my throat. "Seriously. I need a drumroll."

She rolls her eyes but raps her fingers against the table for a makeshift drumroll.

I bring my hand forward with a flourish, the bracelet I made for her lying flat against my palm. I used one color—a deep green flecked with silver glitter. Without a color pattern, the woven design of the rubber bands is more apparent, wrapping over and under each other in beautiful synchronicity.

"I've always loved seeing you in green."

I watch her face closely as she delicately lifts the bracelet from my hand and turns it over in her fingers. Her features are soft, her eyes hooded and unblinking as a slow smile spreads across her lips.

She examines the black alphabet beads with silver lettering. "It says *Gage*," she points out, her mouth quirking up and a question in her eyes.

So everyone will know you're mine, I think. Out loud, I say, "So you'll always think of me when you wear it."

I take the bracelet from her and slip it onto her wrist, making sure the plastic clasp is secure. I let my touch linger, caressing the soft skin on her arm.

Finally, I lift my head and look at her. I'm half afraid of what I'll see, nervous that I'm coming on too strong.

But she's glowing under my gaze, peering at me with a look of wonder and love that echoes what I feel for her.

It's almost too much to hope for, too much to expect, but I push her even further. "Come to dinner with us tonight." My voice is low, infused with a confidence born from reckless, optimistic longing.

Her eyebrows pull together. "Are you sure? I don't want to intrude on your family time."

The way she says it sends a surge of warmth through my chest. A family dinner. Maggie and her husband and two kids are clearly a family, and sometimes I struggle to see where Annie and I fit into that. Sometimes I feel like I'm the one intruding.

But Olivia's simple acceptance of my place in Maggie's family, like it's a given that I belong with them, makes it easier for me to accept it, too.

I lean my forehead against hers. "I'm positive. I always want you to be where I am."

Chapter Twenty-Eight

Olivia

That evening, Gage and I take his Jeep into town to meet his family for dinner. We both wear our new bracelets, looking like a couple of lovesick saps with the kitschy rubber bands on our wrists. An impression I'm not saying would be completely inaccurate.

As we tiptoed around each other in front of our families at the party last weekend, separate but together, all I could think was how much I hated the act. My reasons for avoiding a real relationship with Gage faded into the background, still present, but not what I wanted to focus on.

All of the little moments and hints throughout the summer that have made me think Gage wants more than a fling meld together into a flashing neon sign, especially after our craft session earlier.

If Gage thinks I'm enough, maybe I am.

So tonight, at his request, I'm dipping my toes into the relationship waters and meeting his birth family. It strikes me as strange that though Annie's been my best friend for more than ten years, it's not her that makes this introduction. I've heard all about Maggie and Kent and Duncan and Callie, from both Gage and Annie, but to be meeting them through the lens of my connection with Gage feels significant.

I have a sudden thought, and the resulting question breaks through the silence in the Jeep. "How are you going to introduce me to them?"

Gage glances at me, a teasing smile on his face. "I was thinking I'd use your name."

"Olivia or Delaney? And as what? Your friend? Annie's friend? Your make-out buddy?"

Gage grimaces. "Definitely not that last one."

"I'm serious!" I pinch my bracelet between my fingers and snap it against my skin. I repeat the nervous fidget again as I wait for Gage to respond.

"How would you like me to introduce you?" he finally asks. I don't know how he sounds so calm when I'm drowning in a tidal wave of anxiety.

I spin through the possibilities in my head. "Well obviously Maggie talks to Annie, right? So, I don't want to be too obvious because I don't want Annie to hear about us secondhand."

Gage shifts in his seat. "Listen, about Annie—"

I rush to cut him off, my stomach fluttering. "I'm not saying I'm still determined for Annie not to know about us, but I want to be the one to tell her."

Gage pulls into the parking lot of one of the local restaurants. It's a concrete building with a red tile roof in high peaks like those on the Alamo. A Texas lone star sign hangs on the covered walkway leading up to the front doors.

"I get that, but—"

"So, I think you should introduce me with my first and last name and as a friend you and Annie grew up with." The words tumble from my mouth so quickly that I'm left trying to catch my breath.

Gage parks the Jeep and turns it off. As he removes the keys from the ignition, he lets his hands fall to his thighs. He rubs his palms over his jeans a few times while inhaling one deep breath, then another.

I watch him quietly and feel like a self-absorbed brat. I've been making this night all about me and how I'm feeling, when Gage is the one facing his deepest trauma. After all he's shared with me about his conflicting emotions surrounding his adoption, I should have been more sensitive. Of course he's nervous. It was foolish of me to think otherwise.

I reach over the center console and lay my hand on top of his, stroking gently with my fingers.

"Take your time," I murmur. "There's no rush."

He flips his hand over and interlaces our fingers. I squeeze and lean closer. Gage lets go of my hand to wrap his arms around my shoulders and pull me close.

I wriggle my arms out from between us and rub circles on his back. His heartbeat pulses against my chest as he clings to me.

As the seconds pass, I feel his heart regulate and his breathing even out. His grip on me loosens until he pulls away and shoots me an abashed smile.

I smile back at him. "Ready?"

"Almost," he whispers before brushing a gentle kiss across my lips. "Now, I'm ready."

We get out of the Jeep and make our way toward the restaurant entrance. On a ramp near the door, a couple that look like they're in their late thirties stand waiting with two children. I recognize the family from the picture taped to the wall above Gage's bunk.

Gage rushes forward and throws his arms around the woman—Maggie. Keeping an arm around her shoulders, he high-fives her husband before ruffling his little brother's hair. Callie peeks out shyly from behind her dad's back, but Duncan grins up at Gage with an adoring expression.

His exuberant greeting now is such a change from his uncertainty in the Jeep minutes ago. It's almost like he's performing, the entrance ramp is his stage, and I'm the audience, watching the reunion from a few feet back.

Examining Maggie from a distance, it's disconcerting how much she looks like Annie. Or how much Annie looks like her, rather. Seeing Maggie, I can easily picture what my best friend will look like in twenty years.

Gage turns and beckons me closer. As I approach, he rests his hand against the small of my back. "This is Olivia Delaney," he says, shooting me a subtle wink. "Annie and I have been friends with her since middle school, and she's working with me at Camp Prairie Star this summer. Olivia, this is Maggie Gray, her husband, Kent, and their kids, Duncan and Callie."

"Hi." I wave, smiling broadly. "I've heard so much about you. I'm so glad to finally meet you all."

Maggie looks with amusement between Gage and me. "Olivia Delaney." She smirks, and now her face is pure Gage, where before I saw only Annie. "We've heard all about you, too."

I cram my hands in my pockets. "I'm sure. Annie and I are best friends, so."

Maggie's eyes sparkle. "Yes, *some* of what I've heard was from Annie." I follow her gaze to Gage, whose ears turn suspiciously red.

Kent, who is tall and handsome with close-cropped black hair and rich brown eyes, ushers us forward. "Let's get in the air conditioning before we melt. We can talk more inside."

He takes Callie's hand, and we follow them into the restaurant. Inside, the dining room is pure Texas with its concrete floors and heavy wood tables and chairs with black metal trim. The walls are distressed gray bricks in a running bond pattern beneath high ceilings with dark wood paneling.

The place is busy, but not as packed as I'd expect it to be on a Saturday night. We're seated right away, despite the large size of our party.

Gage and I sit next to each other, across from Maggie and Kent, with Duncan on the end next to Gage, and Callie on the other end between Kent and me. Under the table, Gage lays his hand on my knee right away, like he needs the connection.

After we order and we're waiting for the food to come, Maggie asks Gage about the summer at camp so far, and Duncan soaks in Gage's words. Maggie holds a hand up near her mouth and whispers across the table, "He's a little nervous for his first year at camp."

Duncan hears her, of course. "Moooom," he complains. Maggie winks.

I lean over Gage to speak to Duncan. "Most kids are nervous when they first get to camp, but then they meet their cabinmates and start doing all the cool activities, and they're having fun before they know it. Plus"—I nod toward Gage—"rumor has it that you're going to have the very best counselor at the whole camp."

Duncan's face brightens. "I'm going to be in Gage's cabin?"

Gage grins and pats Duncan on the shoulder. "You sure are, bud. And we'll have a pretty small group. I think there are only six or seven boys in our cabin this week."

Maggie groans, and before I can ask what's wrong, Duncan and Callie chorus, "Six-sevvuhnn!" in a lyrical lilt while making alternating rising-and-falling motions with their upturned hands, like a balancing scale.

Gage rubs the palm of his hand against his forehead. "I walked right into that one."

All summer the kids at camp—and elsewhere apparently—have been obsessed with saying the numbers six and seven this way with the hand motions. It means absolutely nothing, as far as any of the adults can tell, but it's super annoying.

I shake my head and smile at Duncan. "You'll fit right in at camp."

Across from me, Kent's phone starts vibrating from its spot on the table. He glances at the screen and frowns. "It's my brother. He's watching our dog for us this weekend. I'd better take this, in case there's a problem."

Kent stands, and Gage follows his movements. He turns to Maggie. "Holden's back in Texas?"

"Recently. He's staying in that little apartment above our garage."

Callie watches with wide eyes as Kent steps toward the door to go outside, holding the phone up to his ear.

"It's okay, Cal. Daddy will be right back," Maggie soothes. To me, she says, "It takes Callie time to warm up to new people."

"Hey, CJ." Gage leans forward to see his sister better. "Do you want me to come sit by you until your dad gets back?"

Callie bobs her head up and down, the most pathetic little pout on her lips. Gage pops up and rounds the table to take Kent's seat.

I immediately miss the warmth of his hand on my knee, but as soon as Gage is settled in the chair across from me, one of his feet nudges mine under the table. He catches my eye and grins.

With Callie fully occupying Gage's attention, Maggie turns to me. "So, what do you do when you're not working at a summer camp?"

It's a normal question to ask, but also one that puts me on high alert, because *I don't know.*

I rub my arm as I answer, feigning confidence I don't feel. "Great question. Before the summer, I was a kids' soccer coach in Austin. I'll probably go back to that once camp is done." Before I can overthink it, I rush to add, "But I've been looking into becoming a PE teacher. It's a long process to get certified through the state, so I'll start working on that in the fall, too."

Maggie leans in. "Oh, that's awesome! I forgot you're a soccer player." She pauses. "Are you pretty set on working in a public school?"

"Maggie is the school nurse for a private academy in Fort Worth," Gage inserts before Callie pulls him away again.

I bite my lip. "Um, I guess I don't really have a preference. Why?"

"Private and charter schools don't necessarily require the same certification, at least right away. It might be worth checking into if you're wanting to get started sooner."

Before I can ask any follow-up questions, Kent returns to the table, and there's the shuffle of Gage returning to his seat and Maggie checking in on the phone call.

"All good," Kent reports. "He couldn't remember how much food to give her."

Gage squeezes my shoulder as he walks behind me before sitting back down. I look up at him, and he raises his eyebrows, a keen glint in his eyes. I nod at him, trying to downplay the mixture of enthusiasm and nerves I feel thinking about this potential new game plan for my career.

He sits and leans close to my ear. "We can start looking when we get back to camp tonight if you want."

"Let's see how we feel," I whisper back. With how nervous Gage was leading up to this dinner, he might want to decompress after this. I know he's eager to help me, but I'm just as eager to make sure *he's* good.

The server arrives with our food, and conversation dies down as we eat the burgers and steaks in front of us.

The rest of the evening flows from there. Kent is quiet and charming. He seems to be the designated kid wrangler for the night, making it easy for Maggie to focus on Gage. The kids are adorable and funny, especially Callie once she opens up. It'll be fun getting to know Duncan better this next week at camp.

Maggie is sweet and funny. She reminds me as much of Gage in her personality as she reminds me of Annie in her looks. Of course, how could I not love Maggie? She made two of my favorite people in the world.

We settle back into the Jeep after leaving the restaurant and saying our goodbyes to the Gray family until tomorrow when they'll come to drop Duncan off for camp.

Gage is quiet, and I wonder what's going through his head. I run my fingers along his arm and down to his hand, which I wrap up in mine. "I think it went well. Don't you?"

He hums his assent, but he sounds tired.

We drive back to camp with a heavy silence between us in the Jeep. When Gage pulls into the staff parking lot and shuts off the engine, he rubs the heels of his hands into his eyes.

"How are you really?" I ask through the dim quiet. My question is the puncture in the balloon that forces all the air to rush out, and Gage starts ranting.

"It takes so much out of me, being 'on' like that in front of her. I love seeing Maggie, but it's so hard. I hate that everything feels so stilted between us at first whenever we get together, and then it feels like we're both overcompensating by being extra happy, extra energetic to make up for it."

I shift as close to him as I can with the center console between us. I open my arms, and he sinks into them, his back practically folded in half so he can rest his head on my shoulder. He sucks in a ragged breath and continues. "Sometimes I think, 'If she loved me so much, why did she leave me?'"

My heart cracks, thinking not only of Gage and his deep-seated hurt, but also of Maggie and how heartbreaking it must have been to place her babies in the arms of another family.

I think of my own past decisions, including the one I made to walk away from Gage so that he could have something better.

"She probably thought it was for your own good," I murmur next to his ear.

"Yeah, in a lot of ways it was. I can't imagine not knowing my parents, not growing up in Austin or playing baseball with the teams I did. I can't imagine not ever meeting you. But I still wonder who Annie and I would have been if we were Maggie's kids. It hurts thinking about missing out on that."

I don't know what to say to that, so I stay silent and squeeze him harder.

The fabric of my shirt under Gage's head is damp by the time he sits up. He wipes his eyes with the back of his hand and offers me a shaky smile. "Thank you for being here for me tonight. At dinner and now. I lo—" He breaks off, looking flustered. He clears his throat and tries again. "I love that you're part of my life again."

Is that really what he was going to say? Somehow I doubt it. I think he stopped himself from telling me something else, something maybe he's not ready to admit, yet. Something I'm definitely not ready to hear.

"Of course," I tell him, running my thumbs across his cheeks to wipe off the last of the tears. "Let's get you back to your cabin."

We walk together to Gage's cabin, where he gives me a soft good-night kiss outside the front door.

He stops before walking inside, glancing at me over his shoulder. "Oh, wait. Your job search."

The range of up-and-down emotions tonight was exhausting even for me, and I was only observing. From Gage's nerves before we left the Jeep, to being hyped up and charismatic in the restaurant, and then his crash when we got back to camp, he must be totally spent.

I shake my head. "No way. Don't even think about it. I forbid it."

That pulls a small smile from him. "You forbid it?"

I clasp my hands in front of me. "Yes. We'll do it another time. I promise. Get some rest."

"Thanks, Olivia. Good night."

"Good night," I whisper. I stand outside the door until Gage is fully inside. Then, I turn to walk to my own cabin.

I love that Gage is part of my life again, too.

Chapter Twenty-Nine

Gage

I'm feeling chagrined as I watch for Olivia to come into the mess hall for breakfast the next morning. I'm not a man afraid to show my feelings, but I dumped a lot of heavy emotions on her last night.

I feel better about Maggie this morning, though I'm still wrung out. It's always a swirl of mixed-up emotions when I see her. I love Maggie, and I'm excited to spend time with her, but I'm also nervous about trying to contain all the fears it brings up. It gets overwhelming, and I can't always hold it all in. Despite the tornado of conflicting moods seeing Maggie causes for me, I never regret any of the time I spend with her.

I know that pattern of nervousness, excitement, and breakdown is typical, so I probably should have warned Olivia ahead of time. I literally cried on her shoulder while sharing my innermost fears. Plus, I almost told her I love her.

I mean, I *am* in love with her, but I have a feeling saying so would ruin everything. I'm running out of time, though. There are only three weeks left of camp. Three weeks left until the expiration date Olivia originally set for this "fling."

When she squeezes my shoulders in a hug from behind and then sits next to me on the bench, I flash one of the cheerful grins that aligns with what people expect from my normally buoyant personality.

Her eyes are deep with concern. "Are you doing okay this morning?" she asks quietly.

"I'm feeling much better," I assure her.

"Promise?" She leans in and lays her hand on my arm, studying me.

"Promise." I peck her lips. "I'm looking forward to hanging out with Duncan all week."

Her expression brightens. "He's a great kid. They both are. And they *adore* you."

I think about the kids at dinner last night and smile. "The feeling's mutual." I pause. "*And* after you finish breakfast, I'm looking forward to combing through job ads on the computer with you."

Her mouth pops open. "We don't have to do that this morning."

"Don't think I forgot. My cabin is ready for the campers, which means I'm free for the next"—I look at my phone screen—"two hours before they start arriving."

We finish breakfast and walk to the main office to use the computer there. After thirty minutes of searching, we find two positions for Olivia to apply for. One is at a private K-12 school called Virtus

Academy in South Austin, not too far from Olivia's house. The other is at a charter middle and high school focused on science called the Brightline School, but it's all the way up in North Austin, almost to Pflugerville. Both require a bachelor's degree and some relevant experience, and neither expect applicants to have a state teaching license.

As we read through the postings and then the websites for the schools, Olivia grows more and more animated.

"So, these look good?" I ask her.

She beams. "They look great!" She throws her arms around my shoulders from her chair next to mine in front of the computer. Then her cheeks blush pink. "I feel like I can think about the future with hope now. I've ... I've been feeling pretty defeated about how I'm kind of floundering in life since college ended, since soccer ended. I've been taking things one day at a time because any more than that and I'd get so panicked and demoralized."

Is that why she hasn't been willing to commit to anything more than a summer fling?

She keeps her eyes on mine. "Thank you, Gage. For your help. You found possibilities for me that I couldn't see because I was so stuck in my own rut."

I take her hands in mine. "Sometimes it takes someone with an outside perspective to see the answer that's right there. That's all I did. Thank you for trusting me enough to let me in."

I press a kiss to each of her hands. "Now, what next?"

She raises her chin, thinking. "I have to revise my résumé for this kind of job, but once I do, I'll apply for both."

I look back at the computer screen. "Do you need any help with your résumé?" I know that kind of written work isn't the easiest for her, but I don't want to overstep either.

"No, you've helped enough already. I have to be able to do *something* for myself." She laughs, but it's laced with deprecation.

"I'm here if you change your mind."

And I always will be.

Maggie, Kent, and Callie arrive right on time to drop Duncan off at camp. I'm greeting all my kids for the week—helping them get settled and answering their parents' questions—so I don't get to tour the camp with my family. Other than at the prospective family open house Camp Prairie Star holds every January, Maggie hasn't been back since her own idyllic summer session twenty-five years ago.

I'd love to follow her around and hear her recount her memories, but maybe there will be time for that after Skit Night on Friday.

My focus this week is Duncan, not that I'm planning to play favorites with the kids in my cabin. I mean that I'm looking forward to experiencing Camp Prairie Star through Duncan's eyes.

It's not lost on me that Duncan is the son Maggie did choose to raise. I know the situations were completely different. When Annie and I were born, Maggie was barely sixteen. She wasn't married, or even with our birth father anymore. He wasn't interested in being a dad at all. And there were *two* of us.

When Duncan was born, Maggie was thirty years old and in a loving marriage with a supportive partner who was excited to be a dad.

But still, if I had grown up with Maggie as my mom, I would have come to camp for the first time when I was ten, like Duncan is doing this summer. I would have grown up with Camp Prairie Star as a part of me, like Maggie did and like Duncan, and eventually Callie, will.

In my imagination, there's a ghost Gage, an alternate-dimension Gage, who had that experience. Like the many Peter Parkers in the multiverse of *Spider-Man*, I can sometimes see another version of myself in my mind—the Gage that could have been if Maggie had kept me, right alongside the Gage that I am as Ted and Dawn's son.

And the most disturbing part is that sometimes I'm not sure if the me I actually am is the real Gage or if ghost Gage is the true version. I don't know which Gage is better off, though it's easy to look at any challenge in my life and imagine the grass would have been greener in my ghost kingdom.

Being here this summer, and especially being here with Duncan, who is like a shadow of who I might have been, is my effort to combine my current self with the ghost Gage that could have existed if the adults in my life had made other choices when I was born.

That night when all the families have left and it's me, Jayden, and the seven boys who live in our cabin this week, we're all trying to get to know each other better.

One of the boys picks up on the familiarity between me and Duncan and asks, "Do you know each other already?"

"We do," I confirm, nodding my head, but I realize I never stopped to think about how to explain our relationship to the rest of the cabin. Adoption is not the easiest thing to explain to a bunch of kids.

"Is he your uncle or something?" another kid asks Duncan.

I'm about to step in to take the pressure off him, when he smiles.

"Gage is my brother," Duncan says confidently. "My mom had him before she married my dad, but she couldn't take care of him, so he went to live with another mom and dad. But he's still my brother because distance doesn't erase family."

His simple explanation steals my breath, and I suddenly feel ashamed that I've been thinking of him in terms of my ghost self instead of in terms of being my little brother.

He's not me. He's not a version of me from a potential other dimension. He's Duncan, and a pretty cool little kid. I vow to re-member that this week.

I lay my hand on his shoulder. "That's right," I agree. "Duncan is my favorite brother, as a matter of fact."

Duncan rolls his eyes. "I'm your only brother."

I chuckle. He is, as far as I know anyway. No one's kept tabs on my birth father over the years, so maybe I have more siblings out there somewhere.

The answer seems to satisfy the other boys.

"Although," I say to Duncan with a wink, "you should have saved that information for our game of Two Truths and a Lie. Truths that sound like lies are the hardest to guess. Does everyone know how to play? I'll go first."

I always play Two Truths and a Lie with my campers the first night. It's fun and easy to play and helps us all to get to know each other. I usually start, though Jayden does sometimes instead. The idea is for us to model how the game works.

"So, my name is Gage. Let's see..." I pretend to think, even though I always use the same three statements. "I have a twin sister. My favorite baseball team is the Atlanta Braves. And I have never lived outside of Texas."

"That kid can't answer," one of the boys says, pointing at Duncan.

"Fair point." I nod. "Duncan can't answer for me, and I can't answer for him. Now, which of my statements was the lie?"

"I don't think you have a twin sister," a boy with black hair and dark brown eyes guesses.

Duncan giggles.

"Wrong," I say. "I have a twin sister named Annie."

"The Texas thing," another boy shouts. "You're a grown-up so you've probably lived all sorts of places."

"Wrong again. I've only ever lived in Austin, Texas."

"Who's your favorite baseball team, then?" one of the campers asks.

"The Rangers, of course. Who else?"

This starts a cabin-wide discussion of baseball teams, and which ones are the best. There's a pretty even split between Rangers and Astros fans, with a couple of kids with outlier teams like the Dodgers or Yankees.

I clap my hands together to get their attention back. "Okay, who's going next?"

One by one, the boys introduce themselves and share three statements. We all try to guess which one is a lie. Some of them make it easy—like a boy named Liam who says he rides a dragon to school—but most do a great job of making their lies believable and their truths suspicious.

When it's Duncan's turn, the boys remind me that I'm not allowed to guess.

"Um ..." Duncan begins. "I have a dog named Biscuit. I love anything having to do with math. And ... this is my first summer at Camp Prairie Star."

I know the Gray family has a dog named Macy because Maggie made a big deal about naming the dog after a singer she loved when she was a teenager, so that must be the lie. Of course, I know it's Duncan's first summer here, but I didn't know that he loves math so much. That's pretty cool.

I realize that Duncan's become this whole little person when I wasn't looking. I mean, I know he's always been a person, but when he was born, he was the baby, and then I kind of thought of him as a generic little kid. But I've gotten older, and he has, too. At ten years old, he's got interests and hobbies and a whole personality that I haven't gotten to fully understand because I don't see him often enough.

I'm really looking forward to changing that this week.

By lunchtime on Monday, all the boys in my cabin are best friends, including Duncan, whose typical shy demeanor has disappeared. He's wrestling with the other boys, coming up with ideas for pranks, and racing his canoe across the lake.

For Wacky Wednesday, our cabin decides to coordinate outfits. The boys have Nina help them tie-dye shirts during craft time on Tuesday—including ones for Jayden and me—and use up the rest of my mousse the next morning on their crazy hairstyles. Mostly it looks like they had a competition to see who could get their hair to stick straight up the highest.

We eat waffles with whipped cream and bacon for dinner. Duncan, who's sitting next to me, smothers his waffles in syrup while talking a mile a minute. "Mom says waffles are better than pancakes because waffles hold your syrup for you in these little boxes."

"Yeah, but pancakes can have fruit inside them, like blueberries or bananas," I counter.

He looks at me like I'm the biggest idiot on the planet. "You can put fruit in waffle batter, too."

I hold up my hands. "Point conceded. My apologies."

Duncan laughs and looks up at me, his brown eyes sincere and his mouth half full of waffles and syrup. "This has been, like, the best day of my life."

I'm inclined to agree with him. These past few days with Duncan have been my favorite at camp so far—not counting the weekends. It's been almost magical at Camp Prairie Star, and I understand why Maggie clings so tightly to her memories here.

I don't know why those thoughts make my eyes well up, but they do. I hide the sudden onslaught of emotion by shoveling an enormous bite of waffle in my own mouth.

Chapter Thirty

Late Wednesday night, or maybe early the next morning, a finger poking into my shoulder nudges me awake. "Gage?" a little voice whispers loudly, and I open my eyes enough to check the time on my phone. Five in the morning.

"Gage?" the voice says again, and this time I recognize it as Duncan's.

"What's going on, bud? You okay?" I rub my face, trying to wake up enough to deal with whatever this is.

"I don't know. I got up to go to the bathroom, and my face felt weird, and I looked in the mirror and ... look!"

I blink my eyes. Then blink again. Finally, I can make out Duncan's features in the low light. Except they aren't exactly Duncan's normal features.

His face is puffy, the skin around his eyes so swollen that he's looking at me through narrow slits. I touch my hand to his forehead and then his cheek. His skin is warm.

My first instinct is to swear, but I remember myself and instead draw from everything I learned in training and remain calm, at least on the outside.

Through all the training though, if I imagined an emergency at all, it was one involving a kid I was responsible for but didn't really know. But this is Duncan, who I held in my arms for the first time when he was hours old. Who toddled around the yard after me those summers in Fort Worth when I was in middle school. This is my little brother, and it takes all my willpower to tamp down the panic and think through the problem rationally.

I need to get him to the camp nurse.

First, though, I try to reassure him as I climb out of my bunk. "It's okay, buddy. We'll get you taken care of. I'll be with you the whole time."

"What's wrong with me?" he asks in a pitiful little voice.

"I don't know, but we're going to go see Ms. Hannah, and she'll know exactly how to help. Now, go get some shoes on."

He runs off to find his shoes while I shake Jayden awake to let him know I'm taking Duncan to the nurse, and he's in charge. Jayden's eyes widen, but he nods resolutely and sits up in bed.

I slip on my flip-flops and wait for Duncan by the cabin door. When he shuffles up next to me, he hands me a flashlight, switched off.

"I thought we'd need it for the walk to the nurse's cabin," he whispers.

"Good thinking," I whisper back, kicking myself for not being the one to think of this detail.

Once outside, I switch on the flashlight. "Close your eyes," I instruct Duncan, and then shine the light on his face so I can see it better.

In addition to the swelling, his skin looks red, especially in one section of his right cheek. *Did he get bitten by a spider? Is it an allergic reaction to something?* I try to remember if Duncan has any allergies, but nothing comes to mind. *Is it because he's not allergic to anything, or because I only see him a handful of weeks a year?*

I drop the beam of light back to the ground in front of us. "Okay, let's go." I take his hand and hold onto it, even though he's probably too old for such a thing. He doesn't pull away.

We walk across camp to the nurse's cabin and knock on the door. Hannah, an older woman who works as a school nurse during the year and spends her summers treating poison ivy and sunburns at Camp Prairie Star, flips on the cabin's outside light and opens the door.

"Everything okay?" she asks. Her graying hair is piled on top of her head in a claw clip, and the sash of her plaid robe is tied around her waist.

"Um, we're not sure," I answer, gesturing to Duncan's face.

Hannah steps closer and uses her hand under Duncan's chin to tilt his head toward the light. "Oh my. You two better come in."

She steps back through the doorway, and I nudge Duncan inside behind her.

Her cabin is set up as an infirmary, with two cots near the front of the room and a long desk with medical supplies lining the back wall. Beyond that are two doors, one that leads to a bathroom, and one that leads to Hannah's bedroom space.

Hannah has Duncan sit on one of the cots as she takes his temperature from his forehead with one of those infrared thermometers. When it beeps, she looks at the screen and hums. She asks his name and taps on the screen of a tablet, presumably to bring up the medical forms Maggie and Kent must have filled out.

"It says no allergies," she says, almost to herself. Then, setting down the tablet, she snaps on a pair of latex gloves and examines his face. She touches the swollen areas gently with her fingers as she keeps up a stream of reassuring words.

I slump into a chair near the front door. Watching her work and knowing Duncan is in good hands, I'm able to relax.

"Did you go on a nature hike in the woods yesterday, Mr. Duncan?" she asks with a soft smile.

Duncan's mouth falls open. "Yes. How did you know?"

Hannah glances toward me. "Is Gage your counselor?"

"Yes," Duncan answers.

"I'm also his brother," I add, in case the family connection entitles me to additional information.

"Has he ever had anything like this happen before?" she asks me.

I should know the answer to that, but I don't. I lift an arm helplessly. "I'm not sure. We've never lived together."

Hannah regards me with kind but curious eyes. "That's all right." She pulls off the gloves and turns her attention back to Duncan. "Looks like skeeter syndrome to me."

Despite being tired and worried, I crack a smile and exchange an amused look with Duncan. "That can't be a real thing."

Hannah smiles back. "Oh, but it is. Just means that he had an allergic reaction to a mosquito bite. You can see the bite mark here on his right cheek. I'll give him Benadryl and put some hydrocortisone cream on his face. Both are on the list of preapproved medications his parents gave us permission to administer. He has a slight fever, but I'm not too worried about that." She looks at her watch. "I'll need to call his parents and let them know what happened, but it's not urgent so we'll let his poor momma sleep a little longer."

"When will my face get better?" asks Duncan.

"The medicine should help the swelling go down within a few hours, but the symptoms might persist for a couple of weeks. If the Benadryl controls the swelling, I think we can get you out of here and back to your friends by tonight."

Duncan wilts. "I have to stay here all day? I'll miss the color war."

Hannah gives him a sympathetic look. "I know, but I don't want you running around in the heat and sun until we get the swelling down."

Duncan looks at me with pleading eyes. "Gage?"

I don't want him out in the heat right now either, but it's a bummer for him to have to miss the color war. I'd volunteer to stay with him here today, but I can't leave the other boys, even with Jayden on duty.

"I'll come hang out with you here when I can, and what if I send my friend Olivia to see you, too? Remember, from dinner the other night? And she's the counselor who helps with the boats?"

Duncan nods miserably. I pull out my phone and text Olivia a heads-up. I'll stop by her cabin before breakfast.

Hannah has Duncan drink a small cup of liquid Benadryl and applies a thick, goopy cream to his face, especially around the mosquito bite.

When she finishes, he lies down on the cot and extends his hand to me. "You're not leaving now, are you?"

I take his hand and check my phone. I still have time before I need to get the rest of the boys up and ready for the day. "No, I'm staying for a little while longer."

His expression relaxes, and he closes his eyes. I sit with him until I'm sure he's asleep, and then I let go of his hand. I stand and stretch.

Hannah walks back into the room. She changed out of her robe and into her clothes for the day.

"He's asleep," I tell her.

"The Benadryl will make him drowsy. I talked to his mother on the phone, and she confirmed he's had a reaction like this once before, when he was a toddler."

"Thanks," I say. I rub my eyes, weary not only from waking up too early, but also from the emotional stress of the last couple of hours. I wish there was more I could do to make Duncan comfortable.

"Duncan's going to be fine, Gage," Hannah says, as if reading my mind. She rests a hand on my shoulder. "It's a little allergic reaction. He'll feel up to joining his friends again tomorrow."

I blink against the threatening tears and summon a smile. "I know. Thank you." I point toward the door. "I need to get back to my cabin, but I'll come check on him throughout the day. Olivia will probably also stop by."

She smiles at me. "We'll see you later, then."

I step out the door of the infirmary and almost bump into Olivia. She's dressed in the shorts and oversized T-shirt she wears as pajamas, her hair pulled back in a messy bun.

Without speaking, she wraps her arms around me, pressing her head against my chest. I return the squeeze, and we stand in the hug for several minutes. I breathe in the rosemary and mint of her shampoo, and my pulse slows. My worried thoughts quiet down.

"Good morning," I say finally, brushing a kiss against her forehead.

"Morning. How's Duncan?" She leans back to see my face.

I take a breath. "Good. He had an allergic reaction to a mosquito bite. Hannah gave him some medicine, and he's sleeping now."

Olivia brings her hand up to my face to brush away a strand of hair. "And how are you?"

I meet her eyes. "I've been better."

Her lips form a small smile. "I figured."

"I was scared," I admit. "I didn't know what was wrong with him, but his whole face was swollen. I wanted him to be okay."

"I know." Her hand against my cheek, she smooths a thumb over my stubble. "You'll make a great dad someday, Gage."

And oh man, I am gone for this woman, because even with every-thing else going on, my first thought is *I don't want it unless it's with you*.

Olivia and I take turns hanging out with Duncan in the infirmary, and as predicted, the swelling has gone down enough for him to rejoin our cabin Thursday night. Pending a checkup in the morning, Hannah clears him to return to normal activity on Friday for the final day of camp.

Duncan's cabinmates herald his return by making him the star of the skit they'll be performing for the parents. I even let them add a few fart jokes.

Maggie, Kent, and Callie are back for Skit Night, with Mag-gie fussing over Duncan's mosquito bite. Hannah told us that the swelling might not go away completely for another week.

After the skits wind down with the fire and Duncan is packed into the car with his sister and dad, Maggie pulls me aside to say goodbye.

"Thanks for taking care of Duncan this week," she says, squeezing my arm. "You're a good counselor and a *great* big brother."

Her words make me stand taller, my chest expanding. *I'm a great big brother to Duncan.*

Though I tease Annie about being ten minutes older than her, I've never really considered myself a "big brother" before. Now I want to buy a T-shirt with the phrase "World's Best Big Brother" emblazoned on the front. Though I guess getting a shirt like that for myself wouldn't be very meaningful.

"Thank you," I tell Maggie. "That means a lot."

She opens her mouth as if to say something else, then hesitates.

"What's up?" I ask her.

"Well, I wanted to say that while I don't exactly *regret* not raising you and Annie myself—your parents are amazing and did such a good job with you both—I do think about what it would have been like to be your mom. I've tried to be part of your lives as much as possible, but I know our relationship is more like I'm a cool, young aunt than any kind of mother figure."

I shake my head, tears threatening behind my eyes as I hear the uncertainty and sorrow in her voice. "Maggie, no. It's fine. We're fine."

"No, I know you are." She brings her left hand to my other shoulder so that she has a hand on either side of me. She looks up into my face. It's almost comical because I'm so much taller than her, but the moment is too fraught to be funny.

"I want to make sure you know I love you. You're my family, Gage. You came from inside of me. I carried you and nurtured you and talked to you for thirty-six weeks even though I was scared out of my mind and had no idea what to do. I never stopped missing either of you after I placed you in Dawn and Ted's arms. Even when you were with me, right next to me, I missed you. I missed what our relationship could have been."

I sniffle and wipe my wet cheek against the fabric of my shirt. Everything she's saying resonates with the deepest parts of me. The parts of me that have been afraid of burdening Maggie with my feelings. The parts of me that weren't sure if she yearned for me like I do for her.

"I feel the same way. Honestly. I ... I sometimes imagine what it would have been like to stay with you. As far back as I remember I've done that."

The sorrow on Maggie's face about does me in, and I'm hit with a wave of guilt that my admission may have sounded like I blamed her. I shake my head. "I'm sorry. I shouldn't have said that."

She lets go of my shoulders to wipe her eyes. "No, I'm glad you did. You can tell me the truth, Gage. Even if it's hard to hear, I'll listen."

I wrap her in a bear hug, grateful to have the example of such a strong woman in my life. Adoption hasn't been a smooth experience for either of us. Having good parents raise me didn't take away the sting of being separated, but maybe it made it easier for both of us to bear.

Maggie pulls back to look me in the face again. "I'm proud of you, Gage. I'm proud of the man you've become."

"Thanks," I choke out around the emotion clogging my throat.

"Listen," she says. "What if you all came to spend Christmas with us this year? You and Annie, and Dawn and Ted. Even Olivia, if you want. We can all celebrate together, like families should."

"I'd love that. I'll talk to Annie and my parents." I grimace. So much is still uncertain in my undefined relationship with Olivia. I'd love to be wherever she is in December. I'd love for her to celebrate

Christmas by my side with my family. But all I can do is hope. "I don't know about Olivia, though."

Maggie's eyes soften, and she gives me a melancholic smile. "You love her."

It's not a question, so I don't offer a confirmation or denial. I give her a hug and wave goodbye until the car is out of sight.

Chapter Thirty-One

Gage

The week after Duncan comes to camp is Olivia's birthday. It's on a Tuesday, which means I'm limited in how I can celebrate her on the actual day, but I have big plans for the following Saturday, which is also the Saturday before the last week of camp.

I do have a few tricks up my sleeve for her actual birthday on Tuesday, though. With Nina's help, I weave colorful crepe paper streamers around the inside of Olivia's cabin while she's sleeping. I wanted to do balloons, but I quickly learned that getting helium-filled balloons delivered out here to Camp Prairie Star was cost prohibitive, not to mention difficult to hide ahead of time. So, streamers it is.

I'm not there to see her face when she wakes up on her twenty-third birthday, of course, but I'm hoping it's equal parts thrilled and annoyed. I went *extra* obnoxious with the streamer placement.

She won't be able to get out of bed without tearing through a couple of layers. Olivia's a pretty sound sleeper, apparently, because she didn't stir once, even as I was wrapping streamers under her bed and over the covers.

When I take my kids to the lake for their free-swim time, she's waiting for me with a reproachful smile on her face. *Perfect.*

"I felt like a fly this morning," she says in greeting, her hands on her hips.

I puff out a laugh, because I was *not* expecting that statement. I send my boys over to Rocky for their pre-swim safety reminders. "A fly?"

"Or some other kind of insect stuck in a spider's web, all wrapped up."

I grin. "I think what you mean to say is 'Thank you, Gage, for the glorious birthday surprise.'" I raise the pitch of my voice to mimic hers.

Her eyes dance, though her fists remain against her sides. "I do not mean that."

Still using the falsetto, I continue, "It's so nice that you remembered my birthday and took time out of your sleep schedule to decorate my cabin for me."

She loses the battle against her instincts and laughs, pushing on my shoulder. "You're so ridiculous."

Still grinning, I tease her in my normal voice. "You love it."

And as I hold her gaze, her eyes are shining, telling me without words that she *does* love it. That she loves *me*. I pray that I'm not misreading and that I can have more than the next two weeks with her.

I wrap my hand gently around her wrist and pull her into the boathouse. Our lips are on each other the second we're away from prying eyes. I know we don't have much time before we need to help Rocky supervise free swim, so I make up for it with intensity.

I pour everything I feel for Olivia into this kiss. The sweet and gentle love I have for her, but also my more passionate emotions. It's an embrace that echoes down my spine and all the way to the tips of my toes, leaving me wanting so much more when she pulls away.

"Happy birthday," I murmur in her ear, my eyes still closed as I struggle to compose myself.

"Thank you," she whispers.

I clear my throat and open my eyes, managing to shoot her a half smile. "We're going to celebrate for real on Saturday. So, if you have plans, cancel 'em."

She squeezes the back of my neck where her hand still rests. Her eyes, hooded and hazy, lock onto mine. "You're my plans."

Standing in an unventilated boathouse in the sticky heat of a Texas July, I shiver with hope.

Saturday is bright and sunny. And hot, of course. Olivia, wearing white shorts that come up past her belly button and a blue, sleeveless shirt that's tight around her chest and stomach, climbs into the front seat of my Jeep.

"So, where are we going?" she asks, sliding large black sunglasses on.

"You'll see."

"The thing about surprises," she starts, her voice cautious, "is that I always get carried away imagining the most over-the-top things and end up disappointed by the real surprise, which is usually perfectly wonderful on its own."

I chuckle and consider her words. I have a fun day planned but not like we're-taking-a-private-jet-to-Paris fun. I should tell her.

"We're going to the ice cream factory in town, for starters. It's called a creamery. We can see how they make ice cream, and we can eat sundaes as big as our heads."

I glance over at her as I drive to gauge her reaction. She's smiling, her eyes bright.

"And then, there's a park nearby that has an antique carousel. We can ride it and have a picnic under the trees."

Olivia sighs, but the sound is content and happy. "Perfectly wonderful."

We start in the creamery visitor center, where we walk through exhibits about the history of the company and the ice cream–making process. Then we check out the observation deck, where we can see into the factory. We watch machines fill various-sized containers with soft, creamy ice cream.

"Hungry yet?" I ask Olivia with a grin.

"I'm always hungry for ice cream."

I take her hand. "Then let's go."

We find the ice cream parlor with the long list of giant ice cream sundaes they can prepare. The menu is a mixture of flavors and toppings with endless possibilities.

I feel Olivia's eyes on me as I study the choices. "Should we split one?" she asks.

It's a smart question. A mature one. The sundaes are huge, with enough sugar in them to overload our stomachs. And they're not cheap. She knows I'm paying—a gentleman does not make a lady pay for her own birthday ice cream, especially on a date, which to me, this definitely is.

"If that's what you want," I answer.

On the other hand, Olivia and I agreeing on the same flavor, never mind toppings, would be a miracle. I know I can devour one of these sundaes on my own, and with the way Olivia's eyeing the pictures on the menu board, I don't think she wants to share, either.

I'll do whatever she says she wants, but I silently will her to demand her heart's desire. To choose the thing that will make us both happiest, not the thing she thinks is the responsible option.

"Well…" she says slowly, watching my face as if for a clue of how to decide. I keep my expression purposely impassive. "You probably want some sort of fruit-flavored sundae, and I *need* chocolate." She bites her lip, and inside my head, I urge her to say what she wants. "But let's get one to share. It's a lot of sugar."

"Are you sure?"

She nods once, and I hide my disappointment behind a wide smile. "What flavor? Birthday girl's choice."

Olivia orders a sundae that's a hodgepodge of unnecessary compromise—three scoops of various chocolate flavors and three scoops of fruit flavors, topped with peanut butter and hot fudge and rainbow sprinkles and cherries.

But why do either of us need to settle when we both want exactly the same thing in this situation? Why won't she admit what she really wants?

In the back of my mind, a voice quietly asks, *Why won't you?*

And yeah, I guess I could have said, "Hey, I don't mind paying for two, and I really want my own." We would each have gotten our own sundaes.

And I guess I could always say, "Olivia, I don't want a temporary fling. I want a real relationship with you that lasts forever."

But is it too much to ask that she *knows* that's what I want without me having to tell her, and that it's what she wants, too, and she never leaves me because she loves me enough to stay forever?

Oblivious to my mental upheaval, Olivia keeps up a steady chatter on the drive from the creamery to the park with the carousel.

She's having fun on the birthday outing I planned for her, and I'm glad, but suddenly the expiration date for this summer fling is looming heavy on my heart.

Despite the reckless optimism that led me to go along with Olivia's plan at the beginning of the summer, I don't feel much closer to convincing her to make this a real relationship. I'm running out of time.

We have today, then tomorrow morning, and then kids arrive for the final week of camp. By Friday night, the summer will be over, other than the final cleanup Linda will have us help with next Saturday.

Do I think Olivia loves me? I do. I really do.

But something is still stopping her from opening up to me fully. And I don't know what it is.

I could ask her. Tell her I love her and let the chips fall where they may. But I'm afraid I won't like where those chips end up.

Olivia's voice filters back into my consciousness as I pull into the parking lot at our next destination.

"I'll have to take you to this milkshake place in North Austin for your birthday in September. They have milkshakes with entire cupcakes or slices of cheesecake on top."

I put the Jeep in park and swing my whole head to stare at her, slack-jawed. "What did you say?"

My birthday is two months away. Definitely beyond the expiration date she insisted on.

When she realizes she implied a future for us together beyond the summer, her face turns red. But she doesn't take it back.

My heart pounds as I wonder about the implications of her slipup. I play it cool, forcing a smile and holding eye contact. "Yeah, that sounds nice."

Olivia's words are the encouragement I need to get out of my head and enjoy the day with her. Maybe this is progress, after all.

Still, it's on the tip of my tongue all afternoon. As we sit side by side in the gondola chair on the carousel, my arm around her shoulders and her body tucked tightly against mine. As I spread the picnic blanket in a shady spot in the grass. As we lie holding hands looking at the clouds. As I kiss her good night outside her cabin later that night back at camp.

Three words, four if I include her name.

I love you, Olivia.

Olivia, I love you.

I love you.

Simple words, but so difficult to say. I'm not sure if I'm more afraid of her saying it back or of her shutting down, shutting me out again. If she says it back, it makes this thing between us real and gives her the power to crush my heart. But if she shuts down, I'll be instantly crushed. Either way, speaking the words in my heart will change everything, so I'll leave us floating here in the nebulous realm of make-believe, playing at being a couple in love but without the responsibilities.

Chapter Thirty-Two

Olivia

As campers arrive for this last week of summer at Camp Prairie Star, the air feels different. It's still as hot and humid as it was yesterday, but the breeze is tinged with something new. A heaviness, but also a hope. Finality and expectation rolled together and waiting for me over the horizon line.

I feel the change in the air most whenever I see Gage. He's been different, too, starting from my birthday date on Saturday.

While he's always affectionate—never missing a chance to hold my hand or touch me in some small way—he's been clingier. He's velcroed to my side, as if he's afraid to let me out of his sight.

He has to, of course, to do his job and for me to do mine, but throughout the week, he's at the lake whenever he can be—with or without his campers. At meals, he seeks me out, leaving Jayden to deal with the food-induced hyperactivity at their cabin's table.

It's like he's done with camp but doesn't want to be done with me.

Actually, I'm certain that's exactly how he's feeling. If someone gave me three guesses to figure out what's on Gage's mind, I'd only need the first.

He's in love with me.

The good news is I'm also in love with him, and with every hour I become more certain that we could be a real couple.

We haven't talked about any of this yet, but I'm sure Gage can tell how I'm feeling like I can read him.

We've been amazing together this summer, with no shortage of things to talk about. He doesn't act like my opinions are stupid. He's never come close to suggesting that *I'm* stupid. He listens to what I have to say, and more than that, he wants to hear it.

Maybe it's not ridiculous to think he could see me as an equal partner. Obviously, the disparity is there, but maybe if it doesn't bother him, I shouldn't let it bother me.

Especially now that my future is looking so much brighter.

I'm going to be a teacher, of all things, as soon as I can get a job.

I'm antsy that I haven't heard back from Virtus Academy. It's been weeks since I submitted applications to both Virtus and Brightline. While either position would be amazing, I have to admit I have my heart set on Virtus. It's close to my parents' house, for one, which means it's also close to Gage's parents' house where he'll be living starting this weekend.

I decide to call Virtus on Thursday when I'm in between groups of campers to check up on my job application.

I slip into the empty boathouse and lean against the wall as I dial.

The phone rings twice before a woman picks up. "Virtus Academy Austin. How may I direct your call?"

"Um, hi, yeah." Not a great start. I clear my throat. "I recently applied for the physical education teacher position for this upcoming school year, and I wanted to check on the status of that search, please."

"One moment, please." Classical music plays over the phone line while I assume I'm being transferred to whoever is in charge of hiring.

A man's voice finally comes on the line. "Hello, this is Dr. Haught, headmaster of Virtus Academy Austin."

I'm not sure if it's the snooty voice or the showy title, but I immediately picture Headmaster Charleston from the fancy private school Rory attends in *Gilmore Girls*. My sister Nicole is obsessed with the show, and I've watched it all the way through with her at least twice.

"Yes, hello. My name is Olivia Delaney. I recently applied for the open physical education teacher position, and I wondered about the status of that search?"

"We have started contacting the top candidates for interviews. What did you say your name is?"

"Olivia Delaney," I repeat.

I hear the shuffle of papers before Dr. Haught speaks again. "Ah yes, I have your information here. I'm sorry to tell you Ms. Delaney that we will not be moving forward with your application."

I feel my shoulders droop as heaviness settles into all the joints of my body. "Oh, I see. May I ask why not?" I lower myself to sit on the scratchy wooden bench that doubles as storage for the life vests.

There's a pause on the other end of the line. I wipe my sweaty palm against my shorts as I wait.

"Ms. Delaney, we at Virtus Academy Austin have high standards and expectations for our employees as well as our students. We have a specific protocol for employment applications, and we provide detailed instructions for candidates to follow to meet that protocol. You did not follow those detailed instructions when you applied."

Yeah, the instructions were *detailed* all right. Three single-spaced pages of written directions that I tried my hardest to follow. "I didn't?"

"No, Ms. Delaney. The directions clearly stated that applications should be sent as a single PDF file that includes a candidate's letter of interest, résumé, and references all together. You sent three separate files."

"Oh." My lungs and heart deflate simultaneously, taking away my breath and my hope in one fell swoop.

I want to violently press the *end* button on the call, but Headmaster Snooty Pants is still talking.

"We simply cannot hire instructors who don't show the commitment to excellence that we demand of our pupils, who can't follow simple instructions. Sloppy work is not tolerated at Virtus Academy Austin."

"I understand. Thank you," I say, and then I hang up, but my anger has already shifted to defeat.

I can feel my pulse in my throat, a steady, empty *thud, thud, thud*. Hot tears well behind my eyelids as his words echo between my ears, confirming what I already know to be true. *Can't follow simple instructions. Sloppy work.*

Dumb. Stupid. Illiterate.

Being the sporty, fun, cool girl worked for me in high school and college, but out here in the real world, those qualities don't count for much.

I can't even *apply* for jobs correctly, so how can I expect to be successful in them?

Warring thoughts fight for attention as the tears spring free and roll down my cheeks.

You'll never be good enough.

You don't want to work for that pretentious school anyway.

It's not you, it's them—the application process was unfair.

But loudest of all is—*Gage deserves to be with someone better. Someone smarter.*

I know it's true. It was true five years ago, and it's true now. We've talked about some beautiful possibilities lately—dates at the Wildflower Center and celebrating Gage and Annie's birthday together. Possibilities for a future together back in Austin once camp is over.

But there can't be a future beyond this summer fling for us because he deserves more than what I can offer. I lost sight of that these last few weeks, gave into hope and the sheer selfishness of what I wanted.

If nothing else, I *can* do the right thing by Gage this summer and set him free. The decision rolls around in my stomach, threatening to dislodge my pancake breakfast from this morning.

The sound of laughter and high-pitched voices filters through the open door of the boathouse. My next group of campers are coming down the trail for their free-swim time.

I swallow hard. I swipe my hand across my eyes and rub the tears from my cheeks. Pasting on a smile, I walk to the doorway, ready to greet the kids.

I stumble my way through the rest of Thursday and most of the day Friday. By the time Skit Night is over, and the kids are loaded into minivans and pickup trucks for their drives home, I've sunken so far into myself that I'll need a ladder to get out.

Unlike on previous Friday nights, this final one is special. All the staff stay at camp overnight to help with final cleanup on Saturday, and Linda hosts a closing campfire for us to celebrate the end of the summer. Rob and Stephanie, the camp cooks, grill hamburgers and hot dogs, and Troy sets up a table laden with s'mores fixings.

My coworkers from the past three months are a rowdy group tonight. They sing camp songs and recount memories. No one needs the sharing stick because everyone talks over each other. Laughter is the predominant sound.

But through it all, I barely register what's going on around me. I'm in my head.

For me, the last night of camp isn't a celebration; it's a death knell.

I know I need to talk to Gage. I need to put the final nail in the coffin of this summer fling, but thinking about it causes a pressure in my chest so intense that tears leak out of my eyes.

Not surprisingly, Gage hasn't left my side all night. He's sitting so close he's practically on my lap, and his arm is wrapped tightly around my shoulder. His nearness doesn't help me find the courage for what I have to do. It makes me want to snuggle closer, burrow my head into his neck, and stay there for the rest of my life.

I'm sure he realizes I'm not acting like myself, so when I tell him I'm going to turn in early, he doesn't hesitate to stand up with me.

He walks me back toward my cabin on a path through the woods, and he's quiet. The night is all too quiet, and the quiet is what finally breaks me.

I stop in my tracks, causing Gage's hip to bump into mine.

"Gage," I start, my voice cracking. He must see something of what I'm about to say in my eyes, because his face goes ashen, panic flashing across it.

"Look," I press on quickly, not stopping to think out my words or how to say them. "I don't think we need to delay the inevitable. Camp's done. You're heading to school in a week—"

"In Austin," he interrupts.

"—and I'm heading back to my parents' house—"

"Also in Austin."

"—and it's … we said from the beginning what this was, we said it. It's a situationship—"

"No, Olivia." I pick up the agony in his voice, the desperation.

"—and the situation is changing, and so it doesn't make sense anymore."

"Don't do this," he pleads. His blue eyes look like the ocean in the fading light, dark and stormy.

"We said a summer fling. Well, summer's over. The fling is over."

He grabs my shoulders and holds me in front of him, the strength of his grip making me gasp. We're facing each other. He ducks his head to look me in the eye, forcing me to look into his, swirling with pain.

"This thing between us"—he moves one hand off my shoulder to motion to himself and then to me—"was never going to be 'just a fling' and you know it." He lets me go, swiping across his face with one of his sleeves. It comes away wet, but the tears are still dripping down his cheeks. "You know it," he repeats, as if daring me to contradict him.

I do know it. I played with fire. I knew I shouldn't have done it, but I did it anyway. And I got burned.

I hate that I took Gage down with me, but he'll move on to someone better suited for him. He'll be okay.

I stifle a sob, emotion clogging my throat so I can hardly breathe. I try to gulp in oxygen as I throw up my hands and shout, "I don't know what you want me to say. This was always the plan!"

He grabs my hand and intertwines our fingers. He rests his forehead against mine, the warm flush of his skin lulling me into temporary defeat. I should push him away, but selfishly I'm soaking up as much of him as I can before it's too late.

"I love you," he says desperately, frantically. His eyes are closed, and he inhales a ragged breath, his tone softening. "I love you, Olivia," he repeats. "This isn't how we end. It can't be."

I drop his hand and step back, breaking our contact. My foot lands on a stick that cracks as loud as dynamite when it snaps in half. It feels right, sounds right. It's the same sound as my heart breaking.

"I'm sorry." I moan and turn away, trying to get ahead of the tears. I start running. I know Nina's still at the fire circle, so I aim for my cabin. I burst through the door in time to collapse on the bed and sob myself to sleep.

I wake only a few hours later, the night still dark as ink outside. In a frenzied mania, I throw all my things in my duffel bag, careful not to wake Nina.

I type out a vague email to Linda about needing to leave early. By sunrise, I'm passing through the gates of Camp Prairie Star and on my way home.

As I near Austin city limits, my phone pings. It's a text from Gage. I pull to the side of the road to read it.

Gage:

Babe, please can we talk?

I summon the meager emotional strength I have left and block his number. Then, I pull back onto the highway and keep driving.

Chapter Thirty-Three

Olivia

There's no other word for it: I'm wallowing. Thank goodness my parents are away in South Carolina visiting my sister and her husband or else I'd have to explain to them why I've been lying on the couch in the same T-shirt and sweatpants for the last three days. And why I'm eating all the junk food in the house and having more delivered when I run out. I go back and forth between blasting Taylor Swift while singing through my sobs and watching every Emma Stone movie on repeat while sobbing. I sob a lot.

I ignore my phone—the texts from Linda and my sisters, the calls from Annie. I'm sure Gage has told her everything by now, and I wonder if I have to add my best friend to the list of my losses this summer.

On the fourth day, the doorbell rings. When I ignore it—I'm certain the bright daylight of the outside world would permanently blind me at this point—my phone rings. It's Annie again. I ignore that, too. Then I hear another ping on my phone at the same time someone pounds on the door. I check the text.

Annie:

Let me in NOW

I sigh. I'm resigned to my fate. With some effort, I rise from the couch and stumble to the front door. I unlock it, then turn back toward the couch. Annie lets herself in.

My best friend is five feet, three inches of righteous indignation. She stands in front of me with her hands on her hips. Her fierce glare is a drop in the ocean of my misery at this point. But, I made my bed, so, you know.

"You *destroyed* my brother," she thunders.

I shrug. "I destroyed myself, too, if that's any consolation."

Annie balks at my words, stepping back to survey the scene in front of her for the first time. The couch is a mess of blankets and pillows. Empty ice cream containers, cookie packages, and various open bags of chips litter the coffee table. "Last Kiss" is still blaring through my Bluetooth speakers. Who knows what's happening with my hair.

She drops her hands, and her face softens. "I can see that."

Annie moves to the couch and sits down next to me. She rubs my back. I collapse onto my side, burying my face in the blankets. I'm sobbing again. It's amazing that I still have tears left, really. At some point, I'm supposed to feel numb, aren't I? When does that kick in?

Annie continues rubbing my back in a comforting circle. "Gage said … he said *you* dumped *him*." I can't see her face, but I hear the confusion in her voice.

"I did!" I choke out.

"But you love him?" She asks so carefully that I lift my head to face her. I can't say the words, but I nod once, forcing myself to keep eye contact.

I can see the questions in her eyes and between the furrows of her pinched brow. A beat passes as she puzzles out what to say next.

"Delaney, Gage has been half in love with you since high school. He was devastated when you rejected him back then. Why would you do this to him again?"

"He told you all that?" I ask.

"I'm Gage's best friend. He tells me everything." She pauses. "Apparently unlike *my* best friend, who tells me nothing."

"I tell you mostly everything. Except this one minor piece of information …" I wince and sit up, my shoulders tensing. "That I've been in love with your twin brother since I was thirteen."

She sucks in a breath, then shakes her head. "To be fair, it wasn't as much of a secret as you thought. I knew you had a thing for him. But I didn't think it was love, just that it could be. After Gage told me what happened Friday, I figured I was wrong, but…" She pauses. "But it sounds like I wasn't. Honey, then why?"

"It was a summer fling," I mutter, my chest heavy. Maybe if I keep saying it, it will become true.

"No. You're in love with each other."

"Gage isn't in love with me," I insist.

"Um, pretty sure he is."

I shake my head. "He may think he is right now, but it was only proximity. We were all together at that camp for months, and it's not like there were many other single women our age. But he'll meet so many new women at school, and they'll be so much more amazing than me. One day, he'll meet the real love of his life and he'll be like, 'Oh I thought it was love with that other girl, but I've never felt true love until I met you.' She'll be better for him."

"Better for him?" Annie stills her hand on my back. "Honey, I'm trying to understand, but I feel like I'm missing something here."

I guess she needs me to spell it out. "A better match for him. More his equal. Smarter than me."

Annie's face shifts as the pieces all click into place. "You broke up with Gage, broke both your hearts, because you think you're not good enough for him?"

I take a deep breath, and then, for the first time, I tell Annie the full story of what happened at high school graduation and everything that went down this summer, including the phone call with Headmaster Snooty Pants.

While I'm talking, a pit opens up in my stomach as I relive the most traumatic moments of my life, moments I don't want anyone else to see.

But when I finish unloading, I feel lighter, like sharing my memories of the negative moments gives them less power over me somehow.

"Olivia," Annie says gently, and I'm so grateful to hear her use my real name at this moment. "You're not that kid in middle school anymore."

I blink at her, my eyelashes wet against my cheeks.

"The kid," she clarifies, "that never knew why the books and worksheets didn't make sense. You know why now. You know that one in five people have dyslexia. You know it has nothing to do with intelligence. Why are you still letting thirteen-year-old Olivia control your grown-up life?"

"I know," I groan out. I *do* know, but when things like that overheard bathroom conversation or that phone call happen, my emotions take over, and my feelings of inadequacy are in charge.

Annie pulls me into a hug. "You are amazing. You're beautiful and fun. A great friend and sister. Loyal and protective. You're so patient when you're coaching. Everything you do, you give one hundred percent. And you'll figure out what you want to do with your life. Gage would be lucky—*any* man would be lucky—to have you."

I'm shaking my head. Annie's cheeks redden; she's getting frustrated. "You're acting dumb," she huffs.

I puff out a sardonic chuckle. "I *am* dumb."

She grabs my shoulders and holds me at arm's length in front of her. "Olivia Delaney, do *not* talk about my best friend like that. You're smart, but you're *acting* dumb right now. Every woman Gage has ever dated—he compares them to you. And they *never* measure up."

A tiny pinprick of hope pokes through my battered heart. What did the phone call from Headmaster Snooty Pants change, really?

Gage would still want to be with me even if he knew that I didn't get the Virtus job, wouldn't he? All that really shifted was my self-esteem, which I projected to reflect what I thought Gage would think of me.

If he thought I was enough before that phone call—if *I* thought I was enough before that phone call—I can't let one jerk with his unfair hiring practices ruin everything else for me, too.

"Really?" I sniff.

"Really and truly. He loves you, Olivia. So, if you love him, too, why are you making this so complicated?"

"I ... I don't know."

I sit up resolutely, starting a mental to-do list. First, shower and change. Then, rush to Gage and beg him to forgive me.

"I'm going to fix this, Annie."

She frowns and opens her mouth as if to say something. Then, she closes it again.

Her hesitation confuses me. "What? Isn't that what you want me to do?"

"Well, it's just ... slow down. I don't think this is going to be an easy fix." I stare at her through my puffy red eyes. "You have to convince him to trust you again."

"What do you mean?" I know I messed up by not telling him how I feel, but why would it be hard for him to trust me?

"It's been twice now that you've led him on, slammed the door, and then ghosted him. And he already has abandonment issues from being adopted."

Annie still sits next to me on the couch, but she's switched to more defensive body language. Her arms are crossed, and her expression tells me how unhappy she is with me. It's not a side of Annie I see often because she doesn't like confrontation. It signals how serious this situation is.

I let her words sink in, and my heart breaks all over again. For Gage and the pain he's going through because of *me*.

I know it's a cop-out response, but I murmur, "I didn't mean to."

And I didn't, but after everything he shared with me this summer about his feelings around his adoption, I should have realized how it would feel to him for me to *leave* like that.

I realize now how gracious it is for Annie to be here at all. She's giving me a chance to explain and to make it right, when she'd be totally justified in writing me off for the way I've played with her brother's feelings.

Although, again, I didn't mean to. "I was scared," I admit. "I wasn't thinking."

Annie heaves a gusting sigh and pulls me into a hug. "It's not me you need to convince. Do you want my advice?"

My soft voice is muffled against her shoulder. "Yes, please."

"Give him some time right now. Let him start school in peace. While you're waiting, make a plan to show him you're serious about a relationship with him this time. Give him plenty of reasons to trust that you'll stay."

Her instructions feel daunting, but it's the most important assignment I've ever received. I pull in a determined breath. "Will you help me?"

She presses her lips together and leans away. "Here's the thing. He's my brother and you're my best friend. I refuse to be in the middle here. Don't ask me for information about him, because I won't tell you. Likewise, I'm not going to feed him any information about you. This is the last thing I'll say, and then you're on your own. Get your stuff together and get him back."

Annie stays to help me clean up the house. After she leaves, I take a shower and put on clean clothes, and already I feel mostly human again. I make myself pasta for dinner—well, I boil dehydrated noodles and add jarred tomato sauce, but it's a start—and go for a run. I take another shower when I get back and let the hot water blast my skin so long that my shoulders turn pink and my fingers prune.

I go to sleep early, in my bed instead of on the couch in front of a movie. In the morning, I actually feel rested, so I decide to tackle some other tasks I've been neglecting, like clearing out the notifications on my phone.

I unlock the screen, and the first thing I do, after several fortifying breaths, is unblock Gage's number.

I move on to checking my email, where I find a message from the Brightline School for Science, the charter school in North Austin I applied to back at the same time as Virtus.

I have to reread the email three times to make sure I'm getting it right. They want to schedule an interview with me. I check the date stamp on the message and am relieved to see it came in yesterday and not four days ago when I first crashed out.

I email them back right away. By the end of the day, I have an in-person interview set up for next week with a Ms. Carolina Brown, the school director.

Of course, the first person I want to call with this news is Gage, but I don't contact him.

Instead, I think about what Annie said about triggering Gage's fear of abandonment by leaving camp without talking to him. The parallels between how I broke up with Gage at camp and how I rejected him back at graduation are undeniable. I had fear and weak excuses, and I left and ghosted him again. And I lied. Again. I have to stop doing that.

But what it all means is that like Annie said, I need to give us a little breathing room before I do anything else regarding Gage. I need to sit in my insecurities by myself for a little longer, so I don't go to him raw and emotional. I need to be sure and encouraging and solid, so he knows it's safe to trust me again. I need to make sure I *am* trustworthy.

Chapter Thirty-Four

Olivia

Sometimes being the youngest of three sisters is the worst. Teachers and even my parents constantly compared me to my older sisters. It's easy to feel overlooked. I've felt left behind as they've reached milestones I haven't gotten to yet. There are a lot of hand-me-downs.

But usually, being the youngest Delaney sister—specifically being Molly and Nicole's little sister—is one of the best parts of my life, because my sisters are amazing.

When I get on our group text to see if either of them has time for a quick video call, they both drop everything. Of course, asking for facetime with Molly and Nicole isn't something I typically do, so they probably think I'm dying.

Which I'm not, quite yet. I'm back to keeping my head above water as I figure out my next steps with Gage and my career, not to mention my living situation.

"So, what's going on?" Nicole asks without wasting time with pleasantries like saying hello.

"Yeah," echoes Molly. "Are you okay?"

I hold back a smile at their obvious concern. "Hi, Nicole. Hi, Molly. It's nice to see you both." They stare at me expectantly, so I grin and add, "Nice weather we're having."

Nicole rolls her eyes. "Hi, Olivia."

Molly waves. "You're smiling, so this can't be too much of an emergency situation?"

"Yeah," echoes Nicole. "Are you okay?"

"Well." I inhale deeply. "Not really. But I'm getting there. I need some advice."

"Is it Gage?" Molly asks quickly. "Jonathan said he's happy to beat him up for you."

I bite back another smile at the thought of my oldest sister's sweet, even-keeled husband fighting anyone.

Nicole frowns. "Adam's not really a beat-people-up kind of guy, but I'm sure we could figure out another kind of revenge if that's what you need."

That elicits an actual laugh from me, which takes me and my lungs by surprise. After all that crying, it's nice to exercise a different kind of emotional response.

"Thanks, guys. It is about Gage, but actually if anyone deserves to be beaten up, it's me."

"What happened?"

They already know about the whole "summer fling" thing, but I fill them in on everything else, staying vague about the parts—like Gage's feelings around his adoption—that aren't mine to share. I do tell them about my feelings of inadequacy and how I feel like I'm not smart enough for someone like Gage.

"The bottom line is that I need a plan to convince him to trust me again," I finish. "Do you have any ideas?"

My sisters are quiet. I wait to see which of them will have something to say first.

It's Nicole, of course. "I hate that you've been seeing yourself as anything less than brilliant, Liv. I wish you would see yourself the way I see you, and Molly and Mom and Dad see you. You're one of the smartest people we know, especially with the creative ways you solve problems."

I sniffle and blink back the tears that threaten behind my eyes from Nicole's praise. "Molly's the smartest person I know."

Molly's expression is soft. "When you say 'smart,' do you really mean 'good at school'? Because those two things are not the same. I'm good at school because my brain happens to be good at most of the things school wants us to be good at. That doesn't mean those are the only things that are worth being good at, or even the most important things."

"But either way," Nicole cuts in, "stop comparing! Someone else is always going to seem smarter or happier or prettier or whatever, but that doesn't erase the fact that you, Olivia Delaney, are worth knowing and worth loving.

"I'm not going to repeat that ridiculous saying that if you don't love yourself, no one else will, because I don't think that's true at all. All this time while you've been too hard on yourself, lots of people have loved you and will continue loving you. We'll love you so that you can see how worth loving you are."

I have no hope of holding back the tears now, and they're spilling down my cheeks. I didn't realize how much I needed to hear these words of affirmation. First from Annie, along with the dose of humility she served up, and now from my sisters.

"As for a plan for Gage," Molly chimes in, "I'm going to suggest therapy."

"Yes! Therapy. One hundred percent," Nicole agrees.

Back when I was first diagnosed with dyslexia, I had a couple of sessions with the psychologist at my middle school. I was so used to masking my inability to read that I carried that skill over to masking how I was feeling from other people. I insisted I was fine. Though she probably should have, I was relieved when the school psychologist didn't push.

I'm willing to try again. I'm willing to try almost anything at this point.

"By myself or, like, couples counseling? Isn't that for married people who are having problems?" I ask.

"By yourself is a good idea, but also together. Couples therapy could be for any couple who wants to learn to communicate and understand each other better." Molly shrugs. "Jonathan and I have a standing appointment once a month. It's been really good for both of us."

I absorb her words and the idea of couples therapy—assuming I can convince Gage to be part of a couple with me. It feels weird and uncomfortable, but we clearly need help communicating and understanding each other better.

"Okay, thanks."

A plan is starting to form in my mind now. I'll start with an apology, followed by radical honesty. I'll lay out all my feelings and pray Gage isn't too far gone for me to get back.

That settled, I switch topics to update my sisters on another area of my life. "Now, my next news. I have a job interview!"

Nicole and Molly squeal, and I launch into all the details about the Brightline School.

Like I said, sometimes being the youngest of three sisters is the worst, but today I'm grateful for all the love and support that comes with it.

The day of my interview with Carolina Brown at the Brightline School for Science arrives. As I step out of my air-conditioned car into the scorching parking lot, I'm doubly grateful for the gray blazer I'm wearing over my fitted white blouse and flowy skirt. Between the August heat and my nerves, I'm sweating through the blouse, and the blazer hides it well.

The two-story school building stands ominously, all beige concrete panels and dark-tinted windows. It looks more like an office building than a school, except for the fenced-in grass fields in the back, with a basketball court and picnic tables under bright yellow canopies.

My would-be classroom. The thought gets my heart thumping, and though the emotion behind my elevated pulse is still part nerves, it's also excitement.

I walk through the front doors of the main office and am immediately greeted by soft colors and glass display cases filled with student reproductions of DNA strands, cell structures, and solar systems.

I'm also greeted by the receptionist behind the front desk—a short balding man with a colorful necktie and a kind smile.

I give him my name, and he picks up the phone behind the desk, presumably to let Carolina Brown know I've arrived.

Her office must be nearby, because I've barely taken a seat in the waiting area when I hear an electronic beep, followed by a door opening.

A woman who looks maybe two decades older than me with black hair slicked down smoothly on the top and sides, leading to a curly puff ponytail at the back of her head, comes through the open door. Her lightweight dress flows behind her in a brilliant pattern of yellows and oranges.

She offers me a bright smile and extends her hand. "Hi, I'm Carolina Brown."

I shake her outstretched hand. "Olivia Delaney. Nice to meet you."

"Nice to meet you. Do you go by Olivia?"

I pause and make a split-second decision that's been all summer in the making. "Yes. Yes, I do."

She smiles at me again and ushers me through the door. I walk through it, feeling like the movement is too routine for the extraordinary thing I've done. I reclaimed my name. I reclaimed my identity.

I smile to myself and walk taller as we make our way down a hallway and into a small conference room.

The interview goes well. I feel like I have good answers to all the questions, and after a while, the interaction feels more like a conversation than an interview. By the time we get near the end of her questions, we're on a first-name basis.

Carolina sets her pen on the table and closes the notebook she's been using for notes. "What questions do you have about the position or the school?"

I'm ready for this question. My sisters coached me ahead of time, and we brainstormed some questions I could ask that would help me learn more about the position but also help the interviewer see my interest.

"In your ideal scenario, how does the new PE teacher change Brightline for the better?" I ask.

Carolina smiles. "What a beautiful question." She thinks for a moment, and then her words come out hesitantly. "One of the challenges we're facing as a school is getting the kids excited about physical education. Students come here to concentrate on their studies, especially science. Many of them are very focused on their classroom pursuits and struggle to see the benefits of gym class," she admits.

I frown. "My brother-in-law is a scientist, and he loves to swim and play basketball. An interest in science isn't at odds with loving sports."

Carolina smiles. "Agreed. It's not at all antithetical. However, I would say the majority of our students have trouble seeing that."

"Okay," I say as a way to pause the conversation while I gather my thoughts. "What if we emphasized the science involved in exercise? The body systems and how regular movement enhances their effectiveness? We could even turn PE class into experiments with physics and biology, using their own bodies as the test subjects." I realize how that sounds and backtrack. "I mean not in any way that's dangerous, of course."

"No, I love that! I think the students will too." She's quiet for a moment, studying me. Finally, she says, "Olivia, I'll be frank. Our school year starts on Monday. We need a PE teacher, and I think we'd be extremely fortunate to have you."

I suck in a breath. The thought of having only a few days to prepare to teach has my heart thumping.

"You're going to be my hiring recommendation to the board of directors," she continues. "They need to approve the decision, but I don't think they'll have any issues."

My mouth drops open, and I scramble to close it before Carolina realizes how shocked I am. "Well, this is … thank you. I'd love that," I manage to splutter.

"I'm certain the board will add a condition requiring you to work on your teacher certification, but that doesn't need to be in place before you start working."

I nod. State teacher certification in physical education was something I planned to work toward either way. But now I can do it while working a steady, full-time job.

"We'll talk about an official offer letter and discuss salary after the board approves. They have a meeting tonight to discuss these last few position vacancies, so I hope to be in touch by the end of the week."

She stands, and I follow suit. I reach out to shake her hand. "Thank you, Carolina. I look forward to hearing from you soon."

Chapter Thirty-Five
Olivia

I t's the end of August—two weeks after my interview and a week and a half into my new job as the PE teacher at the Brightline School—before I feel ready to approach Gage.

Not only was I working on myself to make sure I can be a partner he can trust, I wanted to give him some time, too. He started school a week ago, and I don't want to distract him while he orients to his new classes and professors.

But I've waited long enough. I can't go another day wondering what will happen. Even if he doesn't want to give me another chance, I'd rather know so I can move forward than stay in this endless Schrödinger's situation. I need to know for sure if the cat is dead or alive.

Despite Annie's warning that she wouldn't act as a middleman, she relents enough to give me a rough idea of her brother's class schedule. I know that on Thursdays, he has some sort of lab class until five, and it's his last class of the day.

So on Thursday, I drive home to my parents' house as soon as the bell rings to signal the end of the school day. I change my clothes and drive to the campus—it only takes a few minutes. It really is right on the edge of our parents' neighborhood—prepared to grovel if I have to.

The school is small for a university—three commercial buildings of sand-colored stucco and large reflective windows on twenty acres that include parking lots and fields of Texas wildflowers—though I know it offers a limited number of niche health sciences programs.

One loop around the parking lot and I find Gage's Jeep parked an easy distance from the back entrance to one of the buildings. Pulling into an empty parking spot nearby, I slowly count to ten to calm my jangling nerves.

I take my time climbing out of the car. I peek into the Jeep, and my memories transport me to the night Gage drove us back to camp after dinner with Maggie and her family. He cried on my shoulder about how much Maggie leaving had hurt him. And then I went and did the same thing, for the second time even.

I won't blame him if he refuses to hear me out. I'll be devastated, but it will be all my own fault.

I fiddle with the green rubber band bracelet on my wrist, tracing the letters with my fingertip. I can't bring myself to take it off.

Leaning my back against the front bumper of the Jeep, I watch the door to the building. I realize that while I am nervous and unsure about how this whole thing will go, most of the trembling I feel down my arms and through my fingers is anticipation.

I miss Gage. Whether he forgives me or not today, I still get to see him and breathe the same air for a few moments at least.

When he walks out flanked by two classmates, my eyes find him right away. A breeze lifts the sandy hair off his forehead as he smiles at something the woman next to him is saying. He's in light blue scrubs, a backpack slung over one shoulder.

He looks so good. It's all I can do to stay rooted to the spot instead of running to him and throwing my arms around his neck. I force myself to wait.

His classmates peel off, turning down the sidewalk that leads to the front parking lot. They wave, and I hear calls of "See you tomorrow!" Gage lifts a hand in their direction, then tucks it in his pocket as he turns to walk toward his parking spot.

I know instantly when he sees me. He stops walking, and his eyes light up. My heart pounds as I wonder what that means. But then, as if remembering, he takes a step back and his expression dims.

He walks toward me slowly, pausing on the sidewalk three feet away from me. I search his expression, but it's unreadable. I can tell he's being cautious about opening up to me, as he should. Still, the pain stabs at my chest, and with anticipation out of the way, now I'm all nerves.

Maybe I shouldn't have waited so long; I wanted to be whole when I stood in front of him and bared my heart and soul.

"What are you doing here, Olivia?" His voice is steady, almost sharp in its indifference.

I swallow and wring my hands together to stop them from shaking. "I ... I got a job."

His expression softens enough to reassure me to keep going. "Yeah?" he asks.

I bob my head, ending with my chin tucked as I look at my shoes. "Yeah. It's the PE teacher job at that charter school in North Austin? The—"

"The Brightline School for Science," he finishes.

I lift my head to snap my eyes to his. He's still guarded, but the fact that he remembered the name of the school must mean something.

"That's great, Olivia. Congratulations." His tone is flat, but it's the kind of monotone that feels intentional, like he's forcing his voice to sound disinterested.

"Um, how's school going?"

Finally, the first ghost of a smile appears on his lips. "Really good." The smile fades as he holds my gaze with an intensity that makes my palms sweat.

"What are you doing here, Olivia?" he repeats.

"I'm sorry." The words rush out of me. I pause, taking a breath to help my brain slow down and focus on the speech I practiced in the mirror ten times this morning before work. "I used you, and I lied to you. I led you on."

Gage is shaking his head. "You didn't really lead me on. You were clear from the beginning what you wanted from me."

I hold up a hand. "But I was lying. I've been in love with you all summer." I pause. "Longer actually."

Gage's eyes widen at the "love" part, but I'm on a roll now and can't stop. "The worst part is how I left. I should have had a conversation with you like you wanted instead of running off in the middle of the night."

There were a lot of should haves and a lot of regrets.

"Why?" Gage asks. His expression is still stoic but his voice cracks, belying some of the emotion he's trying to keep hidden.

I frown. "Which part?"

"Any of it. All of it."

I lift my shoulders. "I guess it's the same reason all around. Look at you." I gesture from his clothes to the impressive building behind him. "You've got your life figured out. You're going places, destined for greatness." I motion toward myself. "And then there's me. Until a week and a half ago, I was unemployed and directionless."

Squaring my shoulders, I admit, "I didn't think I was worthy of you."

Gage shifts on his feet. "So, you're here now because you think having a job somehow makes you more worthy of me?"

I slide my fingers under the Gage bracelet on my wrist, then clasp my hands in front of me. "No. I'm here now because I realized it's not up to me to decide who should or shouldn't be part of your life. It's *your* choice."

His expression softens, and it gives me the courage I need. "And I'm here now because the reality of my life without you in it wrecked me. I don't want a life like that."

Gage takes a tiny step closer. "In each other's lives how exactly?"

I meet his eyes. "I love you, Gage, and I want a real relationship with you."

Gage winces and runs his hand through his hair. "I love you, too, Olivia. I have since we were kids, but I just ... how do I know you won't leave again? Hurt me again?"

I nod, blinking back tears. "That's fair. But I promise you, I'm working with a therapist to deal with my stuff now. I'm all in."

"I don't ... I don't know."

"Will you let me show you? Will you let me try to earn back your trust? Please." My voice breaks on the last word, but still Gage hesitates. "I know I've already struck out twice, but I get one more pitch, don't I? Don't call me out yet."

The cheesy sports metaphor makes Gage smile, like I'd hoped. He takes a deep breath. "Yeah, okay. It's only fair to let you finish your at bat."

I grin. "I'm down in the count, but this next swing will be a home run. I know it."

Gage lifts his hand and strokes my cheek with his thumb. "I've seen hitters come back from worse."

My smile widens, camouflaging the moisture still in my eyes. I'm so grateful for this third chance with Gage, so grateful that he's willing to try to trust me again after the way I took him for granted and hurt him. I'm determined not to waste the opportunity or either of our time anymore.

I'm going to marry Gage someday, and I'm done pretending my end goal is anything else.

He tilts his head down and kisses me, slowly at first, as if he's committing the experience to memory, reveling in the way our lips press together and move. I understand the impulse, because I'm drinking in this moment, too.

He leans in further, and there's nothing slow about this kiss anymore. Gage lets himself get lost in me, and I'm right there with him.

The pressure of his lips, the way his nose brushes against mine, the placement of his hands on either side of my face, and most of all the love and warmth surging between us, is all pulled from my wildest dreams.

Dreams that I'm worthy of having come true.

Chapter Thirty-Six

Gage

"What's next?" Olivia asks, her hands warm on my shoulders and her smile lighting up my whole world.

Man, I've missed her.

After camp, when I realized Olivia was ghosting me again, I crashed pretty hard. After a while, that initial gut-punched feeling where my chest was cracked open and my limbs were filled with bricks faded, in time for me to start school.

My new classes gave me something to look forward to, but I still kept thinking, *Maybe she'll call. Maybe she'll show up at my house.* When I saw her leaning against the front of my Jeep in the parking lot, the scene was like I had pictured it a thousand times. Except better.

Her flowery shorts and white tank top looked bright and fresh against the backdrop of parked cars. Her face looked like a mirage in the desert. And I definitely noticed that she's wearing the bracelet I made for her at camp.

I lift my eyebrows. "Dinner? I want to hear all about your new job."

I look down at my scrubs. I had anatomy lab today, which means if I don't smell like formaldehyde, it's a miracle.

"Give me thirty minutes, and I'll come pick you up at your house."

She starts to protest. "I can meet you—"

I cut her off. "Please, Olivia. Please let me come pick you up for a proper date."

She nods shyly, and this is new. Olivia is not shy. I think back to that first night at Camp Prairie Star when she admitted her fear of vulnerability. But she's being vulnerable with me now. She stripped herself bare, and I don't take the sacrifice for granted.

If she's trusting me with her feelings, trusting that I'll protect them, I can try to trust her to stay. To communicate. To love me the way I love her.

I'm nothing if not an eternal optimist.

If she's *really* ready this time, if she truly wants to become serious, if she actually is in love with me the way I've been suspecting for half the summer, I can't walk away from that possibility.

I kiss Olivia goodbye for now and drive home.

My parents are still at work, so there's no one to see me grinning like an idiot as I take a shower and change my clothes. I'm back out the door in record time, texting Olivia as I lock up behind me. I'm guessing she must have unblocked my number, right?

I drive her two exits down the MoPac to Rudy's Bar-B-Q. To the uninitiated, this Rudy's looks like a hole in the wall attached to a gas station, but it's been a go-to barbecue stop for Olivia, Annie, and me since high school.

I've never had barbecue better than their moist brisket. Add to that the slightly spicy sauce and some cream corn on the side with banana pudding for dessert, and it comes pretty close to my perfect meal.

No, not the fanciest spot for a first official date, but between the nostalgia factor and how much I know Olivia loves Rudy's, I'm certain it will be the perfect choice.

When she hops out of the Jeep and beams up at me, holding my arm like she can't bear to let me go again, I know I'm right. Maybe about more than the restaurant.

We file through the line, picking up our cold sides and drinks, then ordering the hot food from the workers behind a butcher-style counter.

I pay, and we decide to eat outside in the backyard. We sit side by side on the bench of one of the picnic tables facing a castle-themed wooden playground.

Olivia takes a bite of her potato salad in a way that makes me wish I was a spoon. She swallows the food and takes a swig from her bottle of Dr Pepper.

Setting the bottle back on the table, she tilts her head toward me and says, "I'm really happy you agreed to give me another chance, but I have a couple of conditions."

I feel the corners of my mouth edge up as I marvel at Olivia's confidence. "You're putting conditions on me taking you back?" My amusement is evident in the tone of my voice.

"Yes," she answers with a pert nod.

"Okay. Of course you are. What are they?"

I'm suddenly nervous again as she wets her lips. "Well, the first is that I think we should see a therapist together." She rushes ahead without giving me a chance to comment. "I want a healthy relationship with you that lasts for a long time."

The relief I feel at her suggestion loosens a band of anxiety around my heart. I smile at her. "I love that idea." But I have conditions of my own. "I'd want to see someone adoption-competent. Would it be weird for us to go to the therapist I already see? Dr. Francine does couple's sessions too."

"That's fine with me. Can you set it up?"

"Consider it done." I move my hand from the table to her knee, squeezing it. "What's your second condition?"

She chews her bottom lip, and I shove a forkful of brisket in my mouth to soften the blow of whatever she's going to say next.

"Okay, this is tricky," Olivia starts hesitantly. "I'm not even sure I want to suggest it, except that I think it's important and will be good for us in the long term."

"What is it?" I ask around the food in my mouth.

"Well ... I think we should stop kissing."

My sharp intake of breath sucks the last piece of brisket in my mouth down the wrong pipe, and I choke. Olivia starts to stand up to help, but I wave her away and cough violently into my hand. Finally, I take a big gulp of soda to clear my throat.

Through wide watery eyes, I stare at Olivia. "Why?" I rasp out.

Her face turns red, and she pauses as if considering her words. "I don't know if you've noticed," she says carefully, "but we have *a lot* of physical chemistry."

I take another drink of my soda. "Uh yeah, well aware. Isn't that a good thing?"

"It is, but I'm worried we used it as a crutch all summer to avoid dealing with our deeper emotional connection."

She's chewing on her bottom lip again, and I wonder if she realizes that between this whole no-kissing condition and the attention she's drawing to her mouth, she's torturing me.

"You're the one who introduced the word *fling*," I grumble.

She sighs. "I know, and I did it because I hoped to keep things between us surface-level. But now, that's the last thing I want. Is it what you want?"

I take my eyes off her mouth and meet her gaze. "It never was."

Her cheeks turn pink again. "Okay, good. So, I'm not saying forever, but until we work through some of this emotional baggage, let's take kissing off the table."

I smirk, the opening too perfect to pass up. "It doesn't have to be on the table. Could be on the couch, in my Jeep, wherever."

"Gage." She groans. "I'm trying to be serious here."

She really is trying. I can see she's serious about getting our relationship right this time around. I am, too. *But still, no kissing?*

"I know, but I don't see how not kissing will help anything. All summer, our emotional connection grew anyway despite us focusing on the physical."

"Exactly. So, probably our physical connection will grow anyway while we take some time to focus on the emotional."

Despite how much I hate this idea, Olivia's reasoning makes sense.

"Is hugging okay?" I ask.

She looks at me like I'm the biggest idiot in the world. "Of course."

"What about if I kiss the top of your head or your forehead?"

She considers her response to this question. "Yeah, I think we avoid, like, lip-to-lip kissing."

"What about—"

Olivia groans. "Gage," she says, elongating the name so that it's four syllables instead of its usual one. "We're not going to write out a list of dos and don'ts. Let's make sure we're spending our time together talking rather than making out."

"Fine," I grumble, but I still think I'm going to need more to go on. There are an awful lot of possibilities that can include talking, but don't go as far as making out.

At the same time, I don't want to give Olivia the impression that I'm more interested in her lips than anything else. I'm interested in all of her, and her lips happen to be a part of that. I also would never do anything she wasn't completely comfortable with.

"I'm sorry," I tell her. "I'm on board with both of your conditions."

She pats my arm, letting her hand linger. "If it's any consolation, I think that second condition will be as difficult for me as it will be for you."

Knowing that does help, actually. I smirk and lean closer to her, pressing my lips to her temple in the most sensual way I can manage.

I'll need to do my part of the work to build that good emotional foundation Olivia's talking about. And fast.

After we finish eating, I stack our trays and gather the trash to throw away. When I return from the garbage cans on the other side of the porch, Olivia looks thoughtful.

"What's up?" I ask.

"Have you told Annie about us yet?" she asks.

I shake my head. Flashbacks of the summer slam into my consciousness, and I'm worried she'll suggest keeping our relationship a secret again.

My worries evaporate when she grins. "Good, let's stop by her house to announce the news."

I fish my phone out of my pocket. "Let me text her to make sure she's home."

Gage:

Are you home?

"Did she know you were planning to come talk to me today?" I ask.

"She knew I was going to do something on some Thursday because I asked her about your schedule, but she didn't know the details."

My phone pings with Annie's reply.

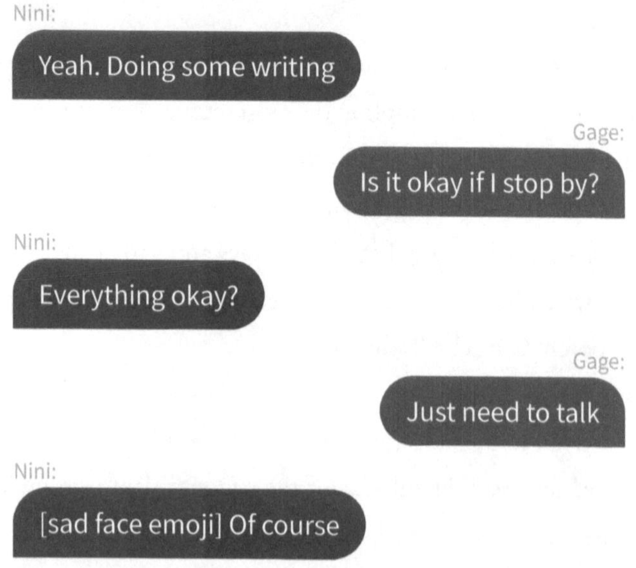

I slide my phone back into my pocket. "I think she thinks I'm moping." *Again.*

It's a fair assumption. Over the last few weeks, I've spent almost as much time brooding on her couch as I have my own.

The corners of Olivia's mouth pull down, and she wraps her arms around my middle. "I'm sorry, Gage."

I raise my eyebrows. "And how have *you* been feeling these last couple of weeks?"

She squeezes me. "Miserable."

As much as I don't like the thought of Olivia being unhappy, knowing she was unhappy because she wasn't with me feels pretty good.

"Then we're even."

I wonder if Annie will see it that way, though. If she's still supportive of Olivia and I getting together. Guess we'll find out soon.

Thirty minutes later, we're standing at the door to Annie's apartment downtown near Lady Bird Lake.

I knock, and when Annie opens the door clad in purple pajama pants and an oversized T-shirt, Olivia and I raise our joined hands and shout, "Surprise!"

Annie shuffles back a step, her hand flying to her chest. Once she gets her bearings, she claps her hands and squeals in a pitch so high that every dog within a mile radius is probably on their way to her apartment right now.

I guess I don't have to worry about my sister being supportive of Olivia and me as a couple.

Annie puts her hands on her hips. "You two crazy kids finally figured it out, huh?"

As we move past her to enter the apartment, I pull her into a hug. "By the way, if you lost your voice, it's in my right ear."

Annie laughs and rolls her eyes. "Okay, Dad."

I cringe, because yep, that is a joke our dad tells all the time.

"I opened a new package of Oreos today," Annie says as Olivia and I settle onto the couch. "Would either of you like some?"

"No, thanks," Olivia answers for us. "We had dinner at Rudy's."

Annie's eyes widen. "You went to Rudy's without me?"

Olivia and I exchange a look. "We were on a date," I explain.

Annie bites her lip. "Oh, right. Of course." She shakes her head. "This is going to take some getting used to."

We fill her in on our evening. Well, mostly Olivia does. I'll admit that it feels a little weird to have the same best friend as my girlfriend. Like Annie said, this will take some getting used to for all of us.

Eventually, we let Annie get back to her writing, with Olivia promising her they'll talk more later.

The sky outside is bright and clear, and the night is still young, so Olivia and I walk the short distance to the lake and sit on a bench overlooking the water.

Olivia lays her head on my shoulder, and I wrap my arm around her.

"We still have a lot to talk about," I remind her. "Going all the way back to high school."

Olivia sighs. "I know. But not tonight."

I drum my fingers against the armrest of the bench. "So, this whole no-kissing thing. When does that start?"

Smirking, Olivia looks up at me. She pretends to consider the question. "Tomorrow?"

"Thank you," I mumble before capturing her lips with mine. "Tomorrow it is."

Chapter Thirty-Seven

Olivia

I take a fortifying breath as Gage and I walk into the waiting room for our first couple's therapy session with Dr. Francine. I know we're going to have a lot to sort through.

Gage and I have talked since we got back together, of course, but so far, we've avoided any of the more loaded topics. It feels like it might be easier to tackle those with a professional to help us along.

When it's time for our session to start, a tall woman with red hair opens a door that I assume leads to one of the consulting rooms. "Gage and Olivia?" she calls, smiling at Gage, who of course she already knows.

We stand and follow her into a small room with a sofa against one wall across from a wingback chair, and a coffee table in the middle.

She gestures for us to sit on the sofa, while she makes herself comfortable on the chair.

"It's nice to meet you, Olivia. I'm Dr. Francine. Now, if you both could tell me why you're here," she says. "You're a young couple, recently started dating. Why do you feel the need for couple's counseling?"

Gage glances at me, and I nod for him to answer. "Olivia and I are in love, and while we've recently started dating, we've known each other a long time. The thing is, we both have some ... I don't know, coping mechanisms from our past traumas that have made it really difficult for us to be there for each other. We want to learn to break those patterns so we can have a long, healthy relationship."

Dr. Francine nods. "That's admirable."

Between the two of us, we explain our history to Dr. Francine. She jots down some notes, and I wonder what she's writing.

If they're already in counseling, these two are really in trouble?

Too messed up for me to help?

Abandon all hope, ye who enter here?

Okay, she's probably writing notes about some of the details we're telling her so that she can remember them, but opening up like this is so hard for me, I can't help but feel judged.

"Thank you," Dr. Francine says when we finish. "That helps me understand the context. What part of your relationship would you like to discuss first?"

Gage glances at me almost guiltily, then swallows. "There's one huge question I have."

Dr. Francine nods. "Okay, let's talk about it."

Gage turns to me. "What happened at high school graduation? I mean we were kissing, and you seemed into the idea of dating me.

Then when you got back from the bathroom, it was like a switch flipped."

It takes most of my willpower to look Gage in the eye as I share these feelings with him.

"Yeah," I say softly, "I'm really sorry about that. You're right that before I went to the bathroom, I was all in. But I overheard a couple of girls that were supposed to be my friends talking about how surprised they were that a smart guy like you would go for a dummy like me. I felt like I was missing something that was obvious to everyone else—that you were too good for me. I didn't want to drag you down."

Gage's eyes are fiery when he responds. "They said that?"

I nod. "They suggested it would only make sense if you were looking for a trophy wife."

Gage's face registers shock and anger.

"Gage, I can see you reacting to what Olivia shared. How are you feeling?"

Gage inhales a deep breath. "Furious," he answers. "How could anyone say that? Especially when they're supposed to be her fr—"

He breaks off, frustrated, and turns to me. "You're one of the smartest people I know."

My cheeks heat. "That's nice, Gage, but come on, you know that's not true."

"Like hell I do! That's one hundred percent fact, babe."

Dr. Francine interjects. "Olivia, why are you doubting what he's telling you?"

"I know I'm not smart. I was lucky to get Cs through school. I wouldn't have gone to college if it wasn't for soccer. I couldn't even read until fourth grade, not really."

"And that made you feel stupid?" Dr. Francine asks.

"It's evidence that I *am* stupid."

"She's not stupid," Gage cuts in, his voice tight. "She has dyslexia."

"Aha. I see," says Dr. Francine. "When were you diagnosed?"

"Eighth grade," I answer.

Her eyes widen. "That's pretty late. No one caught it before then?"

Again, Gage speaks up. "Her auditory recall is amazing. She was able to get through school up to that point by remembering what the teacher said." He turns to me. "That's not something a 'dummy' would be able to do."

I stare at him. I didn't realize he knew that about me, or that he had given it so much thought.

"Olivia, I'm going to send you some links to videos about dyslexia. Dyslexia is defined as an unexpected difficulty learning to read despite high intelligence. Part of how it's diagnosed is comparing reading ability to overall IQ. I'm sorry if no one ever explained that to you."

I nod, my head spinning. I know it should have been a big relief when I finally got my dyslexia diagnosis. *At last! An explanation!* But by then, I'd been called stupid by so many classmates and had so many teachers exasperated with me for not "applying" myself, even when I knew I was trying my best, I think it was hard to internalize anything else.

"Now," says Dr. Francine, "I'd like to steer us back to the conversation around what happened at graduation. Gage, you were surprised when Olivia came back from the bathroom with what seemed like different feelings for you. And Olivia, you put up a wall because you felt inadequate after overhearing your friends' conversation."

I dip my head. "I'd liked you for a long time, Gage. It killed me to let you go at graduation. I thought I was doing the right thing."

"How long?" Gage asks gruffly.

"How long what?"

"How long had you liked me?"

"Since your fourteenth birthday party," I admit.

Gage chuckles wryly and runs a hand through his hair. "Since sophomore year for me," he says. "I wish I had known. You never gave any indication."

"That was on purpose. I didn't want you to know. What if ... what if you didn't like me back?"

"And at camp? You really wanted a summer fling?"

I shake my head slowly. "Not really."

He scoffs. "Me neither, but it's what you said you wanted. It's what you asked for."

"And you agreed," I point out.

Gage groans.

"Okay we're about out of time for today," Dr. Francine interrupts. "But I think it's become clear that the two of you need to work on communicating your feelings to each other better. Here's your homework: every day until we meet again in two weeks, I want you each to tell the other something about what you're feeling. I know you're both busy, and you don't necessarily see each other every day, so feel free to text, call, email, whatever works. Texting might actually be easier at first."

Gage:

What I'm feeling today is that I miss you. Classes are kicking my butt

Olivia:

I'm feeling hungry

Gage:

Hunger isn't an emotion

Olivia:

Still counts

Gage:

Nope

Olivia:

Okay fine

Olivia:

I'm feeling excited about doing a soccer unit with the kids next week

My third period class of eighth graders is gathered in front of me on the PE field at Brightline as I walk them through the context for the soccer skills lesson I've prepared on shooting goals.

"Okay, so the goalie is here." I set an orange cone in front of the goal to the right of the center. "And if a player kicks the ball from here …" I place another cone in a spot about twelve yards away from the goalie, more to the left.

"… what angles are going to work best for the player to kick the ball into the goal, assuming they kick it in a straight line and the goalie doesn't move?" I grin. "Which is not going to happen in a real game, by the way."

The kids laugh.

"Get into groups of two or three and try kicking the ball at different angles. You can measure the angles with these." I pull out a bucket of plastic protractors I borrowed from the math department and set it on the grass in front of me.

The students peer into the bucket with interest.

"Work on this for the next twenty minutes, and then each group needs to report back to me what you discovered."

One boy near the front of the group raises his hand. I answer his question before he asks it. "Yes, Marshall, actually kicking the ball is a requirement for this assignment." Marshall drops his hand with a scowl.

The kids break themselves into groups and start their investigations. I stay behind them, watching as they kick the ball, adjust the angle, and then try again. Some of the balls go way off course, and students chase after them. Many balls go into the net, and the group members high-five each other in celebration.

After the promised twenty minutes, I blow my whistle to call the students back to me. They drop their protractors into the bucket and call out the degrees of angles they found that worked.

Here's a secret: I don't care which angles they found that worked. They were running around, practicing soccer skills, and *enjoying it*, and that's what matters to me.

My watch beeps to remind me it's ten minutes before the bell rings to end the period. I dismiss the kids to change back into their school clothes.

"Coach Delaney," a student named Camila calls as I walk with the class to the locker rooms. I turn toward her. "What happens if the player kicks the ball, so it arcs up, and it's not rolling flat on top of the grass? Or when the goalie moves? How does that affect the angles?"

I stop walking and consider Camila's questions. My body knows what to do to compensate for the varying angles while I'm shooting on goal, but I can't say my brain knows how to explain it.

But maybe I don't need to know the answers, I only need to empower my students to find the answers for themselves.

"What do you think?" I ask her.

Camila's forehead crinkles, and she bites her top lip as she thinks. "In my physics intensive, we were learning about projectile motion, but that formula doesn't take into effect air drag or spin. The Magnus Effect would certainly be in play with an object like a soccer ball."

I raise my hand. "What's the Magnus Effect?"

Still distracted by working through the problem in her head, she gives me a brief answer. "The lift force or curvature of the ball's path."

"Ah." I grin. "In my world, we call that bending it like Beckham."

I wasn't sure she would even hear me with how intense her thoughts seem to be, but Camila stares at me, confusion written all over her face.

"David Beckham?" I ask. "Arguably one of the best and most handsome footballers to ever play?"

Her eyebrows pull together even more. "Football? I thought we were talking about soccer?"

I pat her shoulder. "Never mind. Tell me more about the calculations."

She chatters about initial velocity and projection angle the rest of the way to the locker room. When we get inside, she bounds off, calling over her shoulder, "Thanks, Coach Delaney! I think I found my science fair project!"

I stop short. *My class inspired her science fair project?*

Brightline holds a school-wide science fair at the end of every academic year where students showcase projects they've built bit by bit throughout the whole year. Project plans are due before Thanksgiving break. With only a couple of months until that initial deadline, everyone's been talking about their ideas. The Brightline science fair is a huge deal, and students take it very seriously.

I turn toward my office so I can text Gage, my heart as warm and full as a hot-air balloon. My feet skim across the floor as I float in and retrieve my phone from the desk drawer.

Even though it's via text, my face warms at his praise. And he's right. I am kind of rocking this teacher thing.

I smile to myself as the bell rings and I prepare for the next class.

A week later, I'm enjoying some much-needed downtime. Gage and I have been good about sharing at least one feeling with each other every day. I'm excited to report on our progress to Dr. Francine at our appointment next week.

Gage pulls his buzzing phone from his pocket, looks at it, then turns to me. He raises his eyebrows. "Really, babe? I'm right here."

I hide my face. "It *is* kind of easier to text it to you, though."

He pulls my hands down and cups my face. "However you need to talk to me, I'm here. I'm glad we're talking. And I'm glad you feel safe with me."

"And cozy," I whisper.

"And cozy," he agrees. He caresses his thumb across my cheek.

Sighing loudly, he pulls away and picks his phone up again. He types, and then my phone pings.

Gage:

> Today I'm feeling frustrated by this whole "no-kissing" rule

I smirk and text back.

Olivia:

> You wish your lips were on mine right now? We'd start out sweet and slow, then the tension would build …

Gage reads from his phone and groans loudly, his head collapsing onto the back of the couch. "You're so mean."

I giggle, but my teasing kind of backfired because now I'm struggling to keep my lips to myself, too. "Seriously, though, focusing on the nonphysical stuff right now will make us stronger for the future."

He smooths a hand over my hair. "I know. And I'm committed to that. Besides," he winks, "you're worth the wait."

Chapter Thirty-Eight

Gage

The first thing we do at our second counseling session is report back on our "homework" of communicating with each other about how we're feeling.

"It was really helpful, actually," Olivia says. "It's hard for me to be vulnerable with other people but practicing a little bit every day has made me feel more comfortable."

I shift in my seat on the couch, taking Olivia's hand in mine. "I can see the difference, for sure." I look at Olivia. "When I tell you I love you now, I know you believe me. And it meant a lot that you remembered your promise to take me to that fancy milkshake place for my birthday last week."

I turn back to Dr. Francine. "On my end, I'd been struggling with … not with being able to tell Olivia how I feel in general but trusting that my feelings won't overwhelm her or make her push me away.

When Olivia shared last time about how much her feelings around her dyslexia were holding us back, I felt like I'd finally been given the Rosetta Stone to understand her better."

It was a startling and achingly sad revelation. That she would think even for a second, never mind five years, that I wouldn't want her because of her learning disability makes me furious, not at her, but at anyone in her past who ever put her down.

She's everything I've ever wanted and more.

Dr. Francine nods. "Last time, we talked about what happened at graduation. Today, I'd like to get into what followed. When you talked at graduation, you both agreed to continue your friendship. What happened?"

It feels like she's changing the subject, but I want to talk about this, too. As hard as it was when Olivia rejected me as her boyfriend, her ghosting me afterward is what hurt the most.

"We stopped being friends." I chuckle humorlessly.

"And why is that?"

Olivia speaks up. "It was my fault. It was too hard." She looks at me. "I didn't know how to act around you anymore. I was avoiding my feelings for you. It got easier when we went to different schools a couple months later anyway."

I wipe my hands on my jeans and focus on Olivia. "On my side, it felt like you abandoned me. I was bitter about your rejection, and you ghosting me didn't help. I didn't reach out to you because I felt like you wouldn't want me to."

Dr. Francine taps her pen against her lips, then points it toward me. "Gage, do you think your adoption might have affected how you reacted?"

I consider it. "Yeah," I say finally. "I'm already sensitive about people leaving me because I lost Maggie when I was still a baby. Even though I saw her regularly while I was growing up, and even though I eventually understood *why* she gave us up, it's been a sore spot for me."

Olivia turns to Dr. Francine. "So, my go-to move of avoiding problems played right into Gage's fear of abandonment."

Dr. Francine folds her hands in her lap. "That sounds likely."

Olivia squeezes my hand and meets my eyes. "I'm sorry I wasn't sensitive to your fears. I know I hurt you, but I won't leave you again. I promise. I'm in this forever."

While her words are reassuring, and I trust that she's sincere, it doesn't stop the fear I feel when I think about the possibility of Olivia breaking up with me.

When I say as much, Dr. Francine turns to me. "Gage, I want you to recognize that 'abandonment' implies leaving somebody helpless. An infant, for example, can be abandoned because he can't fend for himself. The infant that Maggie 'abandoned'—or so it felt to your psyche—still lives inside of you and fears being left helpless again. But you can't be abandoned now. You're an adult; you're not helpless. You can take care of yourself. People may leave you, but you will survive it."

Dr. Francine has made similar statements in my individual sessions with her, but today, for some reason, the words hit me particularly hard. I've heard the idea before, and it made sense to me logically, but today I can feel it sinking into my bones.

I'm not helpless. I can survive people leaving me.

Does that make the thought of someone—of Olivia—leaving me easy? No, but it does keep the thought from overwhelming and paralyzing me.

"We're almost out of time for today, but feel free to continue this conversation without me. You're both making a lot of progress in this short time with being open with one another. Can you feel that?"

Olivia and I hold each other's gazes, and she offers me a soft, watery smile. Because we're with Dr. Francine, I hold back from wrapping Olivia up in my arms with her head nestled on my shoulder.

Instead, I smile back at her.

"Yeah," I answer Dr. Francine. "I'm feeling more secure in our relationship every day."

"Me too," Olivia says. "I'm still hesitant to be vulnerable, but I know that if I'm having doubts about how Gage feels about me, I can talk to him about them."

Her words warm me from the inside out. I don't want Olivia to have doubts at all, but when she does, I'm glad she knows she can talk to me.

At the same time, I know Olivia isn't the only person in my life I've held back from because I'm worried about being rejected.

Mostly, I'm thinking about my parents. I've never talked to them about my doubts and fears about my adoption. I didn't want to worry them or make them feel guilty or like they failed somehow.

But if there's one thing I've learned this summer, it's that holding back damages relationships, while honesty, even when it's hard, can strengthen them.

A few days later, my mom, my dad, and I are all home at the same time, so we sit down together for dinner. My dad makes taco soup because the temperatures have dropped into the seventies here in early October, which is as close to feeling like fall as we get in Austin.

Sitting at the table, I wait until everyone's almost done eating before I shore up my courage to start a conversation about my feelings.

"Mom, Dad, can I talk to you?" I start. They must hear something in my tone because they instantly give me their full attention.

"Of course, son." Dad sends me a reassuring smile.

"Always," my mom adds.

I take a deep breath and launch into a rambling monologue about the developmental psychology class I took in college and how it led to me coming out of the fog and processing some of the hard emotions I've held onto about my adoption. I talk about always feeling like I needed to prove to them that I was worth keeping when I was a kid.

I keep my eyes on the plate in front of me because I'm worried about their reaction, and I need to get the words out before I can face the consequences.

When I finally finish talking and look up into their faces, my parents aren't angry. They don't even look hurt or disappointed. Instead, the emotion I see shining in their expressions is ... love.

"Oh, Gage," my mom whispers as she reaches across the table to take my hand. "I'm so, so glad you're telling us."

My dad stretches his arm toward me to hold my other hand. "We always expected one or both of you would have difficult feelings around your adoption. We know that even if we did everything perfectly right—which, let's be honest, we didn't, because it's impossible to be perfect—adoption is still traumatic."

"We knew loving you with our whole hearts wouldn't be enough," my mom continues, "as much as we wanted it to be."

"But, Gage, I want to make something perfectly clear right now. Your existence is not, and never has been, a burden; it's a joy. For me and your mom, but for Maggie, too."

"It's been a joy to be your parents," my mom reiterates.

Like when I talked to Maggie back in July, I feel a weight lift from my shoulders. I know I still have feelings to work through before I can really move past the damage of my adoption—feelings that will probably be around to some degree for the rest of my life—but having everything out in the open now helps me understand that I don't have to work through those feelings alone.

By mid-October and our third counseling session, Olivia and I are sharing honestly about our feelings even when we're not with Dr. Francine.

So, when Olivia texts me that she's planning a special date night for us this weekend after I'm done with midterms, I'm not surprised.

Now that Olivia understands my struggles better, her mission is to show me how committed she is to our relationship. And I do feel more secure in her feelings toward me, but even better, I'm starting to become more successful coping with my fears.

She picks me up for our date on Saturday and drives downtown. When she parks near Lady Bird Lake, I start to get an inkling of what she has planned.

When she starts to get out of the car, I stop her.

"I talked to Maggie today," I say.

Olivia tilts her head. "Yeah?"

I swallow down my nerves. "Yeah. Annie and our mom and dad and I are going to spend Christmas with Maggie and her family in Fort Worth this year."

Olivia smiles. "I love that. You'll have so much fun."

I run a hand down the side of her arm. "Would you ... would you consider coming with us?"

Her mouth pops open, then shifts quickly into a wide grin. "Yes," she breathes out. "I want to be wherever you are."

Visions of our future together parade through my head. Christmases and mistletoe kisses, eventually a wedding and a family. It's everything I want.

I shake my head to return to the present. We get out of the car and rent kayaks, and now I'm reveling in the memories of our past—our second date back in high school. As I expected, we paddle to the Congress Avenue Bridge, like we did back then.

At sunset, the first of the Mexican free-tailed bats who make their home under the bridge emerge, then more and more until they form a rolling dark cloud silhouetted against the orange sky.

We're quiet as we watch them, holding hands the best we can with our kayaks bobbing on the water. I remember the hope and awe and anticipation I felt watching this same scene when I was an eighteen-year-old kid in love with one of my best friends. I'm overwhelmed with similar feelings flooding my senses now.

If I'm right, Olivia has a picnic planned next, where she's packed our favorite foods. Then, we'll lie on the blanket and watch the stars. And then ... well, maybe history will repeat itself.

But I don't want to spoil the surprise, so I'm quiet as we paddle back to the rental shop. I grin at her when she pulls a picnic basket and blanket from the trunk of her car. I help her spread the blanket on a grassy hill in the park between Riverside Drive and the Colorado River. I talk and laugh with her as we eat our favorite foods.

By the time she lies back on the blanket and tugs me down next to her, my heart is pounding. Olivia rests her head on my shoulder, and I run my fingers through her hair as we search for constellations.

"Gage," Olivia whispers, and I lift myself up on one elbow so I can look into her eyes. "I've never felt as close to anyone as I do with you. I love you."

I bring my free hand around to cup her cheek. "I love you, Olivia."

She bites her bottom lip and shifts closer as her gaze drops to my mouth. When she meets my eyes again, I hope she can read the question in them. She nods, her lips stretching into a soft smile.

I'm eager to taste her again, but I don't rush. Olivia is my everything, and this kiss will be one of the many I plan to give her every day for the rest of our lives.

I stroke my thumb gently across her cheek, and her breath hitches. I lean in, hovering above her, drinking in the way Olivia looks bathed in starlight.

"Gage," she whispers again, so quietly I slant closer to hear.

"Yeah?" My voice is as strangled as the last shred of my self-control.

Her eyes glow. "Just kiss me."

Obediently, I erase the last inches between us. When my lips meet hers, the images that dance across my closed eyelids are a kaleidoscope of our past and our future. Of the moments we've shared and the milestones yet to come.

I know it won't be easy; we have more work to do together in counseling and individually as we move through the parts of our pasts that threaten to hold us back. But we're committed to each other and our relationship.

We both know this love between us was always so much more than a summer fling.

Epilogue

Two Years Later

After two years of hard work, high tuition payments, and way too little free time to spend with my girlfriend, I'm finally graduating with my occupational therapy doctorate degree.

I still need to pass the board exams for my state licensure, but I already have a job lined up with an outpatient clinic here in Austin where I'll specialize in working with young kids and NICU graduates. It's a dream, honestly.

I fell in love with this patient population when I worked at a similar clinic in Dallas during one of my semester-long fieldwork rotations, and now I'll be getting paid for it.

On the drive to the event venue where the graduation ceremony is being held, I give my family a heads-up that I'll be getting an award.

Olivia gasps, and my dad asks, "What kind of award?"

"I don't know. Some award, but it means I get to give a speech. Plus, it will look good on my résumé."

"That's amazing!" Annie exclaims.

My mom turns around in the front passenger seat and pats my leg. "We're so proud of you, Gage."

We park at the venue, and my family walks me inside where they'll meet up with Maggie and her family. As we make our way through the parking lot, my classmates stop me for high fives and hugs, offering up their congratulations.

"Congrats on the Luminary Award, Gage. I voted for you!"

"Hey, Mr. Luminary hotshot! Well deserved, man."

"Can't wait to hear your speech!"

Olivia, who's walking next to me, my arm around her shoulder, notices the comments, and the thoughtful look on her face tells me she's processing. She pulls out her phone and types something as we make our way toward the building.

Suddenly, she stops and gasps at something on her phone screen. She lifts her eyes to me and, in one fluid motion, punches me in the arm.

"Ow!" I moan. "Is that any way to treat the graduate?"

"'Some award?' You called it 'some award?'" She thrusts her phone into Annie's face. "Look at this!"

Annie starts reading, then grabs the phone from Olivia's hand. "Oh my gosh! Gage!"

My mom and dad crowd in to read over her shoulder.

Olivia puts her hands on her hips. "Gage Donovan Carter! You won the Hinojosa Luminary Award?"

Without waiting for me to answer, Annie reads from the screen. "The Hinojosa Luminary Award goes to the graduating OT student that best embodies the program values of professionalism, excellence, innovation, and integrity. The winner is voted on by program faculty and peer students from the graduating class."

My dad adjusts his glasses. "That sounds like a pretty big deal, son."

Olivia punches my arm again. "It sounds like a *very* big deal! Why didn't you tell us?"

I shrug, looking between my family members.

Olivia moves her hand, and I flinch, thinking she's going to punch me again. Instead, she puts her hands on my cheeks, squishing my face. She looks into my eyes and smiles.

"I'm so proud of you, babe. I love you so much." She stretches up and kisses my already puckered lips.

"Thank you," I mumble, but it sounds more like "tay koo" with the way she's squeezing my cheeks.

It all bodes well for the surprises I still have planned. Today, I'm angling for *all* my dreams to come true.

When it comes time for the awards part of the graduation ceremony, I wiggle in my seat. I turn around to make sure I know where my family is sitting in the audience. I see Kent first, because he's so tall, and there are Maggie, Callie, and Duncan next to him. On the other side of Duncan are my parents, and then Annie and Olivia.

My eyes linger on Olivia. She looks beautiful in a dress that's lacy and sexy and adorable all in one. And it's white, which is perfect for the occasion even if she doesn't know it yet. Her hair is down, shimmering gold flowing around her shoulders.

We've continued our appointments with Dr. Francine, though we've scaled back to one a month. Even though we've become near experts at communicating our feelings to each other, sometimes it's still easier to tackle hard topics with her impartial mediation.

Both our emotional and physical connections are stronger than ever.

Olivia is preparing to start her third year teaching PE at the Brightline School for Science. After completing the educator preparation coursework required for a teaching license during her first year at Brightline, she passed the certification exams last year, marking this school year as her state-required "internship" period. It's the last step before she can get her official teaching license.

Because her job gives her summers off, Olivia returned to Camp Prairie Star for two more sessions as the activities director. She finished the last week of camp a few days ago, in time for her to come home for my graduation.

Between Olivia being away at camp for the last three months and me living in the garage apartment at Maggie's house in Fort Worth for my second fieldwork rotation the four months before that, our relationship has been sort of long distance for most of the year.

I've hated being apart from her, though it doesn't make me panic like it used to. Even so, if everything goes according to plan today, I'm going to make sure it doesn't happen again.

My attention is called back up to the stage when I hear the university president introducing my mentor, Dr. Carol Decker, to announce the Hinojosa Luminary Award.

She explains what the award is, and I shift in my seat again. I'm honored that my instructors and classmates think I'm deserving of it, but I'm also preoccupied thinking about the speech I'm about to give. I wipe my sweaty hands on the front of my robe and fidget, preparing myself to stand up and make my way to the stage.

"I'm delighted to announce the recipient of this year's award, and to welcome him up on stage to receive it. Dr. Gage Carter."

I edge around my classmates' legs to exit the row I'm seated in and walk down the aisle to the steps on the side of the stage.

When I reach Dr. Decker, I wrap her in a bear hug and try to keep my hands from shaking.

I'm grinning as I step up the podium. I glance back at Dr. Decker. "That's the first time I've been introduced as Dr. Carter, and it feels amazing." The crowd laughs.

I clear my throat to begin my speech. "I'm honored to receive this award, which I consider to be a vote of confidence from my faculty and fellow students. I'd never have gotten to this point without your companionship, patience, and brutal feedback." The audience laughs again. "Thank you."

I look out at the audience and once again find the row holding my family. "I'm grateful for the support of my family. To my mom and dad, thank you for loving me. Maggie, I love that you're part of my life. Kent, I love that you're part of hers. To my little siblings Duncan and Callie, thanks for keeping me on my toes. To my twin sister and best friend, Annie, thank you for being my anchor through everything. And to my girlfriend, Olivia. You're my world. I love you."

This next part is planned but not written down. I lock eyes with Olivia across the rows of heads. I swallow before continuing. "I can't do life without you." My voice catches, and I blink back tears. "Will you marry me?"

A collective gasp lifts up from the audience as Olivia's mouth drops open, and Annie grabs her hand. I'm quiet, staring at her and waiting. "Uh, kind of need an answer, babe." I grin, my heart beating fast.

"Yes!" she shouts, while laughing. The crowd applauds.

I make a show of patting my sides, then say into the microphone, "I have a ring for you, but it's currently in the pocket of my pants, underneath this gown, so I'll have to give it to you later."

Everyone laughs. I know I'm commandeering graduation at this point, but what are they going to do? Kick me out? Besides, the crowd loves it.

Still locked in on Olivia, I gesture her forward. "Come up here, babe."

She shakes her head, but I nod back at her. Finally, her face red, she edges out of the row and makes her way to the stage. I hop down—which is not easy in this long flowy gown—and kiss her senseless in front of everyone.

She's blushing furiously, but I know she loves the attention. We both do.

Bonus Epilogue

To visit the whole Delaney family twenty years in the future, download the bonus epilogue!

https://books.bookfu nnel.com/delaneysin love

Or visit **www.juliemilo.com** and sign up for my newsletter!

Acknowledgements

Writing *Love at the Lake* was an experience that required me to get out of my comfort zone. Olivia is the most *unlike* me female main character I've written, and I sometimes had to stop and reflect—is this how *Olivia* would react to this, or how *I* would react? I did quite a bit of backspacing until I got fully into her head.

I tackled two sensitive experiences in this book: adoption and dyslexia. Like with sensitive topics I've written about before, it was important to me that the portrayal of these experiences were authentic. Though I am an adoptive mother and a parent to a child with dyslexia, the experiences of an adult adoptee or a person with dyslexia are not my lived experiences. To prepare, I read books, some from experts and some from first-person experiences.

For adoption: *The Primal Wound: Understanding the Adopted Child* by Nancy Verrier, *Adoption Unfiltered* by Sara Easterly, Kelsey Vander Vliet Ranyard, and Lori Holden, and *All You Can Ever Know* by Nicole Chung. I also have participated in various adoption-centric groups online for years, with the viewpoints shared in them incorporated into my knowledge base.

For dyslexia: *My Dyslexia* by Philip Schultz, *The Adult Side of Dyslexia* by Kelli Sandman-Hurley, and *This Is Dyslexia* by Kate Griggs.

Thank you to the beta readers who provided helpful feedback on my manuscript: Bailey Blythe, Elizabeth Stevenson, DeAnn Grady, Kyliegh Romine, and Jessica Boomhower. Thank you to Christie Piper for your help in fine-tuning my blurb.

Thank you to Sydney Christensen for once again taking my vision for the cover art and running with it. She truly helps my characters come to life.

Thank you to my awesome book coach and editor, Ruth Shilling (www.rseditorial.co). Sometimes it's hard to get a story out, especially when imposter syndrome is winning. Ruth talked me through the doubts and encouraged me to trust my instincts as a writer. This book is better because of her.

Thank you to Alicia Whitaker (@aliciasalwaysreading on Instagram), who provided proofreading services and also helped connect me with a few beta readers with lived experiences with adoption and dyslexia.

I can never say it enough: thank you to my family. This is Gabriel's book, and he shows up in it through the traits of several characters. He's an inspiration to me in this and many other ways. Ana remains my biggest fan. She's always eager to brainstorm with me when I'm stuck in a plot point. And they both, through their incessant obsession with the numbers six and seven, inspired me to include that obnoxious kid trend in the book. I feel for you, Maggie.

Thank you to my husband, Andy, especially. He knows what he does, and how grateful I am for him.

Finally, thank you readers! It's more fun to write stories knowing you're there to read them. If you've loved this, or any of my other books, consider leaving a review on Amazon, Goodreads, or another bookish platform. Reviews truly make a huge difference for authors, especially indie authors like me!

Also by Julie Milo

Delaneys in Love series

Love in the Stacks

Love in the Lab

Love at the Lake

Second Chance in Asheville

About the Author

Julie Milo spends most of her time reading and writing. When she's not reading and writing scholarly stuff for her day job, she's reading romance, nonfiction, and literary fiction for fun. She writes closed door/kisses only (also called "sweet") romantic comedies.

Julie was raised, but not born, in Florida where she started dictating stories to her parents before she even knew how to write. By kindergarten she was writing and illustrating picture books and subjecting her classmates to read alouds at school. While the illustrating did not stick (her drawing skills never evolved past about third grade), the writing did, and for most of her childhood, her answer to "What do you want to be when you grow up?" was "an author." Returning to writing decades later is a dream come true, and Julie is proud to finally be able to call herself an author.

Julie currently lives on the Gulf coast of Florida with her thoughtful husband, two amazing children, and two dogs (one delightful pit bull and one very energetic black lab). She loves dessert and hates cold weather.

You can learn more about Julie and her books at www.juliemilo .com.

www.ingramcontent.com/pod-product-compliance
Lightning Source LLC
Chambersburg PA
CBHW051258130726

47987CB00004B/1571